Praise for Julianne Lee's
A Question of Guilt

"An interesting historical fiction novel . . . an intriguing saga."
—*Genre Book Reviews*

"Lee's excellently researched novel is written in a fluid, engaging style and is full of intrigue, cover-ups, and plots. Her investigation of this historical mystery provides a vivid theory of what might have happened between Mary Stuart and Henry Darnley, and will keep readers turning the pages."
—*Historical Novels Review*

HER
Mother's
DAUGHTER

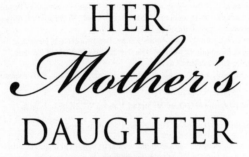

A NOVEL OF
QUEEN MARY TUDOR

JULIANNE LEE

BERKLEY BOOKS, NEW YORK

THE BERKLEY PUBLISHING GROUP
Published by the Penguin Group
Penguin Group (USA) Inc.
375 Hudson Street, New York, New York 10014, USA
Penguin Group (Canada), 90 Eglinton Avenue East, Suite 700, Toronto, Ontario M4P 2Y3, Canada
(a division of Pearson Penguin Canada Inc.)
Penguin Books Ltd., 80 Strand, London WC2R 0RL, England
Penguin Group Ireland, 25 St. Stephen's Green, Dublin 2, Ireland (a division of Penguin Books Ltd.)
Penguin Group (Australia), 250 Camberwell Road, Camberwell, Victoria 3124, Australia
(a division of Pearson Australia Group Pty. Ltd.)
Penguin Books India Pvt. Ltd., 11 Community Centre, Panchsheel Park, New Delhi—110 017, India
Penguin Group (NZ), 67 Apollo Drive, Rosedale, North Shore 0632, New Zealand
(a division of Pearson New Zealand Ltd.)
Penguin Books (South Africa) (Pty.) Ltd., 24 Sturdee Avenue, Rosebank, Johannesburg 2196,
South Africa

Penguin Books Ltd., Registered Offices: 80 Strand, London WC2R 0RL, England

This book is an original publication of The Berkley Publishing Group.

This is a work of fiction. Names, characters, places, and incidents either are the product of the author's imagination or are used fictitiously, and any resemblance to actual persons, living or dead, business establishments, events, or locales is entirely coincidental. The publisher does not have any control over and does not assume responsibility for author or third-party websites or their content.

PRINTING HISTORY
Berkley trade paperback edition / December 2009

Library of Congress Cataloging-in-Publication Data

Lee, Julianne.
  Her mother's daughter / Julianne Lee.—Berkley trade pbk. ed.
      p.   cm.
  ISBN 978-0-425-23008-4
  1. Mary I, Queen of England, 1516–1558—Fiction.   2. Great Britain—History—Mary I, 1553–1558—Fiction.   3. Queens—Great Britain—Fiction.   I. Title.
  PS3562.E326H47   2009
  813'.54—dc22   2009019236

PRINTED IN THE UNITED STATES OF AMERICA

10   9   8   7   6   5   4   3   2   1

To Dr. Michael E. Williams,
for joyful Sunday mornings.
For stories told and retold, that let us know who we were,
who we have become,
and who we might be one day.

ACKNOWLEDGMENTS

When I was twelve years old I began writing fiction for the purpose of entertaining my friends. In the beginning I wrote in spiral notebooks that I then handed off to my buddies and watched their faces as they read. Whenever there was a chuckle or a frown, I'd ask, "What? What part is that?" I wanted to know what had piqued their interest. That was my audience: a single reader. While constructing a story, whenever I wrote something particularly amusing, I chortled over the reaction it would elicit.

Over the past forty-odd years, not much of that has changed. For a while, early on, I wrote short stories that were circulated online among small groups of friends or published in zines with an extremely small circulation. I knew most of my readers personally.

Now that my circulation has widened, I still chortle. Though I can't possibly meet all my readers—and cannot even hope to meet as many as I would like to—I still write with certain people in mind who have supported my work over the years and the decades. They are: my good friends Marie Waters, Nina Lamb, Trisha Mundy, Diana Diaz, Laura Anne Gilman, my father Alan R. Bedford Sr., and editor extraordinaire Ginjer Buchanan.

AUTHOR'S NOTE

For the record, this author is a Protestant of the Methodist persuasion and moderate in all possible things. We Methodists are extreme in our moderation. I have no agenda in writing this book, either pro-Catholic, pro-Protestant, sexist, racist, or political. I make no excuses for the policies of Mary Tudor, nor do I condemn anyone. My only purpose in writing about her is to take a peek inside the head of a woman who has been reviled throughout history as evil and/or insane. That history having been written by those with far more agenda than I, I have a sense that perhaps there is more to her story than might be imagined by those of us with only a twenty-first-century perspective. We live in a world where religious freedom allows us, as a viable philosophy, that of a Jedi Knight, and we have lost the pervasive certainty that characterized religious thought during the medieval period. We tend to judge the past through the glass of modern ideas.

In my research, and taking into consideration human nature, I find Mary less psychotic than neurotic, and the circumstances of her life, her times, and her particular reign—the very first of a woman in her country—support events in ways that belie the tradition that she was a bloodthirsty nutcase fit only for the rubber room. This is a story of many points of view. Each character or historical figure sees these events through a scrim of personality and experience, and draws his or her own conclusions about them accordingly. I trust that Gentle Reader will take a moment to let go of the idea of agenda and also see things through their eyes.

Julianne Lee

www.julianneardianlee.com

HER
Mother's
DAUGHTER

PROLOGUE

None of the girls could sleep. They whispered to each other and giggled at everything. A couple of them attempted sleep with eyes shut tightly against the noise and the wandering shine of Annette's flashlight, but nobody had even a prayer of going unconscious. The light flitted here and there, probing the room and creating shadows everywhere it was not. Gracie was the only one not in the seventh grade, and she didn't count because she was Karen's sister and only a fifth grader. Karen was the birthday girl, it was her slumber party, and she had to let her sister be there. Hardly any of them paid Gracie much attention, especially whenever she blurted little kid stuff.

Karen kept shushing her friends, so Mom wouldn't come into the room again to make them shut up. Annette whispered things to her about Sharon, who dressed like a nerd and was only invited because Karen felt sorry for her. Sharon was ignored even worse than Gracie and lay in her bag off to the side near the ceramic statue of a Dalmatian dog with her mouth shut and tears standing in her eyes. Nobody wanted to know, so they didn't look at her. But Karen did try to get Annette to shut up. They all lay in sleeping bags arranged on the living room floor, rustling with restless energy. Nobody was likely to sleep much tonight. Everyone was too wired on birthday cake and punch.

Karen and Gracie's mom's muffled voice came from the hallway for about the millionth time that night. "You girls go to sleep! I'm not going to say it again!"

"Good," whispered Annette, and the rest of the girls burst out in giggles. Then they fell silent to hear if Karen's mom had heard it. There was no response from the hallway, so Annette sat up and leaned over to whisper to Karen, "Hey. Look at that reflection in the mirror."

Everyone rolled over for a look at the mirror hanging on the wall over the sofa. It was huge, with a fancy gold-looking frame and an etched design around the edge.

"What about it?" Karen sat up, too, to see.

"It looks weird."

Karen shrugged. It had been there all her life, and she realized she'd hardly noticed it before. "It's just a mirror."

"Maybe not."

"What do you mean?"

Annette's voice took on a low, ominous tone. "I bet I can show you something."

"What?" Karen was so gullible. Annette grinned but then bit her lip so she wouldn't give it away.

"It's magic. I can summon a ghost."

"Yeah, right." Karen lay back down on the floor.

"Really. Honest to God. I know how."

"How?"

The other girls were listening, and Sharon said in a voice from elsewhere, "There's no such thing as ghosts."

"Yeah, there are. Go over to that mirror, and I'll show you."

"Oh, I know what she's going to do. And it's fake," said Gracie.

"Shut up. It's not fake."

"Is, too. I saw it once, and it's fake. There's no ghost."

"Is, too. Go over there, Karen, and I'll show you." Annette waited while Karen hesitated, then said, "Go on. It's really cool. Don't be a chicken." Annette leapt from her sleeping bag and took Karen by the hand to pull her over to the mirror. She went, but slowly and without much enthusiasm. Mom was going to come in any second and get mad at them for being so noisy. But she went and looked into the mirror. Annette stood behind her, trying not to grin.

"Okay, where's the ghost?"

"You've got to summon her. Chant over and over the words 'Bloody Mary.'"

There was a general murmur of recognition among the other girls, and one said, "Oh, yeah. I know this."

Karen looked over at her, then back at the mirror. "Bloody Mary?"

"She was, like, this old-timey evil queen. She executed a whole bunch of people. She was really awful, and burned them at the stake." Her voice went low and ugly, filled with dark relish for the evil of it. "Alive. She burned them *alive*. She was really, really ugly and looked like an old, nasty witch. And she was crazy. She went around yelling, 'Off with their heads!'"

Gracie said from her sleeping bag, "It won't work unless you light a candle in the room. When you say the name, you've got to be able to see a candle in the mirror."

"Oh, yeah. We need a candle."

"There," said Karen, and nodded to the squat, fat candle standing on the fireplace mantel. It was red and smelled of cinnamon, left over from Christmas. A wreath of plastic holly, with little red plastic berries all through it, lay around the base, the leaves covered with a thin film of dust where Karen's mother hadn't reached with her dust cloth. A rim of sagging wax surrounded the short, black wick. Annette took the fireplace lighter from the mantel and clicked the trigger to produce a genteel butane flame, then held it to the wick and lit the candle. Another click extinguished the torch, and she set the lighter back on the mantel. She clicked off the flashlight now that they no longer needed it. Karen indicated the coffee table. "Put it there. I can see it in the mirror, I think."

Annette set the candle on the table, then returned to the mirror. The rest of the girls giggled and shushed each other. The candle threw dancing shadows all over the room, particularly on the mirror in front of Karen. The girls gathered close.

"All right," said Annette. "Go."

"What?"

"Say the name. Over and over. Just keep saying it, and she'll come."

"Nuh-uh." Karen shook her head and tried to back away from the mirror. But Annette held her hand and made her stay.

"No, you gotta do it. Don't be a chicken. Scaredy."

"I'm not afraid."

"Then do it."

Karen looked sideways at the mirror.

"Go ahead."

For a long moment Karen looked like she would just go back to her sleeping bag, but then she said to the mirror, "Bloody Mary."

Everyone giggled. She said it again. "Bloody Mary."

Annette said, "Oh, I forgot to tell you. If you summon her, she'll reach through the mirror and pull you into hell with her."

Karen's eyes went wide, and she stepped away from the mirror. "Forget it. I'm not doing this."

"Chicken!"

"I don't care about any old queen."

Annette snorted in disgust, tossed her hair, and turned to face the mirror. "I'll do it."

Karen backed away, moving toward the door. Gracie figured she was ready to run down the hall to Mom and Dad's room, and wanted to go with her. But she was too curious about what would happen to Annette if the evil queen appeared. When Annette started chanting, she joined in. "Bloody Mary, Bloody Mary, Bloody Mary . . ." All the girls joined and said it together. "Bloody Mary, Bloody Mary, Bloody Mary . . ." As it went on, nobody was giggling anymore.

A few more times, but nothing happened. Even the candle stopped flickering so much in the still air of the living room. This was just totally boring. The girls stopped chanting, and there was no sound. The house was silent, and there was no ghost in the mirror. Totally boring.

"Oh, well," said Karen, and she sounded relieved. "Okay,

let's go to bed. I'm tired." The thrill of being awake this late at night had seeped from the room, and everyone seemed to sag a little. Even more boring. Maybe it was time to sleep after all.

The rest of the girls agreed, and made their way back to their sleeping bags. Annette blew out the candle before slipping into her bag. Gracie sat up, staring at the mirror.

Nothing there. All she could see from where she sat was a bit of the dark corner where the ceiling met walls.

She lay back down, and finally the room went quiet. In a few minutes there were soft sounds of girlish snoring. The moon outside slipped behind a cloud, and even that small light dimmed until there was nothing to see in the room, even had anyone been awake.

Then a flickering light blossomed in the mirror. The candle on the coffee table remained dark, but from the reflection of that candle in the mirror came a yellow, dancing light that threw shadows on the living room ceiling and walls and highlighted the faces of the sleeping girls.

A face formed in that light in the mirror. A grim visage of a woman. Her jaw was square and clenched, her lips a thin line, and her eyes filled with deep grief. She looked through the mirror frame at the room filled with sleeping girls, then behind her at the reflections of those girls. She picked up the skirts of her red velvet dress and went to the reflection of the nearest one, to brush a lock of hair from the slumbering face. The girl slept on, undisturbed. Tears rose to the woman's eyes.

"So innocent," she whispered to herself. "Bloody Mary . . ." she said and pressed her lips together again. Then she whispered in a voice choked with sorrow, "Wretched, undeserved name. Would that I could tell you and you would listen."

CHAPTER ONE

They call me "Bloody Mary," an appellation I abhor. My name has been stained, painted with a black brush by my enemies. For hundreds of years they have called me this. "Bloody." "Tyrant." History of little fact and long agenda. Tales told first in barrooms, then around the supper table, eventually in too-warm classrooms by men who know less than they imagine, and finally the stories are cast in iron and passed off as truth of printed word. Shadows of truth, as I have been naught but shade these past centuries. Reviled in the name of "religious freedom" I could never have imagined while alive. A freedom that simply did not exist for me or my subjects. Ever.

I was England's first sovereign queen. Had I been born male, so very much would have been different. My mother would have been praised for furnishing the kingdom with a proper heir and not set aside for a vile whore. I would have been groomed for the throne all my life and risen to it on my father's death without question. I would have been hailed as a strong leader. Mine would have been called a firm hand. My legend would have been not of "Bloody Mary" but "Defender of the Faith."

My earliest memory is of my father. He was a majestic man— the greatest king England has ever known.

Mary Tudor's earliest and fondest memories were of being carried in her father's arms. He loved her more than the world—she was sure of it—and she returned that love with a child's utter lack of reserve. At public functions and private celebrations her guardians would take her to him, where he awaited her with joyful anticipation. She saw his eyes light with pleasure at sight of her, a smile splashed across his ruddy, handsome face. She would throw her arms wide and run to him, for him to sweep her up from the floor in a rustle of silk, linen, and fur, and swing her around once before settling her against his shoulder like an arquebus, cradled in the crook of his arm. Her father was a robust man with strong arms and wide shoulders. He ever smelled faintly of horse leather, for he was a great knight and formidable in the lists. Bards throughout the kingdom told great tales of his prowess with a lance, and even at a tender age Mary knew how skilled he was at unhorsing his opponents. All her life she would love that smell, for it meant safety. In her father's arms she was safe.

There she held his strong neck, and the ride would begin. Down the center of whatever great hall held the gathered crowd he would stride. Men and women in glittering costume would smile and applaud. Braziers all through the room would throw light and warmth inside heavy stone walls hung with rich tapestry and wood carvings. Mary was Henry's only daughter and best beloved of the realm after her father and mother. She was, as her father often said, "The greatest pearl in the kingdom." Most beloved, and she loved them all in return. They were her family and her people, and therefore they were Mary, herself.

Her father would present her to anyone he wished to impress with the beauty of his daughter, and each dignitary so honored would express his or her pleasure at the flattery. Often there were presents, and Mary loved receiving them. A gold pomander. A jeweled ring. A measure of silk. Tokens of affection and regard that defined her world. That world shone with pleasure.

"Are you ready to meet the princess, Your Majesty?"

Charles V, emperor of the Holy Roman Empire, stood near the head table at one end of the great hall at Windsor and turned to the speaker, his interpreter, Montoya, then to the original speaker, Cardinal Wolsey, who stood near the dais, and nodded. Then he returned his attention to the English king, whose proud smile betrayed his expectation of Charles's reaction to his daughter. King Henry's clothing of rich silks and furs glittered with golden and jeweled ornaments, and his eyes sparkled in anticipation of showing off his daughter.

There was never any subtlety to Henry. Everything he thought and felt was there for the world to see, for he thought himself invulnerable. The English. So pleased with their Englishness, and so despising of everyone else. Henry behaved as if all of Europe should feel the same. Charles regarded the

English king with hooded eyes. Big, loud, rude ... his very self-absorption and overconfidence made him vulnerable to manipulation. For the sake of marrying off his daughter to the most powerful man in Europe, he would go to war on behalf of Charles's own interests, pay for that war from English coffers, and Spain would reap the benefits.

The musicians playing softly in the shadows off to the side fell silent, and a herald trumpet sounded, a crisp series of notes announcing an important arrival. All those nearby looked to Charles expectantly, for the time had come for him to meet his future bride. A formality, since the marriage treaty was what it was and wouldn't be affected, regardless of how this meeting went. The purpose of his visit was less the betrothal than it was England's declaration of war against France that would follow, and that was the way of things. But also the way of things was that life was filled with pomp and formality; without ceremony, the ordinary folk would never know what to think about anything. Nor often the extraordinary folk, for that matter, and one after all must have the cooperation of the nobility, who could cause so much trouble if they wished it. So Charles turned with a wide smile to have a glance about for the girl he expected to marry six years hence and prepared himself to appear pleased regardless of how pretty or plain she might be.

Across the enormous hall, she stood with her mother, his aunt, in the arch of the doors at the far end. Even at this distance he could see the joy shine in her. Her sunny smile brightened everything around her. Not just pleasure for the moment but eternal happiness for everyone in the room and perhaps in all the world. She looked across at him, and he could see her instant affection for him. It touched his heart, though he was a man of twenty-three and she but a child of six.

She started toward him, the throng parting before her and her mother the queen. She strode at Catherine's side, without need of holding a hand, as confident and pleased with herself as her mother. As she drew closer, Charles saw her eyes were lit with genuine intelligence. That was to be expected, since her mother was Spanish. Indeed, she was his mother's sister. Fine intellect could hardly be avoided in his own cousin.

As for her looks, Mary's face was too square for true beauty, but she was a comely enough child, and her smile was wide and infectious. She might grow to a handsome woman, and with her joyous demeanor there was no reason to believe she shouldn't. He couldn't help but smile in return, for she seemed to expect it of him. Her eyes never left him, and when she arrived at the dais, she gave a perfect little curtsy. When she stood again, she gave a bit of a bounce of barely contained energy. Such life in this child! As Queen Catherine presented her to him, the girl's hands lifted a little as if she expected him to pick her up. He was almost tempted to do so.

Instead he bowed to her and took her small hand in his large one calloused by years of riding and war campaigns. He kissed a tiny knuckle and greeted her as was proper. She returned the greeting as properly and perfectly. She asked after his health and the ease of his travels, and he replied as graciously, saying his journey had been a pleasant one, though that was a lie. It was never pleasant crossing the water to Portsmouth.

"Would you care to hear me play the virginal for you?" The sincerity of her desire to play delighted him.

Charles allowed as he would be most pleased at that. From

the corner of his eye he noticed Henry's glowing countenance. The English king's chest pushed forward like a knight in the lists about to charge, and his already ruddy cheeks were even more pink with pride. Charles had noticed the small keyboard instrument prominently positioned and had been told she expected to play for him. In all politeness, he would have brought it up himself if she'd not asked.

With a bright smile reminiscent of her father's, Mary went to the instrument and sat herself before it happily to play. Charles was relieved to see she played well, with a facility rare for such a young musician, even a girl, who would be expected to play well. For how else would she spend her days but to learn the graceful arts? Her fingers were a child's and played with the simplicity of a child, but they were light on the keys, and the tune she plucked was a lively one. She had a flair, a style that was almost dance, and her happiness shone through in the music. It lightened his habitually morose heart in a way that made him wish he could feel this way all the time. Impossible, but one could dream.

Throughout my life, Charles was a delight and my mainstay. They called him ugly, with a jaw too heavy and a dull look of stupidity in his eyes, but I knew him to be as intelligent a man as any I've ever known, and with a stalwart heart unmatched in any realm. Those years I dreamed of being his wife were joyful to me, though I was sorely disappointed to learn he'd married another.

Mary looked out the carriage window toward Ludlow Castle in Wales. It had been a terribly slow journey from London, with stops in Coventry and Thornbury. There had been a pageant and gifts for her along the way and much ado made of her passage, with crowds waving and cheering whenever she passed through a town of the least size. Everyone was to know of the new princess of Wales, and that for the first time in history the succession was designated to a daughter. Even tiny clusters of hovels here and there brought out the curious if the road passed near enough, and on learning who occupied the lead carriage, most burst forth with spontaneous affection. These small groups Mary loved the most, for she could hear their individual voices and the words they shouted to her: an old wife blessing her, a young man extolling her piety. She blessed them in return and waved as she passed. Her heart filled to bursting with goodwill.

But the journey wore on, and she was glad to finally be at Ludlow. She was heartily sick of traveling, for even in the yearly progress there was opportunity to rest. Now she looked eagerly to the castle to know what comforts it might offer this weary wanderer.

The castle loomed above the trees, a vast stone fortress surrounded by a goodly amount of wooded acreage. The small village of Bewdley stood below the drawbridge, and of course the peasantry turned out to see their princess pass. Princess of Wales. That was Mary, since recently her father had come to acknowledge she might be his only child to survive. Mary had no brothers, her mother had stopped having babies, and without a legitimate prince to inherit the throne, the kingdom might fall into disarray after her father's death because of the number of potential claimants. That would never do—for all her father had established in his kingdom, and his father before him, to come to nothing.

Some said it would be impossible for Mary to sit on her father's throne. They said it was against God's law for a woman to rule men. But Mary knew better and felt in her heart they were wrong. God's will must be done, and if Mary had not been meant to rule, there would have been a prince to take the throne. After all, Mary's grandmother had been queen in her own right. Isabella, queen of Castile. Everyone knew Mary would be a fine queen one day, and as she gazed up at the walls of her property and listened to the well-wishes of her father's people, she looked forward to learning the things she would need to know to fulfill that destiny.

That was the very purpose of this trip. She was to represent her father's authority in this distant corner of his kingdom, where customs were strange, the people dressed and spoke oddly, and her court would bring a taste of civilization to this backward land. The carriage rumbled across the wooden drawbridge and clattered across paving stones through the gatehouse and into the bailey of the castle. There she waited for her council and guard to open the carriage door. She descended with one leather-clad hand supported on the riding glove of chamberlain Sir John Dudley, filled with bright anticipation of the months ahead. As she was escorted through the newly renovated great hall on her way to her privy chamber, her head aswarm with excitement and curiosity, there were bits of broken stone and sawdust everywhere about. She barely noticed and paid no attention to the mutterings of her council and her retinue behind her. She was exhausted and quite ready for sleep.

"Pray to God for a miracle, Philip. The king must have an heir." John Dudley and Philip Calthrop stood near the dais in the presence chamber. The furnishings were sparse compared to the lavishness of Henry's London palaces. This room felt cold and hard. Mary's chamberlain and vice-chamberlain whispered to each other, though nobody could hear them over the murmur of voices while they all awaited the girl.

Everyone thought of her as "the girl," and not even so very much a princess. This exercise in Wales was proving a waste of time, and nobody believed Henry would succeed in foisting a female heir on them. It was, after all, called a *king*dom. Were it a queendom, he was certain it would be named that. The very sound of it was awkward and unnatural.

"Whatever do you mean?" asked Calthrop.

"She can't possibly ever rule England."

"And why not?"

Dudley peered at Calthrop and wondered whether the man was genuinely stupid or merely putting on a face of loyalty to his mistress. "You know bloody well why not. 'Tis wrong for a female to rule. Against God's plan. Furthermore, I remind you she's promised to the emperor. If, God forbid, the king should depart the earth tomorrow, allowing her to ascend the throne would be to hand the entire realm over to Charles. Which, of course it would please the Empire no end to subsume England and make her naught more than an outpost of Spain to surround and cow the French." He shrugged his shoulders in an irritated gesture. "It would be disaster for us. We'd all be speaking Spanish by Christmas, I vow."

Calthrop chuckled at the levity, dry as it was, then shook his head, adding a glance about the room so as not to appear too much in conversation with Dudley. He said, "You've no need to worry about that, sir. She won't be marrying the emperor, I'm afraid."

Dudley's eyebrows went up. "And why do you say that?"

"Because word has come he's to marry someone else."

Dudley blinked, but wasn't all that surprised. He'd known for years Henry's interest in alliance with Charles had waned, and he was hoping for a way out of the marriage treaty. "So, who is the emperor going to marry?"

"Isabella of Portugal."

"Ah." Good. "But if the princess inherits the throne, it matters not who she will marry. Or, rather, it matters all too much; she'll be ruled by her husband, and it will go badly for us all."

"Well, then, the thing to do would be to have an eye for who she would marry, yes?"

Dudley grunted a noncommittal reply and fell into a fit of thinking. Calthrop spoke truthfully, he thought.

A pair of trumpets announced the arrival of the princess, and everyone in the room came to attention. The ten-year-old princess entered through the archway from the direction of the castle chapel. More than likely she'd spent the greater part of the morning at Mass, as had many of the dozens of attendants and functionaries in her household. Like her mother, Mary devoted most of her energies to spiritual matters. Mary had always been close to Catherine—too close, to Dudley's mind—and had been raised to piety of a degree more Spanish than English. She even dressed more in the Spanish style than a proper English princess ought. Dudley considered himself devout, but even he couldn't match the utter, abject devotion of Catherine and her daughter.

With the aid of a small step stool, the girl took her seat on the dais, nearly dwarfed by the enormous chair of ancient Welsh oak, and gazed out over the gathering of councilmen, supplicants, guards, and onlookers, all of whom waited expectantly for her to speak. She was small but seemed not childlike at all. Like a queen in perfect miniature, her tiny feet clad in embroidered silk slippers resting on the stool as if they were squarely on the floor. With a square face not unlike her father, she seemed almost mannish, and Dudley had to admit that was a mark in her favor for the role she played here in Wales. A year ago, when she'd first arrived, she'd been wide-eyed and unsure. Now she appeared a small adult, familiar with what was expected of her and poised to make her own thoughts known. Not that it was her own thoughts she would speak today, for her counselors had nearly total sway in these decisions. But she spoke them as if they were her own, a skill she'd only acquired since bringing this court to Wales. Perhaps this expedition into the hinterlands was serving a purpose after all.

Welshmen in awe of finding themselves in the presence of royalty stood before her, waiting to be called forth. They brought suit in the court, to be heard by the blossoming princess. All was orderly, all predetermined by her council. Dudley observed her polished manner. Royal. She gave the impression of control and satisfied those who saw her. In truth, that had been one of Henry's goals in sending her. Unfortunately, those who did not attend her did not observe her, and those who did not recognize her authority were the ones she needed to sway and could not. Each case brought before the court was dispatched with alacrity. As the afternoon wore on, issues were resolved exactly as expected.

Once the proceedings had wound down and the last suit concluded, while Mary conferred with one of her ladies to her left, Calthrop whispered to Dudley, "What of the fugitive?"

Dudley held up a finger for the vice-chamberlain to wait for his reply while the rest of the court withdrew from the room and Mary returned to her privy chamber with her women. Then he turned with Calthrop to follow the others into the great hall. He said in a low voice under the general murmur, "Holed up in Bewdley still. The presence of Her Royal Highness is not impressing these savages in the least, and they're adamant their sanctuary will hold."

"He's killed two people. His wife's parents, for God's blood! These people kill each other and steal from each other more than any I've heard of in England, I vow!" Calthrop was a rather plain man and more gentle than most. He, more than anyone on the council, struggled with understanding the primitives living in the far reaches of the realm. These Welshmen spoke an uncivilized language, and their laws were as unformed, but Calthrop insisted on thinking of them as equal to the English. Dudley found little patience with this sort of naïveté.

"They're an independent lot, indeed. They'll govern themselves rather than be ruled from England. Particularly by a little girl."

"Something must be done about it. This lawlessness cannot continue."

"It hasn't helped that Henry's own functionaries still question her warrants." And they would surely continue to, no matter what authority Henry might bestow on his daughter.

"You don't say! Who, then, this time?"

"Brereton's kinsman, Randolph. He looks after the man's affairs and has questioned a warrant for a deer to be taken from Shotwick Park."

Calthrop sighed at the pettiness of the behavior, and Dudley was quite in agreement. "Only one deer," he said. "One would think he could let them have one deer for the sake of

averting rebellion." He made a clucking sound of disparage-
ment with his tongue, then added, "You know that sort of thing
only undermines her authority and thereby also weakens the
king's. If only they would see that. If only they would also see
that weakening the king's authority does naught but weaken
themselves."

"Tell it to those who would have as much of that authority
for themselves as they might garner and to hell with the Crown.
If she appears weak, there will be those to take advantage, particularly at his eventual death." He crossed himself and added,
"God forbid."

The vice-chamberlain also made a perfunctory sign, then
allowed as that was true. The murderer who had taken refuge
in nearby Bewdley was a spectacular example of locals denying
the king's authority.

Dudley continued. "The landholders in Bewdley, and some
elsewhere, threaten to withhold their taxes."

Calthrop paused in the gallery and said in a low, shocked
voice, "They'll end up in chains, is what!"

Dudley paused with him and murmured close, "They
threaten to run off into the woods."

"And all join Robin Hood's band of merry men?" Calthrop
chuckled at his own joke, and Dudley smiled in appreciation,
though he didn't find the idea terribly amusing. It was all too
possible, given the insane stubbornness of the Welsh.

"Robbing from each other, more than likely, for the truly
rich won't come near."

Calthrop laughed out loud at that, for it had been a running
joke for the past year that Wales was no place for the civilized.
The entire court had suffered during their exile from the gentle society of England, and living among these tightfisted, clan-

nish, incomprehensible louts had worn on everyone. "I will be glad to go home one day."

Dudley's eyebrows rose. "You may get your wish sooner than you think."

Calthrop tilted his head in inquiry.

"Indeed. We may be returning home before much longer. The Welsh are proving themselves too unruly, and His Majesty is likely to recall his daughter for a failed mission."

The vice-chamberlain didn't have a ready reply for that, so Dudley added, "You can see why I say Mary cannot ever rule England. She hasn't the authority, and won't so long as she remains female."

Calthrop had even less reply to that and only gaped at Dudley, who left him and proceeded on to the great hall for his supper.

There Dudley found the princess just arrived at her table, having entered directly from her privy chamber, in a dark mood far removed from the cheer she'd demonstrated earlier. Instead of the bright and confident persona she'd displayed in the presence chamber so shortly before, she now bore a countenance of dark eyes and tight, white lips. Calthrop's wife, who served as one of Mary's ladies, making her way through the throng of courtiers taking their seats now that the princess was seated, passed near, and Dudley gestured for her to wait. She paused in her exit from the hall, and he asked her what troubled her mistress.

She glanced toward the head table with soft, sympathetic eyes, then told Dudley, "She's only a moment ago had word that Charles has ended their betrothal." She glanced at Mary again. "I'm afraid she's not taking it well at all."

"Did she think he loved her?" Dudley thought it terribly

silly for women to imagine they were loved by their husbands. It made for much difficulty in managing what should be a purely economic and political arrangement. He'd often expressed the opinion that marriage would go so much more smoothly if only women weren't involved in it. But for the moment he held his tongue on that account.

The gentlewoman replied, "She's still a girl, John. She's spent half her life expecting to marry the emperor, and now he's forsaken her. She's too young to fully understand the complexities of this, and one can hardly blame her for being disappointed. In fact, I could hardly blame her for tears, were there any." An edge entered her voice, and an eyebrow rose ever so slightly. "But the princess is well-mannered and has said nothing against the emperor. She shows better form than I would expect to see in a man so used."

Dudley blinked at the sharp comment but let it go. He gazed across the room at Mary, whose own gaze focused on the plate before her, though she didn't seem to see it, and he said, "Well, perhaps it's for the best."

Calthrop's wife said, "One can only hope."

Dudley had meant that it was for the best that Mary wouldn't have a Spanish husband, but he sensed the silly woman was thinking something entirely different.

CHAPTER TWO

Losing Charles as a fiancé was my first heartbreak, though it certainly was not my last. What a terrible shock it was to learn God could inflict such punishment on a princess. Surely even those poor souls who received alms from my table could not have felt so low as I did then. But God had a purpose. Though I never married Charles, he remained my cousin and my ally throughout my life. Had I known what was to come, I might have understood even at a young age that being forsaken was an ordinary thing, and far worse could happen to anyone, even such as myself. Also had I known, I might have despaired.

Mary returned to her father's court to find it changed. Her mother didn't seem part of it anymore, and there were murmurings amongst the courtiers of a liaison between her father and one of her mother's maids of honor, Anne Boleyn. Mary only knew her slightly, but knew her to be flighty, sharp-tongued, and not particularly devout. Mary's ladies said little on the subject, and the men around her said nothing, but she gleaned the gist of the situation from the occasional sly jest or veiled comment meant to fly just above her understanding.

Anne Boleyn had never been well-liked in Catherine's household, and now was liked even less. To Mary it all seemed a little silly, for Henry had been with mistresses before. There were two illegitimate sons, and nobody thought his previous affairs so scandalous as this new interest. Mary didn't take much alarm over this one, either, until shortly after her arrival from Wales when she first heard the thing that brought her an inkling of her perilous situation.

That day when she was eleven found her out riding. It was an ordinary day, and she was partaking in an ordinary pastime. The horse she rode had been a gift from her mother, for Catherine knew how she loved to ride. The warmth of the summer sun on her face, the feel of a strong, responsive creature beneath her, the jingle of bit and thud of hoof on warm earth, even the smell of the beast and its leather trappings appealed to her. Many liked to hunt and hawk on horseback, but Mary enjoyed the ride for its own sake.

Today she sought in physical exertion a distraction from too much thought about her marriage prospects. She sat the side-saddle in a habit of subdued red decorated with black piping and garnets set in gold, and pushed her mount so that some of her guard were hard put to keep up with her. The sergeant called out repeated requests that she slow down and made dark warnings of the possibility of an assassin about, but she knew it for laziness on the part of the guard and her attendants, so she ignored them. She would have her outing, and her health would be better for it. Her physician had told her so.

Nevertheless, the approach of a fast rider coming from the direction of the palace curtailed her day. The fellow shouted as he galloped, waving his hat and nearly acting the fool with it. His desperation for the party to halt so he might catch up let them all know something important was at hand. Reluctantly Mary held up and waited for him, and immediately he reined in his horse to a walk. Mary prayed to God for patience as she then waited for the messenger to make his leisurely way toward her.

It was a servant to her mother's chamberlain, who swung down from his mount and made his obeisance before speaking. Somewhat out of breath, he said, "Your Highness, I have a message from your mother. You're to come immediately to her gallery."

"Whatever for?" She had seen Catherine that morning at Mass and would see her again later that evening at supper. "What could be so very pressing?"

The man hesitated, and Mary knew he was about to lie. He then said, "I know not." A common enough fable. Mary was old enough to understand that hardly anyone told everything they knew, and most told nothing at all worth hearing if they could avoid it. In her life, information was often hard to come by. He added, "She only made it clear she desired your presence at once."

Mary let go the questioning for the sake of not ruining the pleasant day and went with him back to the palace.

There, in a small alcove in the queen's gallery, she found her mother surrounded by a very select few of her ladies. She sat in a cushioned chair, the ladies sitting and standing near and speaking to her in Spanish in low, soft voices. With a large silk handkerchief the queen dabbed swollen eyes and looked out the open window to the river below. At her daughter's hurried entrance she nearly broke down afresh, but instead contained herself and looked to Mary's attendants to address them.

"You all may retire to the presence chamber. Your mistress will rejoin you there shortly."

The men and women bowed to their queen and made their retreat. Mary carefully folded her riding gloves as she watched them go, then turned to her mother.

"What's so terribly wrong, Mother? Why have you been weeping?"

Catherine gave a glance to her ladies who, without a word, also retreated along the gallery to be respectfully out of earshot. Then the queen gestured to a nearby chair that Mary should sit. The princess obeyed, and though in the back of her mind she wished to return to her ride or to some other more pleasant amusement, she attended to what her mother would tell her.

The queen said slowly, in a voice thick with grief and a diction tinged by her native Spanish, "I've had a conversation with your father this morning."

Mary nodded. Though her parents hadn't been close for some time, and she understood they were even less so of late, she knew they were not entirely estranged and still spoke often.

Catherine continued, "I've been informed that your father wishes to seek a divorce from me."

Mary could only blink at that. Divorce was for men who were evil and wished to renege on their responsibilities to their wives. It was for men with no regard for God's law. Certainly it was not something her father could ever want. King Henry was a pious man, prided himself on it, and he was ever concerned to live according to the wishes of God. It was the thing Mary admired most about him. But her mother had said he desired divorce, so it must be true. Catherine was even more pious than Henry and would be in terror of damnation to stain her soul with even the tiniest lie. Mary could only utter one word in reply. "Why?"

Catherine pressed her lips together for a moment as she considered her answer. Then she said, "The reason he gives is that he believes our marriage is not valid by reason of my previous marriage to his brother."

"But there was a dispensation. Surely if the pope allowed the marriage, it must be valid."

"Indeed, he did. But now Henry claims that marriage was consummated, and no dispensation can forgive that."

"But if that were true, he would have known it. He would have known it the day you were married." Mary's thought was that her father couldn't possibly have said what he did, and that confused her. For her father to lie was simply not possible, but now she was hearing two different stories from people who were both supposed to be incapable of falsehood.

"Yes. He would have, were it true."

"But . . ." Mary faltered, and grief welled up in her as the implications began to gather and swarm in her head. "If the marriage was invalid, then you both would have known it from the beginning. He's saying you knew you were living in sin all this time. He's called you a . . ." Mary found she couldn't utter the word in reference to her mother. It was unthinkable anyone could call her mother a whore.

Catherine nodded, and fresh tears rose to her eyes.

Mary opened her mouth to continue, more and more distressed as she put together the pieces her mother had laid out for her, but her voice was choked off by the appalling realization. For her piety, Mary's mother was nothing if not an honorable woman. Catherine's devotion to God was the center of her existence, and to deny it in her was to eviscerate her soul. Everything Catherine had ever done in her life, as princess, queen, wife, and mother, would be for naught were she thought to be a whore.

Finally Mary was able to speak. "He can't possibly mean to say it in public."

"He's set Cardinal Wolsey to find proof to take to the pope."

Mary stared at the floor, thinking hard. It was all too confusing, to think her father capable of such a shameful thing. "He cannot do this to you."

"He already has."

Mary looked to her mother. "What will you do?"

The queen sat rod-straight and raised her chin. "I will answer him. I must maintain my honor, for without it I cannot live. My immortal soul is at stake, and his as well. I love my husband, and will by whatever means necessary protect him from this folly."

"What will he do?"

Catherine seemed to sag, then she turned up her palms on her lap. "I don't know. I think it does not matter what he does to me, but what he might do to you."

Mary blinked at that, for she couldn't imagine her father doing anything untoward to her. Catherine reached out to take her daughter's hands in hers.

"Mary," she said softly, "you must be prepared for what is to come. You understand that if the marriage is annulled, you will be declared illegitimate."

That struck Mary in the pit of her gut, and a sudden bout of nausea nearly made her gag.

"You would no longer be a princess, and most particularly not princess of Wales. He will marry again, and he will want any son from that marriage to have a clear right to the succession."

Mary was puzzled again. Why couldn't she still be a princess? Any boy born to her father would have precedence over any girl. But then she remembered that the son would have to be legitimate, and that couldn't happen so long as the first wife was alive and the first marriage valid. After a long moment of thought, she said, "What will become of me?"

Peter Barnacle slowed as he neared the throng gathered by the king's gallows at Tyburn. He set down the bundle of firewood he carried, in theory to see what was going on, but the truth of it was his back needed a rest, and he reckoned he couldn't take another step under this load. He was a young man but wouldn't be one long if he ruined himself. So he took the blocked street as a sign from God to go no farther for the time being, even though an alternate route around the convent would get him home quick enough, and craned his neck to observe the goings-on.

It appeared there was about to be an execution. Someone of note, by the look of those nearest the scaffold. Not terribly often one would see such finery at an execution, and never at the death of a common thief. This was surely a political execution. Though Peter ordinarily took the position that the upper classes had naught to do with him, and they should be left to do away with each other as they pleased, he was nevertheless curious what the crime was and who was about to pay for it. This might make a good story for his family once he arrived home.

He spotted a friend off among the onlookers, and waved. "David!" he shouted. "David Wheeler! Oy! Over here!"

Davey turned to see who called his name, and Peter continued to wave. When Davey saw him, he waved back and began to make his way toward Peter through the press. Once his friend reached reasonable earshot, Peter said with good cheer, "Davey, lad, who's the unlucky one today, then?"

Davey's eyes were wide with interest and excitement. The young lad was a nearly womanly gossip, and he always knew everything going on. A handy friend to have, for just by speaking to Davey, Peter's curiosity could be assuaged with very little work. His friend replied, "'Tis a nun, it is."

"You don't say!" Peter looked up at the scaffold, then off to the side, seeking the woman prisoner. She hadn't been brought out yet, and he didn't see her or the wagon. It hadn't yet arrived. "Who'd want to kill a harmless nun? What for?"

"Treason, they say. But she's only to be hung, and not the rest of it."

That was a bit of a relief. A traitor's death was often difficult to watch, for all the screaming and blood and carrying on. Hanging was far more orderly an event, and sometimes there weren't even a struggle at the end of the rope if the neck was broke good and proper. "What's she done, then? Refused the king, has she?"

Davey laughed at that. "Nae, and don't we all wish that were a hanging offense?" Everyone within fifty miles of London knew the new queen had long refused the king, and that was why the pathetic old man had been forced to marry that Boleyn whore and set aside his rightful wife. Then Davey continued. "No, the charge is for compassing the death of the king."

Peter nodded. Everyone had done the same at one time or another, but nobody ever did it out loud. Not even in jest, lest one be overheard and misquoted. "What did she say?"

Davey made a disparaging noise with his lips. "What didn't she say? It was all grand pronouncements he'd go to hell for divorcing his wife and that sort of thing. I've heard tell, and from folks who would know, she's a true seer. People have heard voices from her innards."

"Her innards?"

"Aye! From deep in her belly, it was! 'Tis angels speaking through her, they say, and when them angels had things to say about the king, he became uncommon interested."

Peter chuckled. "I expect his ears perked right smart, they did."

"That nun says the queen is in conversation with the devil."

"And you think she ain't?"

Davey paused and looked to see what Peter might have meant by that, and gave a hesitant laugh. Both men adhered to the old religion, having no truck with the Lutheran heresy that had come into favor since the king had made himself head of the English church. Most folks shied away from the subject, even among friends, lest things said should one day be deemed treason. "I'll be shutting my gob on that, if it's all the same to you." He quickly and perfunctorily crossed himself. "God save the queen and her baby princess as well." Then he shook off his alarm and continued. "In any event, the nun says Henry is no longer king in the eyes of God. That the people would rise up and depose him." Davey leaned close and whispered, "She even says she's seen the very place prepared for him in hell."

Peter thought about that. If the woman was a genuine seer, it was possible she could be telling the truth. And he could easily imagine the king in hell for taking a second wife while the first still lived. But he said nothing, for fear of being overheard and his words passed to unsympathetic ears.

Davey continued. "Folks all over London and everywhere is saying the queen's child is a girl because of the sin they've committed. 'Tis punishment, she says. Like the poor harvest last season. God has punished us all for the king's sin."

That much was true. The entire kingdom suffered from the deathly poor harvest last fall. It was still spring, and the cost of corn was so high his own family was reduced to eating horse fodder. He was glad to have the oats, for many townsfolk had none at all. It had been months since any of them had tasted meat. Peter nodded, and that was as talkative as he wanted to be just then, for his resentment of the king's behavior rose to anger when he thought of his parents and sisters and his own growling belly. He wished to marry Ruth Thatcher, but would never afford it in the absence of a miracle.

"Oh, there she is!" Davey gestured toward a wagon pulled by a plodding donkey making its way through the crowd toward the scaffold. A small woman stood in it, her wrists shackled together and chained to the cart rails. She was dressed in a gray shift that was too large for her by far and hung by only one shoulder, and her cropped dark hair stuck out all over her head. Her face raised to heaven, and her eyes were closed as if in prayer. She probably was praying and in all likelihood would continue until the rope broke her neck.

Peter was glad she'd finally arrived. He could watch the execution, then be on his way home with his wood in good time. The family awaited, and as always there was work to be done.

The years of Anne's marriage to my father were torture for nearly everyone. Not only those of us who were displaced but all the English people. They had their religion stripped from them, their beloved queen taken from them, and the Great Whore hadn't even the grace to provide us with the prince we all needed so terribly. For three years the entire kingdom teetered on the verge of civil war, the good Catholic subjects loyal to my mother ready to take up arms to defend their rightful queen and their proper religion. It was only by my mother's condemnation of war that there was no bloodshed. No matter what indignities my father visited on her, she remained a pious, honorable, obedient wife to him, so long as his wishes did not conflict with God's law. I followed her example, as I had followed her throughout my childhood. My mother was a great queen, and her mother before her. I would be a great queen as well, if God willed it. I had faith in that, even when his king's majesty declared me bastard and transferred the succession to my half sister, Elizabeth.

"If the king wishes it to be so, I submit. But I protest in due form against whatever might be done to my prejudice." Mary stood in the room that passed for a presence chamber in this tiny, dank keep, having just been informed the Duke of Norfolk had arrived with a message from the king.

It was winter. In autumn she'd been forced to move here from her residence at Beaulieu. In all her seventeen years, she'd never lived in so miserable a castle. Her already fragile health suffered from the cold and rain, and there wasn't enough wood in all of England to stave off the winter frost in this place. Eustace Chapuys, Charles's imperial ambassador, stood by her as she received the news there was a visit from the duke, who had been sent by her father. Her words were the standard response to each slight and every indignity attempted on her so she might accept a status she couldn't tolerate. Were she to acquiesce to being treated like a bastard, it could be said she deserved the treatment. Each day she trod a fine line between disobedience and forfeiting her rightful place. At any moment she might be arrested and sent to the Tower for Henry's displeasure. Mary drew courage from Chapuys, who guided her in how to behave under these pressures.

To her chamberlain she said quietly, "John, please gather the household in this chamber." She sat in the carved wooden chair on the plain dais. Her household of well over a hundred would fill the chamber, leaving just enough room for Norfolk and one or two of his attendants. Henry might do his best to intimidate her with his messengers, but she would make equal effort to show she was not intimidated. She set her elbows on the arms of the chair and set her jaw against the emotional assault she knew was coming. She drew in her chin and struggled to appear as regal as was in her power. She was the daughter of Henry VIII, England's greatest king. Nobody could take that away from her.

Chapuys stood to the side, near enough to prompt her if necessary but far enough away not to appear too influential.

Thomas Howard entered the room, followed by a large number of attendants. His well-known lack of honor made him especially hateful even beyond his association with her stepmother. But first and foremost, the man was Anne's uncle, and that alone made him Mary's enemy, regardless of his ambitious and ruthless nature or his mission from the king. She regarded him as she would a snake in the garden.

Lack of room forced many of his entourage to remain in the antechamber, and once Norfolk and three of his men had entered the presence chamber, two of Mary's guard shut the doors behind them. Norfolk watched them, then turned to Mary with a strained expression. The room was quite close with so many people, but Mary pretended not to notice. She sat as straight and regal as her mother had taught her. She was a princess, and even if there were those who would deny it, she wouldn't let them forget it.

"What business have you, my lord?"

"My lady—"

"Excellency," Mary abruptly addressed Chapuys. "Am I not a princess?"

"You are, Your Highness."

"Then why does he not address me as such?"

"I cannot fathom it, Your Highness."

Norfolk's face flushed a dark red of anger. He'd been through this with Mary before, since the birth of Elizabeth last September. He said to Chapuys, in order to not be interrupted again, "My lady Mary must understand that in all obedience to her father she must now acknowledge her status as lady. The true princess is Elizabeth, daughter of the queen."

"Norfolk," said Mary, "I know not of any Princess Elizabeth. I am the only legitimate daughter of King Henry. What silliness do you speak?"

With a tone sharper than customarily used toward Mary in

the past, Norfolk said, "The silliness I bring today, my lady, is that you must prepare to move to Hatfield."

A ball of sickness sank in Mary's belly, and nausea rose. Hatfield was Elizabeth's residence. As poor as this small keep was, it was still her own, but now she was hearing she would share a house with that monstrous, unnatural child everyone called "princess."

Norfolk continued. "You are to enter the household in service to Her Royal Highness, the princess of Wales."

Panic nearly froze Mary's heart. In *service* to Elizabeth? The idea stopped her breath. Her lips pressed together as she stifled sudden tears. Weeping before this minion of her father was unthinkable. She sat, silent, until she could once again breathe. Finally, she said, her voice choked with anger, *"I am the princess of Wales."*

"You are not, my lady. It would be best for all if you would acknowledge that."

"I cannot deny what God has ordained. Neither can I agree to a lie. I will not stain my soul with falsehood, even were it to save my own life."

"I do not wish to argue."

"Then I invite you to refrain from argument, Your Grace."

Norfolk snorted an impatient sigh, then said, "I come only to relay the king's wishes. You must present yourself at Hatfield within the fortnight."

Mary struggled not to show how the short notice distressed her. But then a thought struck her, and she looked to Chapuys. "Excellency," she said. He gave an ever so slight nod. It was time to make a formal, written protest to her father. They'd discussed it often, and now she knew the time was appropriate. Perhaps, even, a protest would convince her father to think again about the advisability of putting her in the same household with the bastard Elizabeth.

"My lord," she said to Norfolk, "I will require some time alone before I give my answer."

"There is but one acceptable answer, my lady."

"What lady?" Mary glanced around at her household as if Norfolk had suddenly begun to address someone else in the room.

He quickly said, not bothering again to express his impatience, "There is but one acceptable answer." His tone implied a form of address quite inappropriate for any honorable woman.

"Regardless, I must have time to think on it. Retire with your men to the hall, and I will speak to you again before you leave."

Norfolk wasn't happy with her request, yet had no alternative but to give her some time to prepare her reply to her father. He made his obeisance, as did his men, then retreated to the outer chamber. Mary descended from her dais and retired to her privy chamber.

There she requested her table desk, from which she took stationery, quill, and ink. She turned to Chapuys. "Where is that draft you spoke of?"

The ambassador reached into a pocket of his surcoat and pulled out a rather well-used scrap of paper. Covered with scribblings and scratched-out bits, it was somewhat hard to read, but Mary flattened it on the surface of the desk and began to copy from it.

The paper was a protest to her treatment, more or less what she'd just gone through with Norfolk, but this would be read by her father. It was the first real communication she'd had with him since the birth of Anne's child, and she hoped he would listen to reason if it came directly from her in written form.

Returned to the presence chamber, she passed the folded and sealed document to an attendant, who then passed it to one of Norfolk's attendants. The missive disappeared unread into a pocket, but Mary knew it would be thoroughly examined before Norfolk reached London. Before the king's minions could make their exit, Mary said, "I wish to know what arrangements will be made for my own household at Hatfield. My sister's household will need to make room for mine." The word *sister* was ashes on her tongue, but she uttered it rather than call her *princess*.

"My lady will find servants enough at Hatfield and will need few others."

"Who will?"

Norfolk gave another impatient snort, then amended himself. "You will find servants enough."

Several of her favorite servants had been dismissed the month before by her father, the reason given that they'd encouraged her disobedience. How many would she have left at Hatfield? Her voice quavered as she asked Norfolk who she would have to leave behind. "What of my maids and chaplain?"

"You'll need but two maids."

Mary's jaw fell open. "Only two?"

"Furthermore, you will not be allowed to bring your governess, the Countess of Salisbury."

Mary looked to Lady Margaret, who had been her governess as long as she could remember. Aside from her mother, Margaret was closest to Mary's heart and nearly like a mother herself.

The countess gaped, astonished at the king's cruelty. She glanced at Mary, then said to Norfolk, "Surely His Majesty doesn't mean to separate us."

"Indeed he does." Norfolk spoke with a matter-of-fact tone devoid of the least hint of sympathy.

"But that would be akin to separating a mother from her child. Cruelty beyond measure."

There was a long silence in which Norfolk's reply was a hard stare. They all knew Mary was unlikely to ever see her real mother again, and at the king's command. This order would strip her of everyone who had ever been dear to her in her life. Finally he said, "His Majesty will allow aught but the two maids."

"I would serve at my own expense, my lord. And for the sake of relieving His Majesty's burden, I will pay the wages for all the household."

"Two maids, Lady Margaret. That is all, and the king will be unmoved in this." To Mary he said, "Begin your preparations. Take little, for your quarters will not accommodate many possessions."

Mary's heart pounded with rage and frustration. Her palms went slick with panic. Her lips pressed together as she held back indiscreet words better left unsaid. Once she was able to recover her voice, she said, "You are dismissed, my lord."

Norfolk nodded, for everyone in the room knew the interview was over, and nothing useful could be said further on the matter. He made his obeisance, then turned and also made his exit.

For a long time Mary sat still, gripping the arms of her chair, resisting the urge to run from it. Where she might go, she did not know. She was trapped. And once she was at Hatfield, she would also be alone. Alone among vipers who would as soon see her dead as to speak to her.

Her household stood attendance until they might be dismissed, and finally she returned to herself and rose from the chair to retreat to her privy chamber. There she went to the table bearing the washbowl and vomited into it. Then she sank into a nearby chair and wept as Lady Margaret and her ladies gathered around to comfort her and wipe her lips with a damp cloth.

Lady Anne Shelton stood in the entryway at Hatfield Palace, just outside the quarters of their new arrival, Lady Mary. This was a small errand ordinarily accomplished by one of the lesser maids, but Lady Shelton wanted a close eye on Mary, who struggled with her new situation. Often over the past three months there had come weeping from that chamber, and though she only heard silence for the moment, Lady Shelton knew the poor young woman would take a very long time to recover from her trials. There had been not one smile since her arrival just before Christmas. Lady Shelton hesitated for a moment but then raised her hand to knock on the door.

One of Mary's two young maids answered. The chamber was small, tucked behind a stairwell on the ground floor of the palace. It contained Mary and her attendants, had no windows, and was barely large enough to hold the bed they all slept in. It hadn't even a proper armoire, and the floor was stacked with trunks of clothing and belongings. No wardrobe rooms for Mary anymore, and no attendants to maintain her dresses. No need of them for the few belongings she had been allowed to bring.

Even those trunks were by now half-empty, for each time Mary made protest against the loss of her title, she was denied an item of clothing or a jewel. Lady Shelton wondered whether she would give up the resistance before she ran out of things to wear. She suspected not; the girl was as stubborn as her mother.

The maid curtsied to her superior, and Lady Shelton said, "Please tell Lady Mary we have a visitor for the fortnight."

The girl blinked at the word *lady*, but said only, "May I tell her the visitor's name?"

Lady Shelton hesitated, for it wouldn't be good news to Mary, but then she said, "Say she is to make herself presentable to the queen."

A look of confusion crossed the girl's face, and a surge of impatience welled. Only Mary's household ever thought of Catherine as queen anymore. She added, "Queen Anne." The confusion cleared up and was replaced by something like panic. Lady Shelton said a little crossly, "Please have the discretion to allow me to retreat before you address your mistress, so I won't be required to report your form to His Majesty."

The girl nodded and curtsied, then shut the door as Lady Shelton retreated to the great hall, where Queen Anne waited while her guest quarters were readied by her attendants. Anne had changed much over recent years. Lady Shelton had always known her as ever struggling to put on an impressive appearance and most striking style, and now it seemed the struggle was won. Today she dripped with jewels and fur, ornaments decorating varying silks of deep red and rust shades. The woman was no longer young—she was in her thirties now—but was still a glutton for attention to an extent unseemly even for a queen. Indeed, lines at the corners of her mouth and eyes suggested an air of desperation Lady Shelton had never seen before. Somewhat akin to a spinster hoping for a last chance at marriage. How odd, for a woman married to the most powerful man in four kingdoms!

Chatting with her brother and her uncle, Anne barely noticed when Lady Shelton returned. But Norfolk certainly noticed, and he turned his unhappy attention to her.

"My sister! I hear tell you treat Lady Mary with entirely too much kindness."

Lady Shelton was taken aback by this, though this sort of thing was all she could ever expect from her brother-in-law. The Boleyn men were harsh enough, but Norfolk's behavior often bordered on unchristian in his lack of respect for people. She replied, "I treat her as I would any other of God's creatures."

"She's a bastard and should know her place. How will she understand what she is if you treat her as equal to her betters?"

Unseemly anger rose, but she was an honorable woman and swallowed it. "My dear Thomas, were she the bastard of a commoner I could hardly abuse her as you suggest, for by her honor and virtue she has earned good treatment. Whatever the king may have made her, by nature or by decree, during her time here she has deported herself as gracefully as the most well-born woman I know. As much as you would like me to, I cannot deny it." She mentally cursed her brother for marrying this tedious man's sister.

Norfolk snorted in insulting rejection of the notion. "On the contrary, she has not behaved well at all. She refuses to acknowledge Elizabeth as princess and Anne as queen."

"Mary nevertheless is obedient."

"Except in this."

Lady Shelton faltered, for his point was, on the face of it, undeniable. But she said, "She acts according to her faith. I cannot fault her for placing God above the king."

"It is only the pope the witch places above the king."

Lady Shelton flinched at his vitriol. There was no possible reply to that other than shocked silence. Anything Lady Shelton might have said would have been criminally disrespectful. She held her tongue and refrained from speaking.

George Boleyn stepped into that silence and addressed his aunt. "My lady, I would suggest you obey my uncle and my father in this. Remember your mission as governess and make certain Lady Mary learns her place. It could go badly for you if you fail."

"I would remind you that only my husband has final authority over me."

Norfolk said in a voice of granite, "I would remind you Sir John is not so very independent of wealth or power as to protect you—or himself—from the wrath of His Majesty." By "His Majesty" Lady Shelton understood Norfolk meant "myself." A cold chill washed over her.

At that moment Mary entered the hall with her two maids and stopped just inside the door. Nobody spoke. Mary and Anne gazed at each other across the room, each waiting for the other to reveal herself. Mary was pale, as she had been for weeks. Her constitution had never been robust, and lately she'd had trouble keeping food down. It was a good sign that she lacked the feverish roses in her cheeks of consumption; nevertheless, Lady Shelton worried about her charge. Regardless of how she felt about Mary's behavior, it would never do for any ward to die while under her care.

Finally Anne spoke. "Well met, Lady Mary."

Mary looked off to the side, as if in search of someone who might help her. She said, "I protest in due form—"

"Mary . . ." Lady Shelton headed off the oft-repeated protest that did nothing but irritate everyone who heard it.

Mary took a moment to gather herself, glanced at Lady Shelton, then said to Anne, "Welcome to Hatfield, Stepmother."

The queen took a seat in a nearby chair and arranged her gown around her. Once she was settled, she looked at Mary and said, "Come closer, child."

Mary obeyed and moved to a spot in the middle of the room, where Anne wouldn't have to raise her voice to speak to her.

Anne said, "We haven't seen you since our marriage to your father."

"I've been kept away from my father, and therefore away from you." It went unsaid that Mary had not particularly missed seeing Anne, but her point came across that she did miss her father.

"You should come to court and pay your respects to him." Her voice was light and friendly, a style she had brought from the French court in more youthful times. There was a slight pause, then she added, "And to myself." Meaning, of course, she wished Mary to acknowledge Anne as queen.

Lady Shelton would not have thought it possible for Mary to become paler, but she witnessed it. For a moment she worried the girl might collapse to the floor, but Mary held herself straight and answered the queen.

"I know no queen in England but my mother."

Anne's face flushed, but she held back what she might have said at that moment. Mary continued. "However, any intervention with the king on my behalf would be ever appreciated."

The queen straightened in her chair, realizing she was up

against a stubbornness equal to her own. "I would be happy to bring to bear whatever influence I have with your father, were you to acknowledge my rightful title."

"I would that you acknowledge my rightful title."

"You do understand the danger of your resistance, child. Those who oppose your father often don't live long after."

"My father would never harm me. I'm his daughter."

"He would protect the interests of his legitimate daughter. And I would remind you that blood relation has never given him pause in ordering an execution." Her tone sharpened, heavy with implication. "Indeed, there are men who have died on the scaffold precisely for their blood tie to the king."

Now Mary's cheeks brightened with anger. Not a hot flush, but tiny red blossoms that glowed deep within. Her lips pressed together, but when she spoke, her words denied her feelings. She said, "I decline to perpetuate a lie. I will not stain my soul with falsehood. I am helpless in giving you what you want, for it flies in the face of God's law. Tell my father I will obey him in all things except where they conflict with the will of God. I know no queen but my mother, for she is his rightful wife, and I am his legitimate daughter."

Anne stood. "You are a bastard."

"I am the princess of Wales."

"You are dismissed, Lady Mary. Leave my presence."

"I protest—"

Lady Shelton took Mary's hand and drew her from the room as Mary's maids followed in a hurry, their skirts in their fists. As they exited, Lady Shelton heard Anne address her uncle and brother. Mary insisted they stop to listen, and the women paused just out of sight. What they heard made Mary grip Lady Shelton's hand hard.

"The very moment Henry ever goes out of the country and leaves me as regent, I will have that wretch killed. By hunger or otherwise."

In a voice lowered for discretion but still audible, George Boleyn suggested Henry would take exception to such a thing, even for the safety of his younger daughter. Anne made a graceless snorting noise of disgust.

"I would do it anyway, even if I were burned alive for it after. I will bring down the pride of this unbridled Spanish blood if it's the last thing I do."

Mary stared at the archway they'd just come through, speechless, her eyes wide with horror.

CHAPTER THREE

My time at Hatfield was possibly the worst of my life. My father's behavior toward me while married to the Great Whore pulled the earth from under my feet. I felt adrift in the cosmos. I was separated from my mother, and in fact never saw her again. My only earthly friend was Ambassador Chapuys. He kept me apprised of what he and his special ears at court heard regarding my father's disposition to me, and the news was rarely encouraging. Anne intended to do away with me; that was clear. I became terrified of poison and ate nothing I had not seen prepared. Even then, I couldn't trust Anne's aunt to not find some way to arrange an accident for me. The king, for his part, seemed indifferent to the possibility of my death. Some accounts gave out that he actively wished it. Whenever he visited Elizabeth at Hatfield, I was sequestered away from them. It broke my heart to be so hated by someone I

*loved so dearly. It would have been such a small thing to have been
allowed in his presence, even for a moment, but I was denied it.
The monstrous child enjoyed all his company, that which was right-
fully mine. During most visits I knelt in prayer in my chamber.
My only solace was faith that all would be well and that God had
a plan for me. If only I could know what that was.*

Voices outside her door brought Mary to attention in her bedchamber. She rose from her kneeler and clutched her rosary
between her fingers. Its ivory beads and gold filigree, sus-
pended with a crucifix of finely carved ivory cross and gold
corpus, had a patina of long use, and they felt comfortable in
her hands. More than that, they brought comfort to her heart,
a familiar thing from her childhood when the world had been
safe, and it had held people she could trust.

But her heart leapt, for one of the voices she heard was her
father's. It cut through and rose above the others, not just because the king was a hale and hearty man of strong voice, but
because the tenor was so dear to her heart. The men with him
might have been anyone, for all she knew or cared, but she
recognized her father amongst all others.

She gestured to her maids to stay in the room, and slipped
out to the entry hall. The arriving party had already moved
onward, up the winding stairway to the floor above, where
Elizabeth's personal chambers were. She could hear their cheerful, joking voices dwindle as they went; then they were muffled
by a closed door above.

A guard came to her chamber door and didn't see her
standing near the edge of a tapestry at the other side of the
hall. She kept very still, for it was a usual practice during her

father's visits to have a guard on her to make certain she stayed in her chamber. They feared she would disturb him cooing over that monstrous child. Had she thought it would accomplish anything but get her sent to the Tower, she might have considered breaking in on them, but Mary understood her precarious position.

Nevertheless, she would be free to leave her room if she so desired, and slipped away up the stairwell before the guard could learn she was not in her chamber. He stationed himself by the door and never knew he guarded only two young maids.

On the second floor, the one just below Elizabeth's quarters, she went in search of a quill and paper. There was a good chance the plan forming in her mind would accomplish nothing, but she had to try. The alternative was to not try, and to wonder forever whether something might have come of it.

On a desk in a deserted bedchamber belonging to one of Elizabeth's other servants, she found a quill, dipped it into ink, and wrote on a small sheet of paper a request to be allowed to kiss her father's hand. She signed it "Your Daughter." Then she blotted the paper, folded it over once, and carried it up the stairs.

Outside Elizabeth's apartments, she could hear her father carrying on about the baby. Talking to his attendants as if she were the greatest princess in Europe, he sounded as if he had no other daughter. Mary's heart wrenched. She could remember a time when he had spoken of her that way, and his voice had that warmth when he spoke to her. She drew a deep breath and took the paper to one of the two guards at the door.

"Please take this to my father." She hated how humble she'd become, but desperation had made inroads on her pride. When the guard gave her a skeptical look, for he was a king's guard and she but a bastard girl, she added, "I implore you. Take kindly to a motherless girl."

That touched the man, who may have had children of his own or else simply wished to feel like a hero to the king's daughter. In any case, he took the paper and nodded. Then he disappeared into the inner chambers.

Mary waited under the gaze of the other guard, her fingers twisted together and clenched with nerves that neared panic. She bent her head toward the door, nearly touching the heavy wood with her forehead, as if in prayer. Her heart skipped along at a dizzying pace, and she had to force herself to breathe at all. She heard the guard within interrupt the talk and present the message. There was a brief silence; then the king said, "She wishes to kiss my hand."

Mary's heart sank at his tone of ridicule. She stared at the door as if she might see through it and know the expression on his face.

"Who, Your Grace?" asked one of his attendants.

"Lady Mary."

Mary's body clenched, and she choked at hearing the title her father felt she deserved. Not a princess, as if she weren't his daughter at all. She closed her eyes to keep from weeping. The other men in the room chuckled, and that pierced her through, to have her dearest wish ridiculed by men who were privileged to sit with her father where she was not. She wanted him to take her up in his arms. To show her off the way he had when she was a child. To call her "the greatest pearl in the kingdom" once again. But he would not.

The king said, a hint of anger in his tone, "Tell her she may not. She is to remain in her room until we have gone."

Tears sprang to her eyes, and she could no longer hold them

back. Without waiting for the guard to return, she snatched up her skirts in her fists and fled up the stairwell. Were she to stay behind, she might be escorted to her room to be held under guard, and that would be intolerable. From experience she knew how rough the king's guard could be. On the upper floor of the palace she ducked into a narrow gallery and hid behind a large, thick tapestry. There she cried herself out, in huge, silent sobs.

Here the darkness was warm and comforting for its distance from the others in the palace. Especially she wanted to be away from that horrid baby. She hugged herself and sobbed, until she could cry no longer. Then she waited until it might be safe to venture out in the palace again and not be asked about her reddened eyes and puffy face.

She heard voices again, down in the courtyard below, and made frantic swipes at her eyes and face to dry them. Her ears perked to discern who it was and where they were, lest she be found here in the gallery. She peeked from around the edge of the tapestry and found a door opened onto a terrace on the other side of the hallway. The voices came clearer now, all men of good fellowship on their way from the palace. It had been a short visit, and her father's party was leaving, mounting their horses as they laughed and chattered about a recent hunting incident. Mary slipped from behind the tapestry and stepped out onto a narrow terrace overlooking the yard. Four stories below she saw the men on their horses, waiting as the last of them mounted. One glanced up at the movement on the terrace and made a comment to His Majesty.

Henry looked up. Mary's impulse was to flee back inside, but rather than make the coward's response, she held her ground and gazed at him in return. She couldn't read his expression. He gave only a blank stare. Nobody moved or spoke.

Then Mary sank to her knees and folded her hands. At first there was no reaction, then Henry reined his horse around to face her.

Slowly, with great, dramatic, royal flair, he removed his cap from his head, and with a wide, chivalric gesture he bowed to her from horseback like an Arthurian champion to his lady. It quite took Mary's breath away. She choked on her tears and wished she could run to him and hug his neck. She wished he would tell her all was well and he loved her best. But he did not.

With neither smile nor frown to speak of, he replaced the cap, reined his horse, and spurred away from the palace in full gallop with his men hard behind him.

Mary once more collapsed into weeping and sat on her heels as she watched him go.

Lady Shelton took it upon herself to attend to the lady Mary, who had fallen ill. Everyone else who might help the poor girl had thrown up their hands, calling the situation hopeless, her condition incurable. But they all knew it was unhappiness that ailed Mary. Her father's threats had become pointed, and the grief and terror were too much for her. The governess brought broth and cold compresses, and spoke to her in a low voice in an effort to ease her pain, but always out of earshot of anyone who might report to Norfolk or the Boleyns. God forbid the young woman should die while under her care, but there was only so much she could do without incurring the wrath of the queen. It crossed her mind the queen may have arranged for the girl to be poisoned, and that brought a fear of implication in a plot. Even if there were no poison, or even a plot, the suggestion of it could be ruinous. Regardless of what anyone might do or say, Lady Shelton simply could not let Mary die.

She sent messages to the king, begging for help from physicians. Chapuys's imperial physicians were on hand but resisted any action lest they later be blamed for the death of the king's daughter. The English hated Spaniards, and Henry hated Charles, which made them far too convenient a scapegoat. Even so, they liked to mutter and moan that the king wished for Mary to die, and it almost sounded as if they would be happy to lend a hand to that end. Charles, after all, would have simpler relations with England if not for his aunt and cousin. Though in the event of Mary's death he would make great, indignant noises, he probably would not actually do anything untoward. Charles was nothing if not a practical man. Lady Shelton struggled mightily to hide her disgust with all of them, who would let an innocent girl die to save their own political skins.

A message came from the king, saying that his chief physician thought Mary's condition incurable. There was nothing he could do, and so attending to her would be a waste of time and effort. This was hardly a surprise. Lady Shelton tore the paper and tossed it to the floor. To Chapuys's physician she said, "They all insist there's naught to be done."

"That may be true, madame." Dr. Rodriguez shrugged and looked as if he wished he could be elsewhere.

"You know it is not. There's always something to be done. The only question is whether one has the courage to do it." She wondered how this man was able to call himself a student of Hippocrates.

Mary lay on her bed, pale, unconscious, and shiny with a

thin sheen of perspiration. Occasionally she would rise to consciousness, take some broth, then fall back into an uneasy stupor. Whenever sensible at all, she called for her mother. There was never a reply.

"It is my considered opinion, my lady, that were the senorita taken to her mother's physician, she would have a much better chance of recovery."

"Or if her mother's doctor would come here."

Rodriguez shook his head. "Ah, but you know it is not the art of the doctor from which she would benefit. It is the presence of her mother."

Lady Shelton was forced to allow as that must be true. The girl pined for Catherine, and a visit more than likely would save her life. Both their lives, possibly, for it was rumored the dowager princess was also ailing and was not expected to last any longer than her daughter. But a visit would be impossible. The king would never allow it, especially to save the lives of two people he wished dead but could not execute without a rising among the northern nobility. Not to mention all those commoners who also subscribed to the old religion and would go to war to have back their superstition. "She should be moved to Kimbolton, to be near her mother."

"The king forbids it. He fears a coup, should the two put their heads together at the urging of the imperial ambassador."

That was a distinct possibility as well. There was no telling what havoc might be wrought by a well-loved queen, her angry daughter, and a wily courtier with foreign interests.

"Her mother is the only one who can nurse her without fear of being blamed when she dies."

"When?"

"*If,*" Lady Shelton corrected herself. "If she dies."

"The king has said he will only allow her to be moved near Kimbolton. He won't allow them to meet."

"Not much good that will do her. A mile is as good as ten miles, for that."

The physician shrugged. There was nothing to be done in the face of the king's wishes. Lady Shelton took the damp cloth from Mary's forehead, wet it in the basin, wrung it out, and sighed as she pressed it to the poor girl's gray cheek.

I nearly died that winter. When I was told the Act of Succession would be enforced, and I would be sent to the Tower if I continued to answer only to my rightful title, I was so distraught I succumbed to the illness that brought me to the brink of death. Indeed, I no longer wanted to live, for hope had quite deserted me, and there was no longer any corner of the earth where I might live in safety and keep my honor. To live without honor is not life at all, but craven, unholy existence. Far better to go to God than to remain among those so filled with hate, selfishness, and unbridled pride. But in the end I did survive, for God did have a plan for me. I did not see it yet, but I understood I needed to keep faith in it. That thought returned me to the living. Slowly I made my way back to the world, where I would renew my struggle. Then the next assault came from His Majesty, my father, in the form of persecutions of the Church for its support of my mother. Catholic blood flowed like wine on coronation day.

Jack the Rabbit slipped through the crowd like a shadow, unnoticed by those around him. His slight form and short stature made him appear no more a threat than a young boy. It amused him that rich folks disdained him so well as to give him an easy time of moving in close to their purses. The way he figured it, those purses were often too heavy by far, and it was a wonder anyone could lug them about all day. He did the nobility and wealthy merchants a favor by relieving them of their silver to keep it from burdening them.

Weak-Kneed Willie followed close behind, moving among the onlookers with a grace that belied his size. Together they sought a likely target, and this gathering was sure to be rich with them. It was a traitor they were executing today, and nobody watching was watching his purse. They all gawked and gawped at the scaffold, which held a gibbet, table, and brazier, and gossiped amongst themselves about the condemned man. Only one today, but he was terrible important. Traitors found among priests and such was increasing these days, and everyone had seen the guts cut from those monks at Tyburn a while back, but this here fellow was a shocker, he was. Today the king's victim was the bishop of Rochester, John Fisher. Whoever he was, Jack sure couldn't have told; the cutpurse neither knew nor cared. All he cared was that the crowd was fascinated and wealthy and not paying particular attention to their belongings.

Jack had his dagger out, sharpened to a fine edge fit to shave a royal twat. He came upon a large man with his gut hanging over his belt and his purse, with his mouth agape, staring upward. With one smooth move, Jack bumped into him and severed the thong that held the purse to the belt, then passed it behind him to Willie, who stuffed it into his tunic without so much as a glance at Jack, the purse, or the victim.

"Ho!" cried the fat man. "Watch yourself!"

Jack bowed and scraped as best he could in the press, never making eye contact, and apologized as profusely as he knew how, which was considerable, his position in the world being what it was. Then he looked up at the scaffold and said, "Oy! What's that?"

Immediately the fat man forgot his anger and looked up. In an instant Jack and Willie had moved on and disappeared among the spectators, themselves and the fat man's purse never to be seen again.

By the time the condemned man was brought to the scaffold, four more purses had joined the one in Willie's tunic. Time to repair to a dark corner and watch the execution. Too risky to continue the hunt once the crowd had its blood fever. Too easy to be torn to pieces if he should be found out or even suspected. So they stood near the gate and watched as several of the king's guard escorted the thin, bent old man to his death.

"Hard to believe they'd bother killing him, I say," said Willie.

"How's that?"

"He looks as if he wouldn't last much longer in any case, as old as he is."

Jack shrugged. He'd never understood much of the whys and wherefores of the behavior of his betters. It was too dodgy just keeping his own skin intact, never mind fashing himself about them as had power and money for the purpose.

Folks nearby spoke of the condemned, passing rumors that the king would show mercy this time, and though the brazier suggested otherwise, the rumors might be true. By the accounts overheard, Fisher deserved his fate for writing to Charles V that he should invade England and save them all from the

Lutheran heresy. Jack listened to the talk with mild interest as he fingered inside his tunic the purses Willie had handed back to him. It was a good day's work. By the feel he could tell most of the coins were silver, but some were gold and a couple of small, knobby bits suggested large gems.

Willie said, "I hear he's a cardinal now."

"You don't say?" Jack barely knew what a cardinal was. He had an idea from somewhere they wore red robes but wasn't entirely certain. His thought just then was of how wonderfully oblivious he would be that night once they'd split the money and he could make his way to a public room.

"I do say. I heard the pope made him a cardinal, and he got word of it just last week."

"Fat lot of good that'll do him."

Willie shrugged. "Maybe he'll get a better seat in heaven."

"Dunno." Jack chuckled. "Well, I think he's going to find out in a minute or two."

Even Willie laughed at that, a surprise, since the big fellow had no sense of humor that Jack ever could tell. Then they both fell silent along with the crowd, as the condemned made his final speech in a thready voice inaudible from where they stood. The rope went around his neck, and without further ceremony the executioner drew on the rope to raise him from the boards. He kicked and struggled, and his neck didn't break. Too bad for him. Instead of letting him down while still conscious so his belly could be cut open and his entrails burned, Fisher was left to hang.

"Aye, there's the mercy." Jack nodded to affirm his words. It was plain there would be no blood today, and he was hard put to decide whether he was disappointed. He'd seen the monks die at Tyburn, and it had been a long, loud, messy affair with much screaming and struggling from the condemned and hollering from the crowd. Blood had flowed in rivulets from the scaffold. The stench of bowel and burnt flesh could be smelled for miles on the breeze. This was far quieter, for it was only one man and that one not able to draw breath.

But the poor fool lasted a powerful long time. Almost as if he were breathing after all. Almost, Jack realized in a flash of understanding, as if he were taking care about his neck that it shouldn't break. That he shouldn't die too quickly. It was a show he was putting on for the crowd. He writhed and twisted, but not too much, as his face grew purple and swelled. His tongue swelled to fill his mouth and protrude from his lips. His eyes bulged. And still he lived. A murmur rose amongst the onlookers, and Jack began to wonder if it might have been more merciful to have cut him open and let him bleed. No more painful than hanging, and surely it would have been quicker.

The murmur in the crowd grew, and from nearby Jack heard comments against the king. Those monks, and before that the clairvoyant nun, had been bad enough. The executions were too many, and the Catholics in London had become fearful. That Henry could execute a cardinal was appalling, they said. Jack himself didn't care who the king executed, so long as it wasn't him, but he could see where Henry would need to have a care for his own skin, should this crowd take a notion to rise up and put a stop to the killing. It was an ugly mood they were in today.

But then, it was also none of Jack's affair, for he would be Catholic or Lutheran according to the need of the moment. For a certainty he was going to hell in any case, so his life was committed to the struggle of putting that off as long as possible. He elbowed Willie to get his attention and gestured to him to follow him from the yard. They had money, and he was thirsty.

Mary ate her breakfast as always, in her bedchamber by the fire. The household now resided in Hunsdon, a far nicer palace than Hatfield, and her quarters were improved. It was late spring, but even this house was ever chilly in Mary's estimation, and the hearth did little to rid the room of dampness. She was allowed meat this early in the day, though Elizabeth's household in general did not eat it until noon, for Mary's health depended on it. Without meat for breakfast, she would weaken and possibly relapse. There had been times during the year since her terrible illness when she couldn't keep food down for nearly a fortnight at a time. Even now she'd not recovered the weight she'd lost then. Recurrences of nausea and weakness threatened every day, particularly during winter when it seemed she would never see the sun again. The governess ordered she be given meat rather than let her die.

Mary never knew what to think of Lady Shelton, for she never knew from one moment to the next whether her words would be gentle or harsh. Of course she was in terror of her governess, for the woman was a Boleyn, and therefore associated with the Howards, and could be expected to have only their interests at heart. Were she told to murder, Mary was certain her own life would be forfeit, for she'd seen often enough that most people were cowardly and ever bent to prevailing winds.

The Great Whore had been beheaded the month before, the king no longer having to keep the shrew alive in order to avoid taking back his true wife. Catherine had died the previous January. Now that Anne and her brother, George, were dead, Lady Shelton's brother Thomas was persona non grata at court, but he'd been allowed to live and even to keep his title. His brother-in-law Norfolk was still a strong and ill wind. But though Anne and George were no longer a threat to Mary, there was still Elizabeth, and the Boleyn and Howard families both rested their futures on her. That Lady Shelton had moments when she did not ridicule or castigate and sometimes even behaved in a Christian manner meant nothing. Mary lived every day in fear of her and her relatives.

Her meal finished and the table removed, she began to ready herself for the chapel and morning Mass. This was her favorite time of day, for it brought her the only peace she'd been allowed in her three years in the service of that monstrous child. Since the chapel was small and private, accommodating few people, she was allowed to have her preferred observance for herself and her maids. While in prayer, nobody brought her bad news, or threatened her, or scolded her for her obstinacy. Nobody called her "lady" or "bastard." Her time in the chapel was spent only with God and her chaplain, and even the chaplain often seemed nothing more than a fixture of the room. Like the altar or candles, his presence was comforting, there to facilitate rather than influence. When she was with God, nobody could hurt her.

A shadow appeared at the door. It was one of Lady Shelton's maids. "My lady, you have visitors."

Mary received the news with trepidation bordering on alarm, for there was no longer anyone living she fully trusted. Her mother had left Mary alone in the world with only Ambassador Chapuys and Charles on her side, and even they could be expected to have their own goals in everything. Chapuys was ever pressing her to head a rising among the Catholic lords, a thing her mother had abhorred and she herself looked upon with revulsion. War was never to be desired, and her beloved mother had shown her what honor there was in avoiding it. The food in Mary's stomach was suddenly too heavy, and there was an urge to rid herself of it. She swallowed hard to keep it down. "Who is it?"

"A commission from your father. Norfolk, Sussex, and the bishop of Chichester."

Norfolk. Mary's stomach hitched, and the cold sweat of terror broke over her. Her skin went clammy against her shift, and the chill in the room made gooseflesh all across her neck and arms. Norfolk would have nothing to say she wanted to hear. Her first thought was to have them sent away, but these men were emissaries of her father, so in her profession of obedience, she was forced to meet them. "Where are they?"

"The small chamber to the west of the great hall has been reserved for your meeting. They await you there, and you won't be disturbed."

Mary might have wished it. She heartily yearned for more attendants to bring with her, but the two maids would have to do. She dismissed the messenger, then murmured orders for her maids to ready her and themselves to meet with her father's commissioners. Mass would have to wait, though her longing to flee to the chapel was great.

She entered the chamber with her few attendants and stopped just within the door. She paused to see the three commissioners clustered around the room's small hearth, surrounded by their own attendants who numbered ten or so. Three chairs stood against the wall, but they were blocked by the armored, sword-bearing men milling about. Had Mary somehow imagined this could be a social call, the thought would have fled at sight of these stern carpet knights in breastplates, smelling of horses and stinking of pride. She could see in Norfolk's eyes his anger and evil intent. Certainly he would have his revenge on her for what her father had done to his niece, and never mind that Mary had no influence over the king. Someone would pay, and she was an easy target. Norfolk was just that sort of coward.

Mary gestured to her maids that they should fetch one of the seats and bring it to the hearth. She would have her meeting seated and warm, never mind what Norfolk or his cronies would feel about it. The men were forced away from the chairs as the girls moved to get one, then the girls nudged and crowded them away from the fire as they placed the chair. They moved with an offended reluctance. They were impatient to proceed with the meeting and treated these maneuverings as a stalling tactic.

Mary settled herself into the chair slowly, with as much dignity as she could muster in her terror. Then she addressed Norfolk.

"You wish to speak to me?" As if she had been interrupted while on her way to somewhere else. Somewhere she'd much rather be. Which was true.

Norfolk drew a paper from his tunic and unfolded it. "This is my commission from the king." His tone was perfunctory, as if it were already a given Mary would comply with whatever the king had charged him to request of her, and this was but a formality. "I am to ask two questions of you. The first being, will you repudiate the bishop of Rome and accept the king's ecclesiastical supremacy? The second, will you accept that your mother's marriage was invalid?" He thrust the paper further under her nose as if to hurry her along to her decision. Apparently they had more important things to do that day, and she was keeping these men from them.

Rage rose in Mary, and she was forced to turn her face away for a moment to bring her emotion under control. Her stomach hitched again dangerously, and she choked to keep from vomiting her breakfast. Once she was able to speak, she faced Norfolk again and said calmly, "I will obey my father in all things next to God."

"Your father rules as representative of God."

"I think not."

"That is treason."

The word shot terror through Mary's heart like a bolt, but she struggled to keep Norfolk from knowing it. "If it be treason, then my father will be excessively busy executing traitors, for half his subjects believe it as well." The executions had been many, and she knew the common folk had begun to grumble. Chapuys had long been urging her to rise against her father with them at her back.

"You will acknowledge the king as supreme head of the Church, and his marriage to Catherine as invalid."

"I cannot, for it is falsehood. My mother was not a whore. I am the only legitimate issue of my father. The pope is the divine authority of the true Church. Your statements are lies, and I assure you they will weigh heavy on the soul of he who professes them to be true."

Norfolk reddened. "If you don't sign, you may be executed."

"They say my mother was poisoned. Why doesn't my father do the same to me and have done with it?"

"Odd, the way I hear it the dowager princess's heart was

found to be blackened with evil. I think there's no doubt what her punishment is now for her disobedience to her husband."

"Even more odd you should say that, for the king has insisted he is not her husband."

Norfolk's tone sharpened. "But he is her sovereign, and for that was owed even better obedience. She was wrong in denying him, regardless of the validity or lack of validity of the marriage."

"She was an honorable woman, and that is why she would not put her name to a lie. And that is the very reason I also will not. The king, my father, is not God's authority but rather is himself subject to God's law, and my mother's marriage to him was valid according to that law. I am my father's only legitimate issue, and as an honorable woman I cannot in good conscience sign an oath I know to be untrue. You squander your time here, Your Grace, and I suggest you leave at once." Her head swam, and her stomach seemed to tumble around inside her. She struggled to breathe. The room was too warm, and she regretted sitting so near the fire.

"You are a rude, ungrateful child. I am amazed the king has allowed you to live though you persist in your disobedience. You have indulged in treasonous speech with impunity. Your insistence on keeping your superstitious observance sets a poor example for his subjects. You have stood in the way of his attempts to bring religious reform to his confused and restless subjects—"

"He's himself made them confused and restless." A sharp note entered Mary's voice as her temper rose. "It is because of his selfish whim that they have been unsettled in their beliefs. He's brought chaos and suspicion. And *terror*. The king's subjects are afraid. He's murdered men and women of God and will be punished for it by God." There was a dark silence, then she added, "And so will you."

Norfolk's face flushed, and his men looked as if they would speak on his behalf were they free to insert themselves. His eyes sparked with anger, and his voice lowered to a growl. "I do not believe you are Henry's daughter! No true daughter, even a bastard, would be so disobedient to her father. No honorable woman would be so obstinate in the face of his clearly stated desire."

Mary nearly flinched at the insult that cut deep into the center of her being, but she held firm in the knowledge that she was doing right. "I ... will ... not ... lie!"

"Were you my own daughter, I would dash your brains against this here wall! I would never suffer even my own blood to act so unnaturally. You are an aberration, at variance with every womanly virtue. You are a freakish creature, without honor. You should be put to death and never allowed to influence your father's subjects. You are evil!"

Mary, nonplussed by the duke's vehemence and terrified he might actually snatch her from her chair and throw her against the stone wall by the hearth, fell back on her core position, from which she could not move. "I will obey my father in all things except where his wishes conflict with God's law."

Norfolk made a rude noise of disgust and turned a circle to calm himself in his desperate frustration. Mary could see he was fearful to fail in his mission, and that alarmed her, for she knew a desperate man was also a dangerous man.

Silence fell, and strung out for several moments. Mary saw the duke was thinking hard, struggling for words that would convince her, but there were none. Mary had set herself against this. The room was crowded with men much stronger than herself and her maids, but physical coercion would be a fruit-less struggle, and they seemed to sense it, for violence would only martyr her to the masses of Catholics in the realm. She was prepared to withstand any threat and even go to the block if necessary. Norfolk was powerless against the law of God.

Finally he raised his chin in an effort to salvage some dig-nity and said, "Well, then. I see you are determined to disobey your sovereign, which is not just a criminal act but also a sin."

"It is no sin to decline to obey a sinful command."

Another long silence strung out. He looked around at his men, who said nothing. Some looked in another direction. "We waste our time here, then."

When she saw he'd given in, the knot in her gut loosened some. She drew a deep breath and said softly, "I obey my fa-ther and my sovereign in all things that do not conflict with God's law."

Norfolk swallowed even more annoyance. "Very well. I will relay your answer to the king. I daresay he will not take it kindly."

"I cannot in good conscience put my name to a lie. Were the king truly God's authority, he would understand that."

"My lady would do well to take care in annoying her sover-eign."

"The princess of Wales will submit her body to the will of her sovereign, but her soul is subject only to God."

"I take my leave of you, then."

"By all means, Your Grace. Do proceed in all due haste."

With another glance around at his men, the duke then turned and hurried from the room without so much as a hint of a bow to Mary. Two of the attendants hung back to bow, after assuring themselves their master would not see, and then left. Finally only the women remained.

Mary sat in the chair, trembling. Her maids came to hold her hands, but she barely noticed them. It was all she could do to keep her breakfast from spilling onto the hearth before her.

CHAPTER FOUR

Had I known at the time my father's true feelings, I might not have been so fearful. But it was a risky thing to guess at his thoughts on any matter. I doubt anyone ever truly knew the king's mind, even sometimes the king himself. To be sure, Thomas Cromwell made certain nobody outside the privy chamber knew more than he himself wished, and took full advantage of my father's mercurial nature to influence me. In the end, he succeeded.

Thomas Cromwell sat at his writing desk, quill in hand, scribbling furiously at a letter to Lady Mary. The situation was untenable. Appalling. Norfolk had failed in his ill-advised mission and ruined any chance of that bullheaded girl submitting to the king. He'd known the effort would fail, but saying so to the king would have been as foolish as it was fruitless. Too many men had lost their heads for so much less than what Cromwell himself would be blamed for if Mary could not be brought into line. So long as Mary refused to acknowledge Henry as head of the Church and herself as having no claim to the succession, she was a danger to them all. The letter chastised her for foolishness and warned her of the king's wrath. Indeed, the king had worked himself into a state of near apoplexy at the news of Mary's disobedience. There had been great shouting and pacing about the chamber, ranting accusations of a conspiracy backing Mary in a coup to take his throne. Henry had even taken a swing at his chamberlain with his cane. Cromwell had made great efforts to encourage Henry in his rehabilitation of Mary, calling her penitent and obedient, and now all his work was for naught. In fact, his neck was now stuck out so far he might not be able to retrieve it at all. Norfolk had destroyed any chance of bringing Mary back to court and quelling the grumblings of the Catholic lords, and Henry was irate for the discord and the effort it would now require of him to retain control of his realm. Cromwell wasn't the only courtier in fear for his life on this account.

But even as he wrote the letter to Mary, he knew she would ignore it. She was young, idealistic, and unconvinced of her own mortality. She idolized her stubborn mother, and so was irrationally stubborn herself. He needed to impress her vulnerability on her. It crossed his mind what a shame it was there had been no excuse to execute Catherine when she was alive, for it would have made as indelible an impression on the daughter as had her mother's steadfast stubbornness. So much would have been so much simpler, had Catherine died sooner than she did.

His secretary entered the chamber and announced the presence of several members of the privy council. Cromwell's first impulse was to send them away, to give him an opportunity to think through the problem in search of a solution, but instead he drew a deep breath, let it out slowly, and set the paper aside for the time being. He dropped his quill into the ink pot and sat back in his chair.

"Let them come," he told his attendant.

Norfolk and the rest filed in. Cromwell stood, and noted the absence of some council members as each paid his due respect to the earl. "Where are Exeter and Fitzwilliam?"

Norfolk's eyes narrowed, as if to say Cromwell should know the answer to this, but he replied regardless. "We thought it best to discuss this away from ears too sympathetic to the king's daughter."

Cromwell nodded, his real question having been answered. The purpose of this gathering was to discuss their pressing problem. He sat and leaned back in his chair and gestured for the others to find seats or stand as they wished. Most of them settled around the conference table, but Norfolk posted himself by the fire, where he could dominate the room and keep himself warm at the same time.

Cromwell opened the discussion by addressing Norfolk. The man was an arrogant fool, had done incalculable damage with that arrogance, and needed to be put on the defensive. "Norfolk, you were a miserable failure with the girl."

The duke didn't blink, but was ready to defend himself and responded before Cromwell was quite finished uttering the sentence. "She's as stubborn as her mother and doesn't understand the severity of her situation."

"She believes her father's heart is soft." Cromwell knew just how soft Henry was not.

"His heart is a woman's, not to put too fine a point on it. For all his blustering, you know he'll never execute his own blood."

"He has. You remember Buckingham."

"You understand my meaning. He'll never admit publicly she's different—perhaps not even admit it to himself—but Mary is of his own body. Impossible to divorce from him, no matter how intensely even he might desire it. You have children; you know what it is to be a father. Surely he believes if she were executed, he would be the one to bleed."

"Then we must use more subtle means. Stop blundering about in full view like drunken commoners."

Norfolk raised his chin at the rebuke, then said with a cold edge to his voice, "What do you suggest, then?"

"Charles, perhaps? He has her ear."

"He's also smarter than one might think by the look of him. The king has long underestimated the emperor. Charles would never become a tool for Henry. In fact, it is Henry who has more than once served the purposes of Charles."

Cromwell sat back in his large, heavy chair and pressed a finger to his lips. Then he said, "Surely he would understand the benefit of reconciliation with England. He's no money for his campaigns. With the king's goodwill, he could turn his attention elsewhere and not have to watch his own back. Henry would do that for him. Indeed, he's done it before."

Norfolk could barely contain his impatience, but managed to not blurt whatever it was that rose to his lips just then. He hesitated but still spoke irritably. "You've not been paying attention, Cromwell. Have you not noticed how Charles dragged his heels for the sake of his aunt? Surely you're aware he does not wish to appear too sympathetic to the Lutheran cause.

He's no fool. He's as invested in defending the pope as is anyone else. The Vatican is the source of Charles's own authority. You can't possibly not understand that."

"Of course. But the sack of Rome—"

"Was not ordered by the emperor. By all accounts he lost control of mercenaries who rioted for lack of pay. Any more he's clinging to his power with every nefarious means at his disposal, and is not likely to squander it and alienate its source by appearing to harm the cause of the pope. Don't be a fool, Thomas. Charles will be no help to us in bringing his insufferably Catholic, pope-loving cousin to heel."

Cromwell fell silent at this outburst delivered in a hard, angry tone, lest he respond likewise. He needed a more level head than Norfolk was demonstrating at the moment. After a pause to calm himself, he said quietly, "Then what do you suggest?"

A knock came on the door, and the chamberlain was bade to enter. He said, "Begging your pardon, my lord, but Ambassador Chapuys wishes a conference, if you might be available."

Cromwell said irritably, "Do I appear available?"

The chamberlain flushed red and bowed. "I apologize, but I'm afraid he insisted." He had that look of frustration worn by servants caught between two conflicting duties.

Cromwell at first frowned, but then a flash of inspiration brought a tiny smile to his lips. He said, "Yes, in fact. Escort him in immediately."

With a look of profound relief, the chamberlain bowed and left. Norfolk opened his mouth, but Cromwell cut off the objection he knew was coming.

"I have a thought. Bear with me on this, all of you, and be silent for the nonce."

"But—"

"Trust me. This is the very thing we need."

Chapuys entered the room in a bluster of indignation. "I wish to protest," he said.

Cromwell said nothing at first, letting the ambassador's ire falter, then finally deflate, before addressing him. Once the silence had strung out to his satisfaction, he said, "What is your complaint, then? What thing is so terribly important?"

Chapuys blinked at the brusque manner but proceeded with his mission. "I have a message from Lady Mary at Hunsdon. She tells me she's been ill-treated." He looked over at Norfolk, and it was plain the complaint had been about him specifically. But that was neither here nor there as far as Cromwell was concerned.

"She is as well-treated as anyone of her status should be."

"She is the daughter of the king."

"She's *a* daughter of the king. An illegitimate one. She is treated accordingly." Chapuys opened his mouth to press his protest, but Cromwell interrupted him. "In fact, given that she's also a traitor deserving execution, I would point out that she's been treated far better than is her right. She should be pleased to keep her head, after her refusal to sign the Act of Succession."

Chapuys blinked. "The king would not execute her."

"Press him, and learn whether he would or not."

"There would be a rising."

"Convince the king of that. I've tried, but to no avail." Cromwell held up his palms in defeat. "Henry is convinced the only way to rid himself of the thorn in his side is to cut it out. He will bleed, but only a little. And if not, then by the time he learns that lesson, it will be too late for Lady Mary."

A shadow came over the eyes of the ambassador. His lips

pressed together in a hard, straight line. One of the council members sitting before Cromwell bent his head and looked at the floor. Cromwell resisted the urge to glance at him, lest he be found struggling against a smirk, for he wouldn't want Chapuys to glimpse it. He regretted not emptying the room before talking to the ambassador. Finally Chapuys took a deep breath and asked, "How resolved is the king?"

"I would say he could forgive her resistance, should she submit to the king immediately. The king would have her sign a statement couched in acceptable terms."

"And if not?"

"Expect her to be dealt with by year's end."

That brought another long silence, as the ambassador's thoughts raced. Cromwell could not see them in his eyes, for the Spaniard was an experienced diplomat, but he knew what must be going through that wily Continental mind, and he waited. Then he said softly, "I tell you this as warning, in the best interests of the Lady Mary. Be assured I have no desire to see her headless."

Chapuys then said, "I will take your words under advisement. The Empire wishes for a reconciliation between the king and his daughter."

"Very well. Perhaps I can convince the king to stay his hand long enough for you to apprise Mary of her situation. I will have the statement to you on the morrow, to be relayed to Lady Mary at the earliest opportunity."

"I have not said I will encourage her in either direction."

"I will have the statement to you. I urge you to take the wise course and press it on her so that she signs."

Chapuys replied to that with a polite, formal, and utterly noncommittal bow, then he took his leave.

The council watched him go, waited until he must be out of earshot, then a round of chuckling broke out in the room. Cromwell grinned and hoped Chapuys was sincere in his concern for the life of his little friend.

To Norfolk he said, "I suggest you arrange for the arrests of Sir Anthony Browne, Sir Francis Bryan, and Lady Hussey."

"Whatever for?"

"Why, they're friends of Lady Mary. And the king will need to dismiss Exeter and Fitzwilliam from the privy council. He must make a huge, angry show of it. A thorough interrogation of Lady Mary's attendants wouldn't be amiss, either. Norfolk, that would be a task best accomplished by yourself, I think. Let the king's thorn and her ambassador friend know that the king means to excise her and her cronies from his court and his realm. And possibly even from this earth."

Norfolk nodded, and his smile caused even Cromwell to shudder.

Mary stood before the several chests stacked atop a trunk in her bedchamber. The ironbound wooden boxes were old and battered, and they had just been delivered by servants of the king. Mary knew what lay inside them but hesitated to open them, for she feared it would be too much for her. They were jewels belonging to the late Anne Boleyn, given to her by her father. Mary's maids stood aside, awaiting their mistress's pleasure, their hands folded before them and their heads lowered a bit out of respect for this moment.

She sighed. "Please," she told them. "Do wait outside the door. I wish to be alone."

They both nodded with tender sympathy. They knew what

Mary would see when she opened the chests. The two let themselves out the door and left Mary to stare at the chests once more. Finally she reached for the nearest one, lifted the iron latch, and opened the lid.

There, resting on a bed of black velvet, was a necklace that had once belonged to Catherine, which had been among those wrested from her while Anne was queen. Every necklace, brooch, and ring Catherine owned had been taken by the Great Whore. Sight of it brought a flood of memories and an overwhelming longing to see her mother again. The grief of Catherine's passing washed over her anew. Tears stung Mary's eyes, and she touched the enameled gold with a light finger. It felt warm in spite of the cold room, as if Catherine herself still warmed it, though it hadn't touched her body in years.

Then Mary closed the lid of that box and opened another. A collection of rings and brooches, all belonging to Catherine and appropriated by Anne. One by one she opened the boxes, and each returned her to the days when her mother wore these things as queen. Mary quite willingly forgot they'd ever been in the possession of the Great Whore.

She came to a necklace of finely wrought enameled gold roses alternating with the initial *K*. Mary picked it up and held it in her fingers. The links draped over them and hung heavy with gold, pearls, and rubies. She pressed it to her cheek, wishing her mother were there to wear it again. She sank to a nearby chair, curled into herself, and wept.

Everyone at court and at Hunsdon thought my rehabilitation would be immediate and complete the very instant that Boleyn woman was dead. Everyone except my father. Truly I would have submitted all within my power to give for the sake of his regard, but my conscience would never allow the very thing he required. I could never deny the validity of my mother's marriage. I was invited to court and much was made of me on the face of it, but still my father withheld forgiveness. He did not value me as his daughter, though his new wife, Jane, urged it on him. Because I could not give him the one thing he demanded, he would not give me the one thing I desired. Jane understood the political need for my presence in court, but for my father and myself, politics were the lesser concern.

"Understand that I am your friend, Your Highness," said Chapuys. "Always."

Mary gazed at him across the supper table, where he'd just settled to eat. One of Mary's maids stood between them to serve the supper of venison and baked garlic, and Mary addressed the ambassador with her head tilted to the side to see around her. "Of course, Excellency. You are my only living friend, aside from Charles." Though it was true she trusted Chapuys more than nearly everyone, she still held a reserve. One thing she'd learned in recent years was that, aside from God, there was nobody with her best interests at heart, and even God had his own purpose. To God she would bend her will; all others were subject to question.

"I wonder if you have thought of the risk you take by defying your father. Not signing the Act of Succession is technically treason."

"I've been allowed to go without signing the lie."

"That was before Anne's death."

"All the less reason for signing, now that she no longer is whispering in the king's ear. We all should be free now of her oppressive influence."

"On the contrary, Your Highness. Now that she is gone and your rehabilitation has begun, the king must make clear his position on certain points. It would not be good for certain factions to assume too much change. I've been given an Act of Submission for you to sign." From a pocket he removed a wallet of papers tied with a thong and rested it on the table next to the single sheet. "I believe if you will do this, all will be well between you."

"He's always made himself quite clear. He hates me, he hated my mother, and he wishes I'd never been born." The thought made her throat tighten with the promise of tears, particularly when she saw agreement in Chapuys's eyes. She poked at her food, which was a nice bit of venison, but all of a sudden she had no appetite.

"He wishes for a son with his new bride."

Of course he did; everyone knew that, and Mary understood the need for a male heir. Now that her mother was gone to God and her father widowed, she had no objection to his new marriage, and a brother would not be amiss in the greater scheme of things, even were he a Protestant. Jane was moderate in her view of the old religion, and as tolerant as any Protestant in Mary's acquaintance. "His marriage to Jane is valid. A son would succeed to the throne regardless of my status."

"If she gives him daughters, he would prefer them for the sake of his new wife and a Protestant successor. He wishes for a smooth succession. To leave it up to the divided nobility would be folly."

It crossed Mary's mind that the risk would have been a great deal less had the king not split with Rome. But she didn't need to tell Chapuys that, and so left it alone.

He pressed his case. "Understand that his new bride is taking your part. She smoothes the way for you at every opportunity."

Mary nodded. She suspected it had been at Jane's urging that the king had returned Catherine's jewels.

She said, "And if there are no children?"

"Every contingency must be made clear. The status of yourself and the king's other daughter and any future children needs to be understood by all, so there will be no question of who has the right to succeed when the time comes."

For a brief moment Mary wished Jane to be barren, to never have even one child, boy or girl. It was a fate she feared for herself because of her father's lack of interest in making a marriage contract for her. The terror of it was the darkest thought she had, darker than her own execution, for she prayed every day for marriage and children but never for unending time on earth.

Chapuys continued. "If there are no other children, you will have as solid a claim to the throne as anyone living."

Mary looked at him. "Elizabeth?"

"She cannot be declared any more illegitimate than you have been. Given that her mother, even in death, is in bad odor with the king, you are likely to have equal footing at least."

Equal footing with that monstrous child. Elizabeth was not quite three years old. She was as bright a girl as anyone in the household had ever seen, but still was only three. Mary thought of what that might mean, should Jane turn out to be barren. A tiny ray of hope slipped through the overcast clouding her future.

But then that hope died at the thought of signing a blatant lie that besmirched the memory of her mother. Equal footing was still not right, for she knew herself to be legitimate by God's law. Elizabeth was not.

"I cannot sign something I know to be untrue. My mother's marriage was valid. I know she went to her husband intact, because she told me so and because had she not, he would have said so at the time rather than continue an invalid marriage and thereby participate in her lie. Therefore I am a legitimate daughter of the king. To state otherwise would be a sin."

Chapuys considered his next words carefully and cleared his throat before speaking. "My dear friend, there is something else you must consider."

"What is that?"

"I have reason to believe that if you do not comply with the king's wish, he will have you executed."

Her stomach rolled with alarm. She shut her eyes, then opened them to look at him. "He would not."

"I thought that once, but now I believe it to be true. This marriage to Lady Jane has caused him to want all that went before to be gone. To make a clean breast of the future, if you will."

"He wants me out of the way for the sake of convenience."

Patiently, Chapuys repeated his earlier point. "He wishes to make certain there is no difference of opinion about the rights of any future children."

"Who aren't even born yet." Better to murder the extraneous heirs, just in case there would be new ones. Her cheeks warmed, and she laid her fingers against them. She would soon be ill if he continued to press her.

"He wishes to make *certain*."

Mary sighed. It was logical, though the cruelty of it appalled her. "He would execute me if I refuse?"

"If you give him an excuse to execute you. The thing to do is to not allow him any reason. Bide your time, see what the future may bring. God will understand."

She looked at Chapuys and for the first time actually considered the possibility of signing that wretched paper. But she still couldn't bring herself to put her name to a lie. "I cannot."

"I fear you must, to save your own life."

"Then my life is forfeit, as would my mother's have been. For what good is my life without my honor?"

Chapuys held up a finger for the idea he wished to present, and a sly smile lifted the corners of his mouth. "I believe I have found a solution to that." He reached into a coat pocket and drew out a folded paper. Carefully, he unfolded it and pressed it flat against the table. "Here is a statement I've drafted. It says you signed the Submission without ever having read it."

Mary's interest perked. To sign the Submission unread then sign a statement to the effect that she had not read it before signing would not be a lie, and it would clear her of treason. She reached for the paper and turned it toward herself, but carefully, touching only the edge with the tip of her finger, as if it were dirty and she did not wish to smudge herself. Argument could be made that she knew the contents of the Submission, but this statement drafted by Chapuys only referred to the reading of the thing, not the understanding of it.

Chapuys continued. "This would save your life and your honor both."

Life with honor. The thought brought a heady sense of hope that all might one day be well.

Chapuys then said, "I believe—most sincerely—that God has a purpose for your life, Your Highness."

Now she looked at him to read his face.

"By deserting the true faith, your father has done great damage to your country. He's split his people into factions, turned brother against brother, torn families asunder, created a climate of fear, and plundered the Church for his own gain. He's usurped the authority God gave to his representative on earth and used it against the very people who must trust him to rule wisely. He has not done so."

Chapuys paused to let her respond, but Mary kept silent that he might continue.

He said, "You are, by God's law, the only legitimate issue of your father the king. You are the princess of Wales, and nobody can rightly deny it to you. God has made you that. And all things have a purpose in him. That is what we live by. It is the core of our faith."

She nodded. Those facts were the center of her existence and the support of her will to live. She was nothing if not an honorable, legitimate daughter.

"I believe you are not meant for execution. You are meant to one day sit on the throne of England. I believe with all my heart that you are destined to return your countrymen to the old belief, their beloved religion. You are to bring England back to truth."

Mary's heart raced. It was true. She knew the instant he said it, it must be true. Suddenly all the years of fear and heartbreak made sense. It was God's plan to ready her for the destiny in store. Once more life held a future for her, and it warmed her heart to finally know and accept the rightness of what had happened to her, and that her path was clear. In that moment of clarity, all doubt lifted from her like a great weight she'd been carrying and now could put down. She would sign the Submission to save her own life, for it was the only way to accomplish the thing so plainly laid out for her.

CHAPTER FIVE

Even the musicians faltered and gawked when Lady Mary entered the king's presence chamber for the first time since signing that dreadful statement. The full breadth of the great hall conversations dwindled to a halt, and everyone in the room stared shamelessly to see how it would be between the king and his newly obedient daughter.

With his lute on his knee, Niccolò Delarosa paused in his playing but picked back up and smoothly rejoined his fellow players in the music as he watched that young woman cross the room. He'd always thought the girl far prettier than was said of her. Far from the shifty-eyed harridan of rumor, she owned a regal beauty that, though a bit mannish after the fashion of her very manly father, was nonetheless appealing. He wished for her to smile, for he thought it might brighten her face and relieve its edges. But as she approached the king, her mouth hardened, and though the corners of it turned up, it could hardly be called a smile. Niccolò saw fear in her eyes. Her gaze never left the face of the king, and her eyes widened a bit as she drew closer to him.

For the king's part, there was no emotion to be found anywhere on his face or person. He sat his throne as still as marble and as hard. He'd gotten the abject submission he wanted, and yet he remained as distant from his daughter as before. Like a statue without thought, history, or future.

Niccolò thought him a pig.

The king's right hand rested on the cane he used for walking, the rings on his fingers glittering beneath the flickering light of nearby braziers. Especially the one on his thumb danced with an eerie light. It was set with a brilliant ruby called the Regal of France, plundered from the tomb of Thomas à Becket. The thing sparkled and shone as if it were itself aflame, and the king set his hand so all could see it and know his triumph over the Church.

Niccolò hated him for it. The destruction of the saint's tomb was sacrilege. The English king, with his penchant for drama and ceremony, had brought the dead saint to trial for treason, found him guilty in absentia, and burned his bones, dry these past several centuries. All so he could steal from the Church what did not belong to him. It was said the stolen treasure amounted to nearly a ton, hauled away by sixteen strong men. Sixteen of them! So much wealth! The thought was infuriating. The gold and jewels brought by pilgrims for the sake of the martyred saint beloved of God and his people were not intended for the fat English king. They belonged in the tomb, dedicated to the glory of God and Saint Thomas. But now it was all gone. All was now part of the wealth Henry had stolen from the Church.

Niccolò eyed the king, his face bland as always, never letting on his opinion, for opinions—or even emotions—were the death of musicians. He was in the king's court for the pleasure of listeners only, to sing ballads that reflected only the will of the king and never to reveal a thought or desire of his own. His friend Mark Smeaton had not been so circumspect. The poor, unsophisticated English fellow had not been so subtle, and had been a victim of the bloodbath last May that had claimed three other men and the queen. Executed, he was. Tortured and executed for smiling at the queen once too often and because the king needed to manufacture evidence of adultery against his wife. A tiny bit too much pleasure in the presence of a beautiful woman had been the poor fool's undoing. Since then, Niccolò hadn't dared to smile at anyone.

He watched Lady Mary approach the king and never let even his curiosity show on his face. He played his instrument with all the talent and skill allotted him by God, and watched to see how this meeting would play out. His heart was with Mary, and he hoped all would be well with her.

Halted before the dais where her father sat, Mary dropped immediately into a curtsy so deep she must have knelt on the stone floor, her skirts spread around her in a near perfect circle, so smooth was her descent.

"Rise," said the king.

Mary obeyed and looked up at him with a face clearly filled with hope. What she hoped for, Niccolò couldn't imagine. What the cruel king had to offer was surely nothing but pain. The poor girl should know that by now. But she gazed up at her father as if the man still thought her his daughter, and it broke the Italian musician's notably soft, romantic heart.

"How now, Lady Mary?" asked Henry.

A shadow crossed the young woman's face, but she maintained her brave smile and accepted. "I do well, Your Majesty."

"Welcome to Westminster. Have you settled in? Are your accommodations to your liking?" His words were polite, but his demeanor was not. Still no emotion warmed him.

The hesitation to reply was ever so slight. She answered, "They are. I thank Your Majesty heartily for your generosity in allowing me at court."

Henry nodded, plainly of the opinion that he was generous to have forgiven her disobedience. For weeks Niccolò had overheard the raging debate among the courtiers over various political pros and cons of bringing Mary back into the fold. There had been a great to-do over her rehabilitation. Not everyone thought it a good idea, and the king had waffled horribly, as he had on nearly everything throughout his reign. It was plain there was still much yet standing between Mary and her father.

Niccolò gazed at her pretty, young face and wondered if the king would be so cruel to her as to search among his musicians for a match for her. The thought blossomed in his mind as a nice fantasy he toyed with for the moment. He would have believed such a thing of Henry, heartbreaking though the insult would be for Mary, and a brief heat of desire rose in the musician for the king's unloved daughter. He could love her, to be sure. Were he permitted, he would take her to himself and keep her from any more hurt. Protect her from the world. She was a flower of piety, beloved by God, and he could be her sheltering tree if only permitted.

But then he realized how ridiculous that would be, for even the most hated bastard daughter of the most minor king would never go to a landless foreign commoner who made his living by music. Certainly Henry would never allow his own daughter to marry someone such as he. With a sigh of regret, Niccolò turned his attention to his playing and forgot the former princess as he daydreamed about the kitchen wench he would pursue later that evening.

I wanted to marry. With all my heart, I wished it. Marriage and children were the greatest fulfillment I could have hoped for, even greater than sitting on the throne of England. If God made me for the purpose of one day becoming queen and restoring faith to the English people, then surely he also made me to provide the realm with a clear successor. Furthermore, though I was properly innocent of most aspects of relations between men and women, I was not averse to learning about them within the bounds of holy matrimony. When I was very young I dreamed Charles would take me away from England on a white charger, to Spain where I would be his loving wife and bear him many children. Though he married someone else, that dream never quite died. For the rest of my days I clung to the belief that somewhere there existed a man who might love me. My father no longer loved me, Charles no longer loved me, but surely there was someone, somewhere, who would. I prayed every day for God to send him to me.

The masque was well-attended. There was barely enough room in the great hall for the musicians to play without interference from so many dancers. Their backs were all to a wall, and it annoyed Niccolò to be so cramped with his lute. A rest was called, and the players set their lutes, flutes, and drums to the side while the king's guests admired the performance of a mummer at the other end of the hall. The press of people made the room too warm, and Niccolò thought to slip outside to breathe a little. He deftly moved among the revelers dressed in dramatic costumes ornamented with feathers, fur, and extremely costly baubles, keeping an eye to the floor in case there might be a shiny bit fallen from someone's costume he might rescue. All he found tonight amid the scattered reeds were bits of broken feathers and chunks of dried mud from dancers' boots.

Sight of the king's eldest daughter, finally with a smile on her face, brought him up short. A surge of affection warmed him, and he noted the shallow dimples aside her mouth were present. At the moment she was gay enough for a genuine smile that made slight indentations in her cheeks and brightened the room for him. Her eyes sparkled with infectious joy. Plainly she was enjoying herself.

Niccolò was about to move on and take his air, but paused when a man disguised as a wolf in black mask and black velvet costume embroidered with red piping approached Lady Mary and addressed her roughly. Niccolò frowned. He didn't like the sound of it and stood ready to intervene if the rude fellow overstepped too much.

The wolf-man was Francis Bryan; Niccolò recognized the voice and build. Bryan had been at the mead too much and seemed barely able to stand as he wobbled and yawed above Mary. He addressed her with a wide grin and stood too close. She leaned back, but in the crowded room could not step away. Her smile remained, but she seemed confused, perhaps even flustered.

"Oh, aye, what a lovely woman you are!" His grin was over-full of teeth, and his tone was an attempt at seduction, though to Niccolò it sounded smarmy and rude. It carried none of the respect due her, for her innocence if naught else.

Mary blushed. "Thank you, kind sir. You are too generous."

He bowed deeply to her, then straightened. "Not at all. You brighten my soul with your smile." Niccolò frowned at the too-forward man. The urge to interrupt was nearly unbearable, but the musician held his tongue until Mary might indicate she desired help.

Her smile brightened further, but she stammered, as if not certain how to respond. "Good sir, I . . . I find you too familiar by half."

"Ah, but your beauty moves me to be forward. Forgive me, my lady, for I see I've offended you. I would that you might allow me to make apology in private. A room away from the noise and crowd, perhaps?"

Now the smile died. Bryan attempted to take her hand, possibly to kiss it or draw her toward the door, but she re-trieved it and held it behind her back. "Certainly not. Please make your apology at once, then be on your way."

He leaned in toward her again, and said loudly, with an edge of bullying anger, "Do you not think me handsome enough for you?"

"I do not think any man handsome enough to make me for-get myself. Now, leave me, or I will call my father's guard and have you arrested."

A howl of laughter burst from nearby, and the crowd parted to find the king standing with his fists set on his hips, dressed as a harlequin in bright colors, with bells on his hat and shoes, bellowing with hearty amusement. "Well," he said, "it seems the rumors about my sheltered daughter are true."

Mary's eyes went wide, and a deep flush spread over her face and down her neck.

Henry continued. "So, Bryan, it would seem she knows no unclean speeches and is as innocent as they say." Everyone in earshot, which included nearly everyone in the room, began to laugh.

Bryan, quite forgetting about Mary, joined the laughter and turned to address the king. "I would never have believed it possible in this court. As ribald as are this crew, I should think her virtue would have been compromised long before now." He said it as criticism, as if Mary were somehow deficient for her innocence.

The two of them chuckled, shook their heads over the marvel of it, and wandered away, leaving Mary to stare after them with her jaw dropped open and her skin aflame with embarrassment. Others around her found things to take their attention from her, and still she gaped at her father. Finally she looked around for someone to talk to, found nobody, and fled the room.

I was mortified. That anyone would think it necessary to test my virtue, even less that my father should doubt me! And so publicly! I remained in my quarters for an entire day, seeing nobody but my ladies and chaplain, and eating nothing at all. I prayed, and that calmed me, to know I was accepted by God, that he knew I was an honorable woman and did not doubt it.

CHAPTER SIX

Peter Barnacle started out early with his basket of apples from the small stand of trees by his house. It was his house now. Father and mother were both gone, and that left him to care for his three sisters, two older and one younger, and the younger was a handful. She would be pregnant before they all knew it, if he couldn't marry her off quickly. The older ones were nearly spinsters, so their marriages would be hasty and not particularly advantageous. Unfortunate for them, but his betrothal to Ruth was already two years old, and he could no longer afford to bear the burden of three unmarried sisters.

Today he needed to be in London by mid-morning, and the walk was long, the basket heavy. The weather had grown a mite cold, and so he wore his long woolen coat against the wind. Threadbare spots at the elbows let in the cold, but there was nothing for it. No money for new clothes this year, nor last year, and more than likely not next year, either. He hunched his shoulders and trod onward, the basket handles tied with a rope slung over his shoulder, head bent, his back already protesting the weight.

He needed a good price for his fruit, more than most years, because he'd lost nearly half the yield from those trees to vagabonds. Stolen while still unripe. The countryside was thick with thieves plundering fields and orchards. Of course, there were always thieves about. It was the way of things, and as Jesus said, the poor would always be with them. But last winter there had been more than the usual number of beggars wandering the roads. This year they seemed everywhere. One couldn't step outside the house without being accosted by a man with a ragged tonsure begging for food. And the women! Oh, so many women wandering around loose! Nuns reduced to begging and prostitution. Monks and nuns turned out by the destruction of the monasteries, their lands confiscated by the crown and their gold and silver hauled away by the cartload.

Peter had been particularly appalled by tales of recent events in London. Rumors abounded of executions and suicides. It was as if the entire city had gone mad. Lack of respect for the law was giving rise to random shootings and stabbings. Some were robberies but some not. Many killings seemed to be to no purpose. One woman had cut her own throat at the urging of Satan. She lived long enough to repent and so was given last rites and proper burial, but the event made Peter wonder about the sanity of everyone he saw. Sometimes, when hearing people talk and rant about evil in the world, it seemed as if he himself were the only rational man within a day's walk.

Ahead he saw a thin line of smoke rising from a campfire.

For a certainty it was a campfire and not a house. There was no house on this section of road. And until today, there had been no squatters. That unsettled him and stopped him in his tracks. He stood very still in the middle of the path, thinking. Whoever these people were, they weren't from nearby and therefore were not to be trusted. He needed to get past, but didn't know who he might find in the clearing ahead. Trusting too much in the goodness of his fellow man, even when they were former monks and nuns, was getting to be a dangerous game these days.

But he couldn't go back. He'd come too far down this path to circle back and take another. He needed to make it to London and sell these apples.

But if he passed near the encampment and found himself accosted by men with ill intent, he might lose the apples entirely. He turned and looked back the way he'd come and was alarmed to find two men standing there. He caught them approaching, but they halted when he spotted them. They stared at him, unmoving. Then their gaze shifted to something behind him, and he turned again. A woman stood there, having stepped onto the path from the encampment. She wore only a shift, and her short-cropped hair stuck out in all directions. The men wore tonsures and nightshirts. None owned shoes, and all were filthy except for their hands and faces. He stared at the men, thinking they would be the greatest danger to him.

"Ho, good fellow!" One of them raised a hand in greeting. He was hesitant, as if he were afraid Peter might run off. And that was Peter's foremost thought. He glanced around at the surrounding woods for an escape, but there was none. These men had chosen their site well. The woods were thick, and his burden of apples heavy. He was forced to stay and face the vagabonds.

The two men approached, and the woman came up from behind. Peter stepped to the side so he could see all three at once. He nodded a noncommittal greeting and grasped the handle of his basket all the harder.

The other monk said, "Well met, fellow traveler." The three of them had been a long time from the monastery, their story told by sunken cheeks and red-rimmed eyes. Dry lips cracked, and there was a reedy, papery quality to this one's voice.

"Well met, Father."

The first monk came directly to the point. "Might you have a bite of food to spare for three hungry wanderers? We've had none for days, nor shelter for months. I fear we may expire soon except for the charity of good men such as yourself." He glanced at the basket and surely knew what was in it.

How the monk knew Peter was a good man was anybody's guess, for often Peter himself wasn't certain. For instance now, when he stood before three starving people, holding a large basket of apples, and all he could think of was how to get away without being chased.

As the silence lengthened, the monks' smiles faltered, and the speaker nodded. Then, without the least rancor, he said, "I see. Very well, we have faith God will provide." He held on to his pleasant smile, though it was strained. The other two weren't so strong, and Peter could see the desperation in them both. In all three, really, for the speaker's eyes held a terror of starvation of the sort Peter had known, but not in many years.

"I'm sorry," he said.

"I understand." The monk stepped back to give Peter leave. "God be with you, my son."

The other two repeated the salutation and also stepped back.

Peter mumbled, "And also with you." And he stepped between them to be on his way.

But after only a few steps he halted and couldn't go any farther. As much as he wanted to take these apples to market—he *needed* to take them—he couldn't bring himself to leave these people to starve. He turned back. Saying nothing, he set his basket on the ground and untied the handles, then he reached in for six apples and handed them to the monk.

Relief filled the air, palpable as the three realized they would not starve that day. "Thank you. Thank you, and bless you, kind fellow." The monk muttered a blessing in Latin over the food, then portioned out the apples to his companions.

Peter looked back in the basket at the remaining apples and said, "Tell me, Father. Do you think that, in the absence of bread, one might have Holy Communion with a bit of apple?"

The three went still. The nun looked around, her cheek bulging with fruit, as if making sure they weren't overheard, then looked to her companion to know his answer.

The monk frowned, thinking hard. It wasn't the sort of question one answered lightly, for the sacraments were too important to be improperly done. The fate of one's immortal soul hung in the balance. Slowly he said, "I think that God provides us with what we need. If apples are all to be had, then that is what God has provided, and they should be sufficient." There was another moment of hard thought, and he added, "Also, in the end the food becomes the body of Christ. Whatever it may have been at the start, it no longer is when it becomes that."

Peter nodded. It made sense. "Father, would you administer

Communion and take my confession?" It had been ever so long since he'd had the comfort of absolution. A weight of sin made his heart heavy, and he longed for the days when he could have the sacrament and not fear arrest.

The monk's reply was immediate and eager. "Certainly, my son! By all means, I would be honored to serve you."

Peter took a seventh apple, and his dagger from his belt, and cut it into four pieces, then cut the core from each piece. After returning the dagger to his belt, he held the quarters in his palms toward the monk who performed the transubstantiation as best he could, standing on a path in the middle of a forest. Once the pieces had become Christ, the four of them knelt for Communion.

They had no wine, but they made do with what God had provided.

The question of religion was a daily concern. By law the old observance had become a criminal act. Certain privileged people were allowed to have Mass said the old way, and I was able to have my Catholic worship so long as I kept it private. On the face of it one might think it sufficient to be allowed to worship alone. But it wore on my soul to be surrounded by people so disapproving of the one thing that gave me solace in life, and I knew a great number of my countrymen felt the same way.

Mary enjoyed spending some afternoons with her new stepmother. Sensible, pious, kind Jane was a breath of air after the years living in terror of that harridan Anne. Though much of her time was spent in the chapel, and she occupied as many afternoons as she could exercising with her horses, she often sat with Jane and some needlework or reading. It was a restful and sometimes enlightening time. Jane, after all, was closest to the king and, aside from Cromwell, knew his thoughts better than most at the moment. There was much to be learned from her, and Mary was wise enough to plumb that source.

"Have you found a suitable chaplain yet, Mary?" Jane wet the end of her thread and held it to the needle in her other hand. That hand turned a bit in order to have the pale skin of her forefinger behind the needle's eye, the better to find the hole and know where to put the thread. One or two tries, and the thread slipped through. Deftly she pulled it and rolled a knot off her index finger.

"I have. At least, he suits me. I await word from my father as to whether he agrees the priest suits me."

Jane made a noncommittal hum. It was anyone's guess whether Henry would approve the appointment. Furthermore, they both knew he would take his own regal time in deciding, and Mary would make do with her temporary chaplain who did not care for the old rites. "Perhaps," she said, "if you were to comply with the new service, he would allow you more freedom."

Mary pressed her lips together to keep from blurting the disparaging comment that rose. Instead she said, "I prefer to be free to worship as I have all my life. I find comfort in it and would be in despair of my soul were I to change."

"There might be peace in it if you did."

Mary looked up at Jane, wondering if she really believed that. Jane had always seemed an intelligent woman, but sometimes the things she said struck Mary as hopelessly naive.

"There would have been peace all along, had my father held with the religion to which he had been born and not taken up with the Lutheran her . . . the new ideas."

"Do you truly believe your insistence on worshipping the old way is good for the safety of the English people?" She made a pretense of deep interest in pressing the fragile silk flat with her thumb, as if to make light of her critical words. "The example you set is disruptive. It leads them astray."

Mary put her sewing in her lap and lowered her chin in annoyance. "On the contrary, it is my father who leads them astray. It is his example of rejection of authority that has caused such lawlessness in the realm."

Jane's voice remained gentle and perfectly reasonable. "But he is the authority."

"On earth."

"And God's representative on earth."

"I'm sorry, Your Grace, but I must disagree on that point. Only the pope has the authority on earth. He is God's appointed and infallible representative."

Jane fell silent, and that was just as well. Mary didn't wish to hear again the argument that the pope was elected by men and not by God. It often irked her that the Protestants always seemed to wring the certainty from things. Always throwing out the baby with the bathwater, making life too empty, too . . . unfounded. They never seemed to have an answer for anything but would do or say whatever moved them at the moment. Having heard the Boleyn witch often enough on the subject of her religion, Mary reviled every principle held by the Lutherans.

The silence strung out, and Mary hoped the subject was

dropped. She picked up her sewing once more and applied her needle. But then Jane said as gently as ever, "Your father has mentioned a desire for the end of discord between you."

This time Mary's tongue got the better of her. Her work went back to her lap, and her tone sharpened with irritation. "I cannot bear to see what he has done to his people. The executions, murders, rampant thievery . . . he's turned a nation of obedient Christians into unrepentant sinners. It makes my heart sore."

"More often than not the sinners are Catholic."

"When you wrest a man's faith from him, he's naught to guide him in the way he should go. It's no wonder so many Catholics have resorted to thievery and violence. They are cut off from God and have nowhere to turn."

"We believe each man can speak directly to God and know him personally."

A rude comment relating to overweening self-importance and arrogance on the level of delusion rose to Mary's lips, but she bit it back. Jane was not the enemy and didn't deserve rudeness. Instead she said, "Very well for you. Those of us who believe otherwise are ill-equipped to do without our traditional worship."

Jane had no reply for that, or else she preferred not to voice it. Again the two fell silent and continued with their sewing in that silence.

CHAPTER SEVEN

In quick succession, my brother was born, and Jane died. All mourned the loss of the queen, for she was well-liked during her short reign. The king had his heir, and as Edward grew to a sturdy lad, we all became assured he would one day succeed to the throne. The English people gave a collective sigh of relief, and my father was far happier than he'd been since the advent of that Boleyn woman. Once again in my father's good graces, my life improved immensely. Days were spent in worship, exercise, and social duties, and no more thought was given to who would inherit the throne. England had less interest in me than in the king's marriage contract with Anne of Cleves. That time, during his final years, was the last peace I would ever know.

For the rest of my father's reign he pretended to seek a suitor for me, but none ever measured up to his demands, and most negotiations amounted to nothing more than jaded political maneuvering.

To marry me to a foreign prince was out of the question, for the king feared a coup. With Edward yet tiny, it would be too easy to wrest the throne from him. Any Englishman with too much royal blood was equally a danger for the same reason, and certainly anyone without royal blood would be simply unsuitable as a husband for me. I could never bear the insult of being married off to a commoner, and I thank God my father was never quite that cruel. During the following years, hope for me waxed and waned as madness, and it slowly began to dawn I might never marry at all.

Mary was at her virginal, slowly plinking out a new and difficult tune, when the message came. One of her ladies presented it to her, then curtsied and stepped aside as her mistress unfolded and read the paper. The thing was brief, and was from Cromwell. As she read, her mouth dropped open a bit too much for dignity, and she snapped it shut when she realized she was gaping. Duke Philip of Bavaria wished to initiate a suit for her hand, and the king's secretary wished to know whether she was amenable to the idea.

Her heart skipped, and for a moment she found it difficult to breathe. But once she'd caught her breath, she told herself she must not let herself be carried away. There had been other suits, all political ploys and few of them sincere even so.

She read on. Cromwell briefly outlined the political situation, which was not very involved because this was not a political advance. Mary blinked in surprise and thought this promising. Philip was acting on his own initiative, and that in itself intrigued her. No political motive meant his was possibly a romantic suit, and therefore possibly more sincere than suits that had gone before.

Once again, Mary's heart did a flip-flop. Love? The thought made her light-headed. Love. She'd never considered the possibility of a love match, not since she was a child. She wondered whether she would even know what to do in the face of a declaration of affection. A giggle rose, and she had to stifle it.

To her attendants she said, nearly breathless, "Philip of Bavaria is expected in England to facilitate preparations for the king's wedding. Apparently he wishes to marry me."

The several ladies in the room cooed over the idea and gathered around to see the paper. One of the girls, with the unfortunate name of Elizabeth, said, "Whatever for?"

Mary didn't reply, but with a look gave her to know she thought the question rather stupid and insulting. To the group she said, "The letter is from Cromwell." Mary held it out for them to see, though there wasn't much to it. "He tells me it's a private suit."

That brought even more excitement. Elizabeth said, in a vein of apology and explaining her earlier question, "He's not got his father telling him to marry you, then?"

Mary looked at the message again, though she knew the answer was not there. "Cromwell makes no mention of a political impetus. My brother appears healthy enough to one day be king, so it can't be for the sake of the throne itself. Not that Cromwell or anyone else would discuss such a thing with me. That is for the king to know."

"Will you marry him, then?"

"Of course, I will do as my father directs me. If he wishes me to marry this German, I will certainly do so."

Elizabeth shrugged off the form reply and asked the real question. "Oh, but do you *want* him to order it?"

Mary blushed and gave Elizabeth a disapproving glance.

Nevertheless she replied, "I've never met the fellow, and know nothing about him beyond that he's the son of the Bavarian elector."

"He must be terribly ugly to make his suit without ever having seen you."

Mary glanced at Elizabeth with a slight frown and wondered whether she meant that to be as insulting as it sounded. She decided to let it go in all Christian charity. "Be that as it may, I find it an intriguing idea."

"Will you like living away from England?"

"I've no idea. I suppose I would need to learn German."

"He's a Lutheran, you know."

That thought had not occurred to Mary, and it pricked her pleasure at the news. Marriage to a Protestant, particularly a German follower of Martin Luther, would either be a struggle to maintain her Mass or else a wasteland of spiritual loneliness without it. She would marry such a man if her father ordered it, but she viewed the possibility with trepidation. Then again, perhaps Philip would be tolerant of the old religion, and she could worship in private there as she did in England. That was a hopeful thought, at least.

She stared at Cromwell's message, as if its woefully few words would give them the answers to all their questions. "Well, let's not get ahead of ourselves. There's no use in speculating until something comes of it. As many times as there have been suits for my hand that have come to nothing, I fear this may be yet another false hope."

The ladies wilted with disappointment as they agreed she might be right. Mary set the paper aside and returned her attention to her music. One of the other girls picked up her lute and settled on a stool to join in, and the cluster of women tried to forget the exciting news until there would be more to know.

It wasn't a terribly long wait. The following month Philip arrived in England, and a meeting was arranged when Mary went to Westminster for Christmas. He'd sent a diamond cross as a token of his affection, and though she wasn't to wear it yet, she'd seen it and thought it stunning enough to represent a great deal of affection. More, possibly, than she'd ever received from one man. She loved to wear pretty things, and now allowed herself to hope this negotiation would succeed where others had failed.

She couldn't help wondering whether he might be handsome. As much as she struggled for a pure Christian acceptance of her father's choice of a husband, her thoughts insisted on wandering to speculation on what Philip's appearance might be. Bad teeth? Skin? Might he have a pig's nose? Or a ferret's? She couldn't know until she met him, but would know within the half hour. If he was half as handsome as his token, he would make her a happy bride indeed.

As Mary dressed that day, her stomach knotted and her hands remained clammy no matter how many times she wiped them on a kerchief. Her ladies fluttered about her, fussing with her hair and headdress, straightening her ruffles and jewelry, each of them far more excited over the event than she was herself. At twenty-three years of age, she was nearly a spinster and too old to be so giggly over a man. She took a deep breath and held her voice steady, lest someone think her a whore eager to be serviced.

Against the nippy weather outside, she wore her heavy woolen and fur cloak. The better insulation between herself and the prospective husband, as well.

She went with her ladies to the gardens of the Westminster abbot, which lay between the hall and the abbey. By some standards the yard was not large, but it was large enough for privacy of a sort and better kept for winter than some other areas. The fruit trees were bare and bony, and the herbs cut back and wilted into their dormancy. A weak sun hovered over the southern sky, for it was just past the solstice, and the day would be a short one in spite of the cloudless sky. Mary rather liked it there. A certain peace filled this place, and a reverent silence. Even in this sleeping garden one could see God's hand and feel his presence. The cool air freshened her warm face and brought roses to her cheeks to disguise her hot, nervous flush. Her several ladies and her chamberlain proceeded down the path. In the midst of it they encountered Philip and his attendants, who on sight of the women turned and graced them with warm smiles.

Mary's first reaction was disappointment. Hopes of a handsome suitor dashed to the ground, for he was not attractive at all. He appeared older than his given age, and so she thought he might have lied on the subject. Or else Cromwell had lied, which was the more likely, for Cromwell ever had his own agenda. In any case, though there was no specific feature that made him unsightly, the overall assembly of his visage could not be described as comely. The eyes were just a tiny bit too close together, the nose just a little too large, the chin not quite prominent enough for comfort. Mary made her face smile and waited to see whether he was redeemable in other ways. When she remembered his unfavorable religion, she knew it would take a very good soul to overcome his disadvantages.

"A fine day to you, Lady Mary," he said in Latin, bowing quite deeply for a man of his rank addressing an illegitimate lady. On the one hand she hated being addressed as *lady*, but at least he seemed to mean more respect by it than most of those around her. So far, her opinion of him was not ill.

"Good morning, Your Grace." She gave him a slight nod rather than a deep curtsy, so as to not let him get too far ahead of himself.

"Such a lovely lady I find before me. My heart beats loudly, and hope rises for a successful negotiation with your father."

That made her smile a little, and her cheeks warmed against the chill air in spite of herself. Not many people thought her beautiful, for the lines of her face were not gentle. She thanked the duke, and her mind cast about for something else to say. This was not something she did often, and talking to a man with a romantic interest was an alien thing to her. She could play the virginal, read the Bible, embroider as intricately as anyone she knew, but flirtation was quite beyond her, because she'd never had a need to learn such discourse. The Great Whore had been good at it, and all the world had seen where it got her.

Philip, heading off the pause that threatened to grow into an awkward silence, gestured to the path before them and said, "Would you care to walk with me through this lovely garden?"

She glanced around at the gray and brown landscape and suddenly had doubts about his idea of "lovely" as pertaining to herself as well. But she nodded, and they moved away from their attendants. The other men and women followed, but at a distance. Mary could hear soft conversation between them, and suddenly was more interested in what they had to say than in what Philip would discuss with her. She forced herself to focus on his Latin, a language she had mastered well enough but not as excellently as her English or Spanish. A tiny frown creased her forehead as she struggled to concentrate on his words.

He spoke of how he'd heard of her piety and grace from those he knew who had come to negotiate Henry's match with Anne of Cleves. He declared that it was his dream to marry a godly, obedient woman, and take her to his heart as a soul mate rather than a political alliance.

"You mean, it matters not to you that I am close to the English crown?"

He shrugged. "I'm told you do not stand to inherit." His manner was relaxed, as if it didn't matter much whether she believed him or not.

"To be sure, my brother appears healthy enough to take the throne when the time comes. However, in the case of calamity, there is the possibility I would be all that was left. Surely that has occurred to you."

Philip opened his mouth to reply but faltered, shut it, and gestured to his interpreter to join them. The fat, smiling functionary hurried to them at a quick waddle, and Philip spoke to her in German. The interpreter said in English, echoing his master at the end of each sentence, "Let me be clear in this, my lady. There is no denying you are close to your father's throne, and that were your brother to meet a disastrous end too soon you would stand to move into his place. However, I would point out that such a thing would be a calamity, as you say, of far greater proportions than you suggest. I do not hope for it. Nobody should hope for it. There are others who might claim the English throne, and surely the situation would be an opening for civil war."

Mary knew this. She'd been hearing it all her life. But today she kept silent about what she thought of the idea that she could never be queen. Instead she merely nodded in agreement. What he said was true enough, but only because the English were not as enlightened as many on the Continent and would resist being ruled by a woman.

He continued. "I assure you, my lady, that I come with a true heart and honest intentions. I value you for your virtue and piety only. As your husband I will love you and treasure you above all others."

Flattering words, for even a virtuous wife expected a husband to be less so and to tire of her and take mistresses eventually. None of her previous suitors had ever made so extravagant a promise. She pressed him, and tested his sincerity. "You say you value my piety. Are you aware I follow the old religion?"

A shadow came over his eyes, and her heart sank. She had her answer.

But he replied, "I am aware. I hope you would one day see the light and convert, but until that day, I can tolerate your insistence on the old ways."

She would hope for better than mere tolerance, and didn't care for his tone, for it was she who wished for him to "see the light." But she said nothing to that effect. She couldn't forget that this was possibly the only sincere offer of marriage she'd ever received, and to discourage him might cause her to die a spinster. Fear of that made her continue to smile and to remain as gracious as she possibly could. Marriage, even to an intolerant Protestant, would establish a place for her in the world that her father could not destroy. It would mean a security she'd not known since she was eleven. In spite of his shortcomings, Duke Philip might nevertheless be her salvation. She said, "I would do my best to obey my husband in all things that are not the purview of God."

He nodded, apparently satisfied with her answer. He stepped close to speak more privately, as if the interpreter were not there. He said, "Such a pious lady."

"I am nothing if not devout."

Suddenly he bent down to touch his lips to hers, and in one smooth motion she dodged him and stepped back. The kiss met with empty air. Eyes wide, her mouth fell open in surprise. He stepped back also, a puzzled look in his eyes. "My lady—"

"Your Grace! How dare you?"

"I only—"

"I've never been kissed in that manner, and will not be so precipitously!"

"But my lady, I only wished to express my sincere affection for you."

"Your words are quite enough. I need no further demonstration." She felt torn between tears and anger, for she knew she may have lost her prospective marriage by her cross words. But to break down and weep might make things worse. There was nothing for it but to forge ahead and regain control of the situation. She looked around at the astonished attendants. "This interview is over."

Cheeks flushed far beyond what might have passed for winter chill, she strode through the cluster of attendants and onward toward Westminster Hall. Her own ladies followed, leaving the men in silence behind them.

Mary's hopes for the marriage negotiation crumbled.

I was crushed, though I never let on. Duke Philip left England very soon after. Though he subsequently reiterated his suit, my fa-

ther never took him seriously. Indeed, it appeared he'd never given Philip much credence, and the entire episode had been yet another exercise in manipulation and posturing. Or perhaps even, another joke to amuse his courtiers. I might have saved myself some grief and not had the meeting with Philip at all. To salvage my own pride, I was forced to pretend I'd never wanted the marriage. After a while, I even convinced myself. Easy enough, for I only had to remind myself that marriage to a Protestant would have been a constant, lifelong struggle. Eventually I truly believed I was better off without him, even if I died a spinster. I swallowed my fear and readied myself to accept God's will if that were to happen.

CHAPTER EIGHT

My father's final years were the most pleasant of my adult life. Happy with his son and secure in the knowledge the Crown would go to Edward without protest, he was free to favor me with feasting and shower me with jewels. After the execution of his faithless fifth wife—who, I would point out, was another daughter of that vile Howard family—I was asked to step into the vacancy and fulfill the ceremonial duties of queen. Once again I was lauded and praised, and though still deemed illegitimate, I sometimes was allowed to forget my status and enjoy the approval of my father.

But eventually he died, as all men must. My brother ascended the throne at the age of nine.

* * *

John Dudley, Viscount Lisle, earl of Warwick, duke of Northumberland, lounged in his chair at the council table in King
Edward's privy chamber. The young king, though he'd been
taught regal manners, was nervous with this first session of his
council since the coronation, and banged his heel against the
leg of his chair as his uncle explained to him a matter of England's relations with France. Though Edward had been groomed
all his life to be king and was intelligent enough to grasp many
of the finer points of foreign relations, he was nevertheless
only nine years old, and the council recognized his need for
worldly experience. So for now he needed to have things explained and to be told not to bash his chair with his heel. The
lord protector, his uncle, laid a firm hand on his knee. The rhyth-
mic thudding came to a halt, and Edward bent to the matter
at hand.

Dudley looked across at the uncle. Edward Seymour, Jane's
brother, had been made duke of Somerset and regent almost
immediately after Henry's death. Dudley assessed the man from
behind hooded eyelids. Somerset was, as were all the Seymours,
a dull, listless fellow. To Dudley he seemed not much of a man
at all. Always at loose ends, never as alert as he should be, all in
all, he seemed the sort of regent ripe for a coup.

Now, after the rise and fall of the Howards and Boleyns,
Dudley felt it was time for his own family to ascend to power.
The Seymours were not strong enough to hold the council
and the king. Dudley knew he himself was.

He smiled to himself. He looked forward to the contest he
knew he could win, for the prize was the English throne.

The other two members of the council with any real importance sat on either side of Somerset and the king. To Edward's
left was William Paget, a lithe and long fellow, smooth of

voice and thought. He sat erect in his chair, hands folded in his lap, utterly contained and controlled. To the right sat Lord Admiral Thomas Seymour, Somerset's younger and very pretty brother. Seymour set his ankle on the opposite knee, his attention seemingly occupied by cleaning his fingernails with his dagger. Dudley knew it was a ruse, used commonly enough by men who wished to be ignored while they awaited an opportunity to exert influence. He'd done it himself in the past, but now was older and more subtle than that. He waited for Seymour's assault, to resist whatever he might have in mind when it came.

Moving on with their business, Somerset brought up the subject of Church reforms. The boy's interest perked, for he was a devout lad, and issues of religion were a familiar thing to him. He listened carefully to the protector's ideas on what changes might be made to advance the cause of Protestantism in England.

"There is the question of what to do about your sister, Mary." It was well-known that Edward adored both his sisters, and suddenly Dudley's interest in the conversation picked up. His ear perked to know how Edward would react to Somerset's approach to this. Would the boy resist influence concerning something so important to him? This would certainly illustrate the limits of Somerset's power in the council.

"What about Mary?" responded the boy. "Surely she knows she can't go on worshipping the pope forever. One day she's got to come around and realize the old way is empty superstition."

The men were silenced for the moment. Dudley could hardly believe the child had uttered the one thing they all wanted him to think, and there had been no effort on their part. Somerset glanced around, as if not quite believing their good luck. Then, gently, he reached for a paper at the bottom of a stack and placed it in front of Edward.

"Well, then, Your Grace, I've taken the liberty to write out some ideas for new legislation."

"My father made quite a few laws regarding the practice of the old religion. His reforms go a long way toward freeing us all from popery."

"Well and good, I agree. But these are new times. A fresh press for even better reform is in order. For instance, we think it best," he glanced about the council table to include the others in this, "to repeal all laws governing the printing and reading of the Bible."

Edward nodded, as if he'd been thinking the same thing. "Indeed. No need of the priests to tell us what we can read for ourselves."

"And the service in English."

Edward nodded. The Protestant service had long been in English, and it was understood a new law would make it illegal to conduct the Mass in the Catholic manner. Somerset continued, reading from his paper, telling details of what should be made illegal in worship now that the too-tolerant Henry was dead.

Paget spoke up. "Good Protector, I wonder if it might be too precipitous to make such a drastic reform at this time." His hands remained folded, and he moved not a hair. His voice, though he didn't raise it at all and spoke so gently as to be nearly inaudible, insinuated as surely as if he'd shouted. His words found purchase. The rest of the council fell silent to hear.

Somerset sat back with a stern look on his face. Dudley reckoned he'd not anticipated any resistance in this from the entirely Protestant council. "I disagree." Of course, he disagreed. His mistake was in presenting his own list to Edward, without previous discussion among the other council members.

"And if Lady Mary were to organize her fellow Catholics in resistance? It could mean more than civil disobedience."

Dudley was inclined to agree. The specter of civil war had haunted them all throughout their lives. It hadn't been so very long ago that the overthrow of Richard III had put an end to the wars for the throne, and the Tudor claim through an illegitimate female ancestor was still weak. Nobody wanted war in England, particularly Somerset, whose interest was in taking the Scots to task. But Dudley kept his mouth shut and watched what the others would do.

"Mary wouldn't dare to harm our people," said Edward. The men ignored the naive comment rather than go down that road of insoluble speculation.

Somerset said, "Then we must do what we must to keep Mary under control."

Thomas Seymour sat up from his slouch and twiddled his dagger between his fingers before letting it dangle by its pommel between his index and middle fingers. "No, I agree with His Majesty. Mary would never go to war. She's her mother's daughter more than her father's. Catherine would have gone to the scaffold rather than foment a rising."

"What makes you say that?"

"She could have, and she didn't. For years she didn't, though she might have gained the Crown by it."

"She didn't need the Crown. All she had to do to wreak revenge on Henry was to sit in her castle like a dog in a manger."

To head off a pointless debate on what was getting to be ancient history, Dudley said, "Be that as it ever may be, I am of the opinion that it is sore dangerous to rest the safety of the country on the whims of a woman. Any woman. Today she may resist temptation to revolt; tomorrow . . . who can tell? There is also that she is now heir presumptive. Henry made it clear she is to succeed Edward if, God forbid"—Dudley nodded toward young Edward—"he dies without issue. Even aside from the religion question, she poses a danger in the form of those who would assassinate the king and place her on the throne." A scenario Dudley abhorred, for he was planted firmly in the Seymour camp, and even conversion to Catholicism wouldn't put him in a better position than this, were Mary to become queen. "Perhaps it would behoove us to have assurances she won't be able to organize resistance to Edward's reforms."

Heads nodded around the table. Even Edward agreed with his point. Dudley said, "So . . . how might we accomplish that?"

Somerset said, "It seems to me if we simply keep her away from court and out of sight, the people will forget her, and we can get on with things. Mary, for all that she is a woman, is nevertheless a reasonable one and obedient to a certain point."

Seymour snorted a bit of laughter through his nose, and though Somerset threw him a cross glance, he otherwise ignored it and continued.

"I think she only wishes to live in peace, and will give us no trouble so long as she is not widely seen by courtiers and the public." He looked around the table and nodded once as if to confirm his utterly sensible words.

Paget said, "Out of sight, out of mind didn't help any in the case of Catherine."

Dudley snorted. "Edward isn't married to a shrewish whore hated by everyone south of the Shetlands."

Paget narrowed his gaze. "Perhaps for a time it will be a

workable tactic, but eventually I think more decisive measures will be necessary. One would like to believe she could be allowed to live in seclusion and worship as she pleases without becoming a symbol for her faith, but I fear we delude ourselves in our thinking. There are those who would seek her out for the purpose of harming us. No matter how quietly she lives, if she continues to toady to the pope and to communicate with her cousin the emperor, there will be danger. One day problems will arise. It is inevitable, and at that time we should take decisive and permanent action."

The others thought about that for a moment. By "decisive and permanent" Dudley thought Paget to mean execution or at best imprisonment. He thought it a bad idea, for that would amount to martyrdom. Martyrdom for Mary would only make things worse for themselves. England still harbored too many Catholics, and she was already a symbol of resistance to the new service.

"Well—" began Somerset.

"I have a banner suggestion," said Seymour brightly, as if he'd just thought of it. "I'll volunteer to marry the woman. I daresay I'm the man who could bring her under control."

"I think not," said Dudley, blurting without thinking. He cursed himself mentally for the impulse, but then all he could think about at that moment was that Seymour must have the throne in mind for himself. In an explosion of insight, he realized Seymour was his chief rival for the position held by Somerset. Seymour was planning to wrest power from his brother; the tactic was too obvious to miss. Seymour would marry Mary for the sake of being second in line to a throne held by a boy who could not be expected to create an heir for several years. What havoc could Seymour wreak then?

Looking around at Paget and Somerset, Dudley realized they must be thinking the same thing. Somerset wore the frown of an older brother for an unruly younger one, and Paget struggled mightily to have no expression.

But then Edward said, "Oh, yes! Our dear uncle could marry her, to change her opinions! Then if we expire too soon, there will be a king for England who is close to our heart!"

Seymour seemed quite pleased with this declaration, but Somerset actually went pale. His response was immediate and strident.

"My dear brother, I must, as lord protector of the realm, decline to give my approval for such an idea."

"Give your reason, my brother." Seymour was terse, as his plan met what surely would prove to be an insurmountable obstacle.

Somerset held up his palms as if the answer should be obvious to them all. Dudley readied himself to hear a lie. Somerset said, "Why, Thomas, it is plain to me that neither of us was born to be king." Never mind that he himself was currently the power behind Edward's throne. "Neither were we made to marry a king's daughter, even though she might never become sovereign. In recent years you and I have been raised high. Now that we have each found our rightful places, we must know them and treasure them. We must thank God and be satisfied, and serve our king in ways that best suit us. It is not for either of us to marry our master's sister, for that is not service at all."

Dudley nodded in agreement, the most sincere gesture he'd made all year. He heartily did not want Seymour to marry Edward's sister.

Paget also nodded and said, "Additionally, my lord admiral, I hear through various sources that you've already approached both Lady Mary and Lady Elizabeth, and they've each of them turned you down in the most firm words possible. One might even say harsh."

Dudley raised his eyebrows at that. Mary *and* Elizabeth? Far too obvious. And crass. Seymour should be hung just for his stupidity. And Paget knew of these proposals before himself? It annoyed Dudley to be the last to know what Seymour was up to. He eyed Paget and yearned to know his source.

"Well, then," said Somerset, "you have your answer already, don't you, Thomas?"

Seymour's reply was defiant. "All I might have desired from you, my brother, was approval. Overcoming the obstacle of rejection is my own concern."

Paget didn't bother to hide his amusement, nor Somerset his irritation. Young Edward appeared disappointed but nevertheless listened carefully to the words of his counselors. His foot went back to tapping the leg of his chair.

Somerset spoke with a bluntness that made Dudley blink with approval, for it made him glad he didn't have to find a way to say it himself. "At any rate, the question is an academic one, for neither of Henry's daughters will have you, and for that we should all be exceeding glad."

A dark flush rose to Seymour's face, and with furrowed brow he fell silent. For the rest of the meeting he glowered at his brother as if wishing he could take power then and there at the point of his dagger.

After my father's death I remained in mourning for a terribly long time. Somerset neglected to inform me for several days after it happened, and that alone brought nearly unbearable melancholy. I retreated into seclusion and saw nobody. I ate alone and took my exercise alone, keeping with me no more than two or three servants at any moment.

The only exception I made during this time was for the new imperial ambassador, François Van der Delft. During our talk the subject of Thomas Seymour arose, and he asked about the rumor of a proposal for my hand, made immediately after my father died. The very idea seemed silly to me, for I'd never spoken to the man and had not the faintest idea he wished to marry me. He'd recently married my father's widow, and by all accounts they were happy enough, so the question was an academic one and not terribly interesting. Thomas Seymour was the last man I would wish to put so close to the throne as any husband of mine would have been.

During Seymour's short time on the council, in his role of lord admiral, he made himself one of the most hated and corrupt men at court. In league with privateers, he established something of an illicit fiefdom in Scotland. He embezzled funds, abetted pirates, flirted shamelessly with my sister, and it turned out had some nefarious plan involving my brother the king. Nobody was ever quite certain what he had in mind, but one night he broke into Edward's chambers, shot the poor boy's dog when it tried to bite him, and tried to make away with the king. Imagine how bold! And reckless! How he thought he might succeed is a very puzzle! It was later found he'd acquired a stamp of the king's signature and a set of keys to various apartments about the palace. Needless to say, he failed in his coup and was executed without delay. By all accounts nobody much regretted his loss, not even his own brother.

That was the sort of man Edward had on his council, and where things stood throughout the kingdom. The following years proved a nightmare of political intrigue and social upheaval that made my father's reign appear mild and peaceful by comparison.

*   *   *

Jack the Rabbit came out of his burrow at the smell of burning thatching. Thatching smoke had a stench of dirt about it that burning trees did not. And there was dung as well. A stable was afire somewhere; he knew it. He couldn't see the distant fire for the trees, but he heard shouting from well within the forest. The village to the west was not far. The noise seemed to come from there.

He was well out of London these days, hiding like Robin Hood from those who would do him harm, both with authority and without it. He'd angered one too many powerful and violent men in London, who had marked him for death.

Willie was dead. Murdered in his bed with a dagger and cut open like a traitor by those who would illustrate their bloodthirsty power to the rest of London. Jack, no hero he, readily acknowledged their power and fled. Now, like that fellow thief Robin, he lived in a burrow in the forest and robbed from the rich. Well, those richer than himself, at any rate. He had no standard for judging who was rich enough to steal from. As for who to give the money to, in his estimation there was nobody poorer than himself, so nobody more deserving of his takings than himself. Perfectly logical, and perfectly workable so far. Knock wood. In the forest was plenty of wood, a place to sleep that was more or less comfortable, a fire to keep him warm, and aside from the lack of congenial female company, Jack figured he was as well off as he'd been in London. And far safer.

But now the tang of smoke reached his nose, and he wandered in the direction of the village in search of the source. He climbed atop an enormous moss-covered fallen tree, hopped down on the other side, and followed his nose through the tangled undergrowth. Once not long ago, nearly the entire village had gone up in flames. Catholics. Protestants. They were all a bane on the realm, every last one of them. Everyone knew there was a Catholic church here, and they still had Catholic Mass. They had a crucifix and everything, even though the old Mass had been banned. Holy water, baptism, all of it. Protestants often came to harass this village, for with a Protestant king they all reckoned they could do as they pleased to the Catholics, and naught would be done about it. So far they were right.

As he approached, he saw an outbuilding of the church had been set fire to. A goat pen and lean-to, it appeared. The thatched roof of the open-sided structure was yet throwing more smoke than flame, but it would be going well and good soon enough. The three goats ran and panicked, bleating and leaping in terror of the flames. Women who lived in the surrounding houses screamed and wept and hugged each other. Men fought. Some ran this way and that, carrying church furnishings of gold and silver. Crosses, cups . . . other things Jack couldn't identify. They fought over the loot and bloodied each other for it. Jack was no churchgoer, but though he could barely remember the last time he'd been to Mass, he was fairly certain this sort of behavior was frowned upon by even the new religion. He stood just inside the trees, still and watching like a fly on the wall.

Three men dragged the priest from the stone building and began to beat him, shouting the sorts of obscenities even Jack never used. The priest wailed his pain and tried to cover his face with his arms, screaming for help. Jack only watched. No point in tempting fate, and he was certain if there was a hell, these men were headed there. They had the priest down on the ground, kicking and stomping on him. Even once he was unconscious, they continued to beat him. The snap of breaking bones cut through the roar of flames in the goat pen. Then one of the men shoved the others aside and tore the silk robe from the prone, still body. There was no telling whether the man was even still alive. Surely he was broken beyond repair. The assailants continued to rip clothing from the body until he was entirely naked. They threw his rosary onto the burning roof of the goat pen. "There's for your image of God! Ye roaring, howling, monkey!"

A second man shouted that a little holy water would surely cause the fire to magically go out in a puff. The others burst forth in laughter. The first man pulled his willie from his trews and pissed on the still form lying on the ground. That brought another wave of shouting and laughter, and the others followed suit with their own piss.

Jack saw someone run from the church, carrying a large pewter plate. Another man emerged with a candelabra. Jack wondered whether there might be anything left and slipped along the side of the church to a back entrance. He found the dim interior alive with noise. Crashing, breaking. Chairs lay about the sanctuary, smashed to so much firewood. One of the men there had an enormous iron hammer and was hard at work pounding one of the walls with it. Chunks of stone flew this way and that. Jack looked up at the heavy beams holding up thick thatching. With each blow of the hammer the rafters shook, sending bits of straw and dust down onto the men. They would be killed if they kept this up. Jack knew himself to be not the most intensely intellectual fellow in England, but even he had to sneer at this stupidity. He would have to hurry if he wouldn't be caught there when the roof fell.

He looked around the floor for something to take away but found nothing. Everything was either broken or already gone. The altar was in pieces, and if he wasn't mistaken, a pile of turds rested atop those pieces. Three or four, by the size of the stack. If they meant to make a statement, he wondered who they expected to find the defiled altar in the rubble they were about to create. The crucifix was smashed, probably by the same hammer that was about to bring the roof down on their heads.

At any rate, there was naught there to interest him, so he made his exit in all haste for the sake of his own neck.

In the yard, he saw the goats were still in the pen and about to be caught by the fire. They pressed against the wicker fence, as far from the rolling heat as they could get, bleating pitiably. That fence was about to go up as well.

One of those goats would make a few nice dinners for him, so he ducked his head under the thick smoke and went in. The waves of heat blew against his skin. He put up an arm to shield his face as he grabbed for one of the goats, and singed the hair from it. But the panicked animals were too quick for him and bolted through the open gate. He cursed and coughed and chased them. One was slower than the others and wandered toward the forest, suddenly more interested in grazing than getting away from the smoke and excitement. Jack drew his dagger and went after it. The religious folk could fuss all they wanted over crosses and crackers. Tonight he would feast like a king.

It was time for Mass, and Mary headed for her chapel, followed by a cluster of her ladies. They would be required to wait outside during the worship, for the king's allowance made for the traditional Mass was only for her personally and not for her household. Edward had decreed it. Or rather, his council had. Though he was a dear brother and an intelligent boy, Mary knew he couldn't help but be heavily manipulated by his council. That gang of heretics had him outlawing even what had been perfectly acceptable to his father. She chafed at being hemmed in by those who would do such wrong, but she owed obedience to her protector.

This morning she drew a deep breath and calmed herself in preparation for her time of worship. This was supposed to be a pleasant time, when she could be in communication with God and freed of the tawdry concerns of politics and other worldly matters. She needed to attend the service with a heart free of anger, so she stopped thinking about Edward and his council.

In the yard before the chapel, she and her attendants were approached by a single figure dressed in black. Her chamberlain veered off with two of her guards to deal with the uninvited man. He knelt and spoke. As they approached, Mary heard him say to the chamberlain, "I long for the sacraments." By his speech, he was Italian. Niccolò Delarosa, by Mary's understanding, a musician of her father's household who had joined her own after Henry's death. She had always thought him terribly talented, and slowed to listen.

When he saw she was listening, he snatched his cap from his head and bowed. "If it would please Lady Mary, I beg to be allowed the traditional Mass. I am a long way from my home and fear for my soul to be denied confession." She could see his fear was real, for his desperation showed in wide eyes shiny with tears.

Mary's heart went out to this fellow. She saw his terror of

finding himself in hell for the sake of English laws. She approached him. "Signore Delarosa."

His face brightened. "Yes, my lady." He bowed to her, then regained his feet and bowed again. "My lady, I beg of you. Please let me share in the service. It has been so long since I have been allowed Communion and confession, I have terrible fear of dying and going to hell."

"I . . ." Mary wasn't certain what to tell him. Her brother was her guardian, and therefore she owed him her obedience. She felt obligated to follow his laws. "Signore Delarosa, I fear I cannot help you in this matter."

"Please, my lady. Please do not put my soul in this danger. I am a devout man. It wears on me every day not to be permitted this thing. I serve you with all the affection I have to spare after that I have for God. Please do not exclude me from salvation."

Mary disliked breaking the law. She'd done it in the past, but never lightly. Delarosa's plea had her torn between obedience and compassion, two things equally important to her. For a long moment she struggled for what to tell this man, whose soul hung in the balance.

Then she tried to imagine herself going into the chapel alone, leaving her musician and the rest of her household outside and knowing how much they needed that which she insisted upon for herself. She couldn't do it. There was no possibility of peace in her own worship if she knew others were deprived of theirs. It would be like eating a rich meal before the eyes of a starving man.

"Very well, then. Come with us." She gestured that he should follow.

Delarosa gasped with relief. "*Grazie,* my lady. *Grazie.*" He bowed several times in gratitude.

Mary turned to her ladies, nearly smiling with the pleasure of including them. "All of you. Come inside and be with me in celebration of the Mass."

With a surprised flurry of thanks, the women curtsied, then they all followed Mary into the chapel. Hands went into pockets beneath their skirts for their rosaries.

The next day more members of her household gathered at the chapel and asked to be allowed entry to the Mass. And the next, even more. Most of her attendants and functionaries were Catholic, and so were deeply relieved to be able to worship in the way they felt proper. As the week progressed, even the lesser servants about the palace asked to be part of the growing congregation. There were people in the chapel now who never would have been allowed in Mary's presence, worshipping among those of high rank.

By Sunday morning the little chapel was filled to overflowing with the faithful. Before taking her seat at the front, Mary turned and looked over the gathering. Today they crowded the sanctuary with folding wooden chairs, lined up from wall to wall, people sitting elbow to elbow, the lesser folk standing at the rear because no more chairs would fit in the room. A candle stand tilted, then righted, as the press of people nearly knocked it over. The murmur of voices dwindled to silence as she gazed, and her household waited to hear what she would say.

"I am astounded." Mary's heart lifted and swelled at this demonstration of faith. She'd not known there were so many within the palace who disdained the Protestant service. "My heart soars at the community I see here today. It is a joy to have so much company in worship and good fellowship in our celebration of God's Sabbath. I welcome you all, and God be with you."

The congregation murmured, "And also with you."

Mary turned to the front and took her seat with a wide, joyful smile on her face and a song in her heart.

It wasn't long before word arrived at Westminster that Mary was defying her brother's decree and allowing her household the illegal service, and not long after that, Mary received a visit from the duke of Northumberland, John Dudley.

Mary received him with her entire household present, as she always did anyone she either didn't know or didn't like. Dudley was a little of both, having been in and out of court politics since Mary was a child and currently a prominent member of Edward's council. He and his attendants were severely outnumbered by Mary's assemblage of ladies and liveried servants in the confines of her presence chamber. She sat atop the dais, as regal as she could manage in her current status. She'd never had her rightful title returned to her and was only heir apparent by virtue of her father's will, which had ordered the succession after his death, but she was determined to behave as the princess she knew she was.

Dudley and his attendants made their obeisance respectfully enough. It was to be expected, since Edward personally held his sisters in far higher regard than had his father. She was in exile from court but was not ill-treated.

"My lady Mary," he began. "I have been sent by his king's majesty to have a word concerning your worship service."

She knew what was coming. It was expected. Indeed, Dudley was exactly on schedule with this complaint. "What about my service? My brother has allowed me to worship as I please within my own establishment."

"He has, my lady. However, he has specified that the service be limited to only yourself. No others are allowed to indulge in the Catholic Mass. I have reports that even your lowliest kitchen boy has been to Mass with you." He made it sound as if she were carrying on an affair with the commoner in question, so disgusted it made him.

Mary drew herself even more erect than she had been and raised her chin. "I have no choice in the matter."

"Oh, come. Are you not the mistress of this household?"

"I am my brother's ward."

"Then why do you not obey him?"

"I obey his king's majesty in all matters other than those belonging to God. I cannot, in good conscience, bar my household from the celebration of Mass. It would condemn their souls to hell, and I cannot have that on my own soul."

"They have their own worship service."

"A Protestant service, which is no service at all but rather an apish mockery of Mass led by men who might well wear bells on their toes and hats."

Dudley bristled at that, and it amused her to see his back up, his chin up, and his face reddened. His eyes hooded, and for a moment his lips pressed together. There was an edge to his voice when he spoke again. "It is the lawful service. You break the law by allowing the popish Mass to those not included in Edward's exception made for you."

"The servants and attendants who come to the chapel do so at the peril of their bodies. Far more important to them is the integrity of their souls, for which the Lutheran heresy is no help. They come to me, begging for the sacraments I enjoy in safety. I cannot bear to watch them suffer."

"They suffer not."

Her hands gripped the arms of her chair with white knuckles. "Have you seen them? No, you have not. You do not see the poor supplicants, in terror of going to hell, beseeching me to allow them to partake in the only worship they know will save them from eternal damnation."

Dudley opened his mouth to speak, but Mary's anger at his insensitivity got the better of her, and she rode over him with raised voice. "My lord duke, have you ever seen a burning?"

Of course he had, for enough Catholics had been burned lately for it to be impossible to miss. He gave a slow nod to that effect.

"Then you've seen what happens to the heretic. The screaming, the pain, the agony they suffer for their error. That is what my dear servants fear in eternity. Never-ending fire, unrelieved by death, for that is the reward for disobedience to God. I cannot describe to you the joy in every face I see in that chapel each day, knowing that we all are safe from such horror. Knowing we all are right with God, and that we will not earn for ourselves unending suffering."

Again Dudley tried to speak but was once more interrupted. "John Dudley, I charge you and all of your Protestant ilk with the destruction of the faith of the English people. The advent of the Lutheran heresy has caused confusion. Error. Rampant lawlessness. Too many people don't know right from wrong, and they go about doing whatever they please."

Dudley finally got a word in. "They know the pope offers only empty superstition and lies."

"My household knows no such thing. I know no such thing. I know in my heart the truth of this. For the sake of the souls of those near to me, I cannot acquiesce to my brother. I can forgive him his error, for he is but a child and not entirely formed in his wisdom. But I cannot comply with his wish to condemn my people to eternal suffering. I will not go against

God and cannot disobey him for the sake of obedience to my brother."

"There will be consequences."

"All things bear consequences. We make our choices, and we live with them. I will live with mine."

Dudley stepped forward to speak more stridently, but Mary's voice rose. "That will be all, Northumberland. You are dismissed."

"I—"

"*Dismissed*, I said!"

Dudley stared at her, dumbfounded, his mouth open to speak but no words forthcoming. He snapped it shut, glared at her for a moment, then turned on his heel and made his way through the cluster of his attendants and out the hall door without the slightest pretense of obeisance. His men followed as quickly.

Mary took a moment to calm herself, gripping the arms of her chair and drawing deep breaths. Dudley was a fool. Even more, he was evil for expecting her to betray her faith. It was several minutes before she returned to herself and dismissed the household before making her way with her closest attendants to her privy chamber.

I was so very sure of the way of things. In a world where nothing was ever certain, the one thing I knew to be true and unchangeable was my own faith. It was the only thing I controlled. My father, then my brother, had sway over my body and my behavior concerning worldly matters, but nobody, nothing, could ever take my faith from me or cause me to betray God. As much as I loved my dresses and jewels, as much as I loved my father and my brother, they were never so dear to me as my faith, for it was as myself. Without it, I could not exist, just as my mother could not. But over the next several years, Edward's council convinced him to disallow the Mass even for me. Of course I couldn't obey. I could no more comply with the new laws than I could take up a dagger and do away with myself.

Visits with Edward were discouraged by the council. I learned to instruct messengers to deliver letters directly to his hands. Any message from Edward not in his own hand was assumed to be from Dudley, and it was easy enough to hear the voice of Dudley's secretary in them. During one visit, when I failed to hide my grief that Edward was so betrayed by his advisors, he broke down in tears along with me. His people were in revolt. His council was feeding on itself and on him. He had nobody to trust, not even a cousin on the other side of the channel as I had. As Edward grew and the council corrupted, poor Edward lost his way among the Protestants. Ultimately, he was lost forever.

Dudley was accompanied by several of his attendants, Paget, and Somerset to a meeting in Edward's privy chamber. Nobody knew what the matter was; they were only summoned and no explanation given. He felt a foreboding, for Edward had become increasingly unhappy with his role in government. His uncles had both been eliminated from the council, one of them having been found to be as corrupt as a cardinal and in league with pirates. Dudley entered the privy chamber to find the thirteen-year-old king sitting at the head of the meeting table, his arms laid along the arms of the chair, staring blankly at the floor. On one hand he wore his hawking gauntlet, and on it sat the falcon he kept in his chamber, well tethered to the glove and wearing its hood. Dudley and his men paid obeisance and were ignored. They all waited for the boy to acknowledge them, and finally Edward gestured they should all sit. Dudley, Paget, and Somerset took chairs at the table, and the rest stood attendance. Edward told the attendants to leave, and they did so without protest or even hesitation. Dudley fidgeted uncomfortably in his chair. The air stank of anger. Edward had a look on him that did not bode well for any of them. This was not going to be a smooth conference.

"We can no longer threaten our sister." Edward eyed them all in anticipation of an objection. The men seated at the table all knew Edward would lose the argument. He was still very much under the control of his council, still too much a boy to have his way in more than his supper menu.

"Mary." Paget said what they all knew. Mary was a problem.

"We must allow her the Mass."

Paget drew a deep, patient breath and spoke in the most perfectly reasonable tone Dudley had ever heard. They all needed patience with the king; lately he'd been more contentious even than his sister. "We cannot, Your Majesty. To allow her to ignore the Act of Uniformity would be to suggest it is not valid. The English people already resist it. To allow her to set the wrong example would be to invite anarchy. The public welfare is already jeopardized. It would take little to move the Catholics to complete revolt."

Edward fell silent, then looked up from the floor. With his free hand he reached for the falcon, and plucked a feather from it. The bird cried and flapped its wings. The bells on its jesses tinkled madly. Tied to the gauntlet, it went nowhere. Dudley noticed the creature already had a bald spot across its back; the boy had been plucking away before they arrived. Apprehension crept up Dudley's spine. Edward's face betrayed no emotion. He only gazed blankly at the bird as it settled down and tried to peck at the hand on which it perched. But the thick, padded leather was like armor, and its beak and talons did nothing.

Then Edward deftly plucked another feather and dodged the beak as the falcon tried to find its tormentor. It repeated its dance of fear and pain and tried to peck its way free. But Edward held it well, and it remained on his gauntlet.

Another reach for a feather, and the bird tried to peck that hand. But the boy shook his gauntleted hand, threw the bird into a flurry, and snatched two more feathers. Then he waited for it to settle down again. The feathers drifted down to rest with the others. A growing pile fluttered in a draft near the wooden floor.

To the appalled gathering he said, "I would be obeyed."

Paget said, "Majesty, I remind you according to your father's law you must obey your council until you reach your majority. You haven't gained the maturity to weigh the risks of coddling your sister. She is a danger to us . . . to *you*. She would have the entire country in revolt with her papist ways, and you in the Tower. If not worse."

"I have to wonder," Edward said as he plucked more feathers, "how many lies I swallow in a day. I think I should be full up with them." The keening cry of the falcon filled the room, and its wings flapped. The bald spot across its back grew larger. Edward continued to pluck the bird, dodging its beak and ignoring its attempts at escape. The men watched in silence. Disgust curdled Dudley's gut, but he did nothing to stop the king. None of them did.

Soon the bird was in a frenzy of pain, struggling to get away. Edward shook it until it was dazed. Then, in a fit of anger, he grabbed its head and yanked. One yank, and the neck was broken. A second, and its head came off entirely. Blood spurted everywhere, but Edward ignored it. It dripped from the table and splattered on his knees. Still the men sitting nearby did nothing. Then Edward took the gauntlet from his hand. One by one he yanked the wings from the body, and threw the pieces on the floor.

The group sat in silence, aghast. Edward stared at the dead bird lying in its blood and feathers. Then he said slowly and quietly, "I am like this bird. I am plucked for my feathers until I am naked and cold." There was a silence as he struggled to control his emotion, then he continued. "But I will pluck those who do so to me. I will one day have in my power everyone who now has power over me. I will make them also naked, and I will tear them also into four parts." He looked up at his councilmen, looking as if he might dissolve into tears. "That will be all, gentlemen."

Nobody moved. All were stunned at sight of the bloodied king, until he shouted for his chamberlain and a washbowl. Finally Dudley was able to climb to his feet and retreat from the room. His mind tumbled with puzzlement and plans. Something had to be done to control this child who might never be a competent king.

CHAPTER NINE

The struggle with Edward and his council seemed never ending. They knew they couldn't arrest me without risking revolt, but they also knew they couldn't simply let me alone. While I had no desire for violence, neither could I comply with their wishes. So they attacked my householders. One of my chaplains was indicted for performing the service in my absence and was forced into hiding. Another, also indicted, remained in the household and continued to serve under my protection. The uproar from the council was intolerable. All my attendants and functionaries lived in fear of being sent to the Tower. Then I was expected to relinquish the traditional Mass for myself as well as my household. Dudley and the council threatened me with execution if I did not comply. I was invited to London for the sake of keeping me under the watchful eye of the council, now led by John Dudley, but I declined to go. Once again I

was in fear for my life. Escape to the Continent and the protection of my cousin Charles seemed the only safety for me.

Mary was in the company of several friends when her chamberlain announced the arrival of the imperial ambassador, François Van der Delft, and his secretary, Jehan Dubois. Up to that moment their conversation that evening had been lively, touching on gossip from abroad and a bit from Edward's court. News was plentiful, though often skewed in ways that made little sense to her. It seemed the men of Edward's court had all gone mad or stupid, for the bits of information she received now and again never fit together sensibly. Living away from court was frustrating and sometimes puzzling.

The one thing she did know was that she was in danger from Dudley. He would have her dead tomorrow if he could, for he was embattled, and the people hated him. That much she was sure of. Her householders reported what they heard in the village. The devaluation of currency and the corruption of the council, as well as the discontent raised by the Act of Uniformity all had him desperate to keep her under control. Anymore, it began to appear the only way to keep her from being a problem was to do away with her completely. Mary knew it, her household knew it, and they all knew Dudley knew it. Once again she lived as a prisoner, never eating what she had not seen prepared and never comfortable around anyone she didn't trust with her life.

Van der Delft and Dubois bowed, and she gestured to available seats nearby. It was long past supper, and the evening had grown quiet. The old man eased into the chair with a soft grunt and leaned on his cane so hard it trembled. Dubois took a chair to the rear of his master.

"So, Excellency, are you entirely ready for your long journey back to the Continent?"

"The real question, my lady, is whether you are ready."

A chill of apprehension skittered up her back. She must flee her brother's tyranny and escape to Flanders. The time had come, and now that it had, she wasn't certain she was ready at all.

Van der Delft looked toward the chamber door, then to the two men who sat with Mary. Her controller, Robert Rochester, the servant Henry, who stood at attendance a short distance away, the musician Niccolò with his lute in a dim corner, and her chaplain, Dr. Hopton, as well as three of her ladies. He said, "Lady Mary, may I speak candidly?"

She thought about that for a moment, not eager to discuss a move that frightened her deeply but unable to put off the possibility any longer. Van der Delft was leaving for home, and this would be her last chance to speak to him before his departure. His retirement had been decided on the basis of his illness, which made him pasty and bloated, barely able to stand sometimes. He licked his dry lips as he awaited a reply.

Mary turned to the others in the room. "Ladies, Henry . . . Niccolò, please leave us."

The servants filed out of the room, leaving Mary, Van der Delft, Dubois, Hopton, and Rochester. Once the servants were out of earshot, the ambassador leaned forward in his chair. Not happy with that, he scooted it forward a few inches and encouraged the others to do the same. Mary leaned forward to hear. Hopton and Rochester sat at the edge of their chairs. Dubois stayed where he was, seeming to know what was going to be said.

"What have you in mind?" she said.

"I leave for the coast in the morning. My ship awaits me off Maldon. Once my replacement has gone on to London, I will wait to receive you and take you away to your cousin. However, my lady, I am instructed to relay warning from Charles."

Mary sat up, a bit taken aback. "Charles? Warning?"

"My master wishes you to put off this drastic measure for a time. I am to remind you that if you leave the kingdom and Edward dies, you may lose your right to the throne."

"I cannot ascend if I am dead or imprisoned."

Van der Delft gave a slow nod of acknowledgment. "Above all things we wish to save your life. But an escape attempt carries enormous risk as well. We must weigh that risk of going against that of staying. There are rumors Edward is in ill health."

"Excellency, I am also ill nearly half the year, but have survived these past three and a half decades. Rumors of Edward's health have been rampant long enough to cast doubt on them, for he clings to life nevertheless. There are many who only wish it so, and say it, though they have no knowledge of the matter."

Again Van der Delft acknowledged her point with a nod.

Mary added, "Besides, all things considered, I have no reason to believe Dudley and his pack of dogs will ever allow me to ascend the throne, even were I at Westminster with all my supporters on the day of my brother's death. The council fears me, as well they should, and I believe before word of Edward's death left his chamber, they would find a way to do away with me. I will not wait here like a trapped rabbit for them to come after me at their leisure."

The ambassador considered that for a moment, then seemed to decide something. "Very well, then. I'll inform your cousin you will not be persuaded in this. Once my replacement has come and I have taken my leave, I will return and wait for you in the waters off the coast. You will need a boat to take you from Maldon to my ship."

Rochester spoke up. "I know of a man I can trust."

"You need not tell him who his passenger will be."

"I said I can trust him. Besides, he will guess it."

Van der Delft didn't appear to like that, but said, "Be that as it may, discretion is utmost in importance. Do what you can." To Mary he said, "We know there is a spy here in this household. The council knows too much for it to be otherwise. They know within hours your every move. Once you leave here, you will be committed and cannot pause or even slow down until you are safely on my ship. It's widely known they watch the coast. They've set every householder from London to the shore to look out for you. Every road, every crossroad, path, and waterway is guarded by Protestant eyes. No place is safe. On the journey to Maldon you will have to travel by foot, with only one or two attendants and in disguise. If you are caught, they will surely send you to the Tower. In that event, you will never see daylight again and will never be allowed to live beyond the king."

If Van der Delft was trying to frighten her into staying, it nearly worked. She began to tremble at that. To be caught and sent to the Tower was a terror as intense as assassination. More so, in fact, for death would be the end of troubles, and she would go to God. For a moment she thought she might break down in tears and wished there were somewhere safe for her. She wished she could fly to the Continent, far above her tormentors, and be free of this nightmare without the dangers set between herself and safety.

But she swallowed her fear, drew a deep breath, and said, "I will walk to Maldon, and Rochester's friend will take me in his boat to meet your ship. We will go quickly, and God will protect us from Edward's foul knave.

I cannot comprehend how soldiers go to battle or the martyrs to the stake without fear. I wished myself to be so brave, but even with the knowledge that what one does is right, threat of death is a terrifying thing. When one is lost in the world among evil people, sometimes it's hard to see the path of good.

Alas, poor François never returned for me from Flanders. Age and illness did him in, and he died before he was able to fulfill his promise. I was left with only his secretary to help me. Jehan Dubois did return for me, but by then the risk had become so very great and my terror overwhelming. Circumstances changed as well.

Jehan Dubois didn't like any of this. He'd worked out the plan with the emperor's sister, but he had little faith in anyone involved. There were too many vaguenesses, too many people without any idea of what the dangers were, and too much ambivalence on the part of those involved. It was a bad business all around.

Mary herself had a history of vacillating on the issue of escape. His master's predecessor, Eustace Chapuys, had been terribly frustrated in his attempts to free her from her despotic relatives. Not to mention that Charles wasn't at all fond of the idea, and therefore his sister was little help in the matter. Mary, as was her mother before her, was too convenient a spy and political pawn for him to want her anywhere but at the center of English politics.

Dubois felt naked out there on the sea, watching the horizon and the shore with one hand shading his eyes, praying Edward's navy would somehow overlook his presence. The deck beneath his feet rose and fell as he wished he could take a boat ashore and hide under a bush until Mary had boarded and they could set sail for home on this perilous journey.

The official explanation for the eight ships he had with him was that they were after pirates, and that was the story they would give should they be boarded by the English. His own ship was a merchant galley with a shallow draft, which he could take up the Blackwater to Maldon. It held a cargo of grain to be sold to Mary's household. The idea was to smuggle her aboard while the ship was being unloaded. If she could get away from Woodham Walter undetected and reach Maldon in a timely manner without being stopped, once she was at the ship well-disguised, nobody would suspect a poorly dressed woman at the docks.

At a leisurely, perfectly innocent pace, the galley carrying Dubois made its way up the estuary, leaving their protection behind. The other ships browsed among inlets, as if in search of pirates hiding in the estuary. On arrival at Maldon, Dubois's brother-in-law, Peter, was sent to contact Mary and bring her onto the ship.

But he did not return with her.

Dubois looked up from a letter he was writing to Mary's controller to find Peter outside his cabin, hat in hand. Just beyond him, barely visible through the narrow cabin door, stood a liveried man of Mary's household.

"Who is he?"

Peter indicated him with a tilt of his head. "His name is Henry. He's a trusted servant of Mary's."

"And where is she?" He glanced hopefully at the doorway, but it was silly to think she would be standing out there by herself.

"She is not ready to come yet."

Dubois couldn't help the disgusted grunt of frustration he emitted then. "Why not?"

Henry bowed, a little white around the eyes for having to deliver unwelcome news. "I'm afraid I do not know, sir."

"The tide is at its highest now. We must leave soon or be caught when the water recedes."

Henry bowed again. "I will tell my mistress—"

"No, wait for this letter and take it to Rochester." Dubois returned his attention to the letter he was writing, changing its tenor to one of urgency. He pointed out the extreme danger of the situation and explained in detail the plan for escape. It crossed his mind as he wrote, that the plan was now for his own escape as well as Mary's. He urged an immediate exit from England, and pointed out that the longer they stayed, the more people knew of his presence, and the more likely Edward's council would be made aware of Mary's intention. The waterway would then be blocked, and they would all be arrested. This attempt might even provide an excuse for her to be arrested. Perhaps even executed, but she at least would be sent to the Tower. That would never do for anyone's purposes except Dudley's.

Henry hurried away with the letter to Woodham Walter.

Rochester's reply was to request a meeting with Dubois in Maldon. The secretary received this with more frustration and impatience. Time was fleeting; they needed to get Mary onto the boat and depart. Anyone seeing him with Rochester would be alerted to the escape plan.

But there was nothing for it. The alternative was to simply take his ships to safety, leaving Mary to fend for herself. He had to exhaust all possibility of fulfilling her wishes before he would be free to depart for Flanders.

He rubbed the back of his neck, which had gone stiff with the past days' tensions, and sighed. Perhaps a discussion face-to-face with the controller would move Mary and her people into action. He left his ship and went to a house in the village, where he and Rochester conferred on the matter.

The garden of the villager named Schurts, a Catholic friend of Rochester, in high summer was ablaze with flowers and abuzz with bees and butterflies. Herbs threw their scent every which way, mingling thyme, rosemary, onions, and some slightly more exotic plants from the south unfamiliar to Dubois. Fruit trees bore green apples and green peaches just in first blush. He and Rochester moved among the paths as if enjoying the afternoon and chatting about nothing more dire than the weather. Schurts himself could know who they were and what they were discussing, but the household need not be alerted to the conspiracy at hand.

"We need to leave immediately," Dubois told Rochester. The time had come for candor, for excess politeness could get them all killed. Really, they needed to leave yesterday, but at this point, Dubois had to settle for what he could accomplish.

Rochester shook his head. Firmly, his frown indicating without doubt that he deemed the entire enterprise folly. "It is impossible for Mary to make her way past the king's watch-men without detection and arrest. We could not possibly risk her life so recklessly. There are spies in her household. She believes all her servants to be loyal Catholics, but the heretics have no shame and pretend to a faith they do not own. They attend Mass with nary a flicker of guilt, though they do not believe, so they can report to that arch-heretic Dudley. Her household is not so free of enemies as she imagines."

Dubois frowned. "We are here to save the life of the princess." God certainly knew that was the only reason his ship remained in the harbor. He wondered why a decision couldn't be made one way or the other whether Mary intended to leave or stay.

Again Rochester shook his head. "Mary is not in particular danger yet. She will have her Mass, probably for months yet. If and when that occurs and the council appears ready to arrest her, then there can be another rescue attempt."

Dubois nearly groaned. Instead, he bit his tongue until he could speak rationally. "But I was summoned at the desperate plea of Mary for help. You recall at her last meeting with His Excellency Ambassador Van der Delft that she was adamant rescue be made. My master, in fact, explained to her the dangers you just mentioned, and she insisted on leaving England regardless. Even after that meeting, I asked her if she was without doubt willing to go, and she assured me she was. Now you tell me she has changed her mind."

"I would give my hand to see my lady in safety. I say not that she does not wish to go, but she wishes to go if she can."

Dubois pressed his lips together at his rising frustration, but his patience crumbled. "Yes or no, is Mary coming with us when we sail out with the tide? Our situation becomes more perilous with each passing hour, for our ships have surely been sighted and possibly the council has been informed of our presence. They will not be fooled by our claim of searching for pirates."

It was plain there was something Rochester wasn't telling him. "Come speak to Mary. Come to Woodham Walter."

"I cannot possibly. Tell me now whether Mary will leave England."

"It is not for me to say."

Dubois made a disgusted noise in the back of his throat, and thought about it. One more day's delay wouldn't trap them in the estuary. If he spoke to Mary and she told him she was staying, then there would be no blame in simply leaving, and he would be free to go. He assented to the plan.

That evening at sunset, Mary's servant Henry guided him and Rochester by a convoluted, hidden route to Mary's residence. There, having eaten and refreshed himself, the three stood in an antechamber while waiting to be received by Mary.

Rochester, so not to be overheard by the servants and guards in the room, sidled close to Dubois and murmured in a voice overly pleased with events as Dubois saw them. "There is a mighty secret you should know."

Dubois only gazed at him, waiting for him to continue. Rochester did so.

"Edward is on his deathbed."

Again, Dubois did not respond with more than facial expression, but raised eyebrows did put across mild curiosity. He hoped the king was down with more than a head cold.

Rochester elaborated. "I daresay the king will not see the New Year. The horoscope tells it."

This interested Dubois. "Who has made the reading?"

"Several. Many. All who read the stars are telling it. And they persist in saying so, in spite of the many arrests among Edward's courtiers."

"Edward's own household? That is remarkable." Dubois began to have a feeling he wasn't going to have Mary with him when he returned to his ship.

"You should also know that great danger threatens us."

Dubois knew that and wondered why Rochester thought this would be a surprise to him. But he thought there might be something else afoot, so he asked, "Have you details?"

Rochester put a finger to his lips and indicated with a glance the others in the room. Dubois fell silent, realizing he wouldn't know anything of value until he spoke to Mary herself.

Eventually he and Rochester were escorted into Mary's privy chamber, where she stood by the fire. One of her ladies stood by the door, a trusted lookout to make certain there were no eavesdroppers at the keyhole. A small stack of hopsacks stuffed with belongings stood in the middle of the floor, and Dubois thought perhaps he'd been wrong about Mary's intentions. But hopes of a decisive Mary were dashed by her first words. After formalities, she came to the point. "I am ill prepared to make this journey just now." Dubois glanced at the hopsacks, then looked to Mary for her to continue.

She obliged. "I cannot say I definitely will not go, for I do not know how the emperor would take it if it turned out to be impossible to go now, after I have so often importuned His Majesty for rescue."

Dubois took this to mean all the other times she'd said she would go and then did not. If she thought Charles would be put out if she decided to stay, she needed to be disabused of the thought. He opened his mouth to say so, but she spoke over him.

"You can see I've begun my preparations. I wonder whether

you might oblige me and take my rings back with you, and I will follow at a later date." It was a token to assure Charles of her intention to go to him, a token he didn't need, for he didn't particularly want her to leave England in any case. She added, "Then at least they will be safe, should the council have a notion to plunder me as they did the monasteries."

Dubois boggled. Somehow she'd gotten the notion that she would be safer without her jewels to tempt an arrest. An interesting concept, but he was sure the rings would have small influence over the council concerned with far greater issues regarding her.

"My most gracious lady," he said, "it is my sincere and considered opinion that no better opportunity will arise for this venture. We stand at a juncture where all is as favorable as is likely ever to be. Indeed, each passing moment brings us closer to calamity, should we be discovered. I daresay, if you think it safe enough to send your rings, you may as well go with as after them."

Mary considered that for a moment, her hands clasped together with white knuckles. Then she went to her maid by the door and gestured to Rochester to join them. There they conferred in hurried whispers, Mary with her knotted hands pressed to her bosom, almost but not quite as if in prayer. Dubois waited patiently, hoping this discussion would result in a decision of some kind. Any kind.

Finally Mary returned to him by the fire. Now her manner was calm and confident, and Dubois was relieved to realize she'd made a decision.

"Very well, we will go on Friday. I and my ladies will have an outing at the beach, for our amusement and for me to purge my stomach by the sea. I do that often, and so it will be not suspicious." She went on to describe the plan and set Henry to continue packing the hopsacks as she spoke of two royal galleys that had lurked on the Blackwater the day after Van der Delft made his departure. "Things grow worse than ever."

A knock came at the door. Everyone in the privy chamber fell silent. Rochester went to answer. When he returned, he'd gone quite pale, his eyes wide. He was followed by the villager Schurts. Rochester said, "Our friend has ridden hard with news the bailiff of Maldon and some others of the village wish to arrest your galley."

Dubois went cold.

Rochester went on. "They suspect you have something to do with the warships lurking about. They mean to arrest you and your crew and find out what your purpose is."

That was it. There was no longer any chance of getting Mary safely to the ship and away from England. Indeed, Dubois would be lucky to make it out alive himself. Nobody on board the galley had been told their true mission, but there had been rampant speculation, and questioning could only lead to discovery.

Mary laid a hand across her mouth, her eyes wide and her breathing strained. "Oh! What shall we do then?" Tears sprang to her eyes. "What shall become of me?" She held her stomach, bending forward, apparently in pain. Dubois thought she might vomit onto the floor.

Rochester told Dubois he must leave at once, and the secretary agreed with whole heart. The controller added, "These men of the town are not well disposed. Our friend has told me he's learned they will double the watch tonight. Further, they will have men on the church tower, where they will see all the country for miles. Nobody approaching the shore will go unnoticed."

There was no doubt about what to do now. The king's men had decided for Mary whether or not she would go; it was now entirely out of the hands of everyone else.

Rochester continued. "Schurts here will escort you back to your ship during the stillest, darkest hours."

Mary sat on her bed, hands to her face and sobbing. "What is to become of me?" she repeated, over and over. Dubois felt sorry for her, but not so much that he didn't realize she would be safely away by now if she'd met the ship when it had arrived, as previously planned. Her maid went to comfort her, so Dubois deemed her in good hands.

"I'll take my leave, then, as soon as our horses can be readied." It was past midnight, and so the best time to make the journey to Maldon by dark, unfrequented paths was near. He and the others made their obeisance to Mary, who pulled herself together enough to stand and address Dubois.

"There will be another attempt to leave," she said.

Dubois didn't reply, thinking only that he hoped he would not be the one sent to retrieve her.

She went on to tell him the next attempt should be from Stansgate, closer to the open sea. She would return to Beaulieu, then send instructions to him in Flanders. Dubois nodded, then bowed again before turning to leave. "Do give my best wishes to Charles," she told him. He nodded, and she added, "You see, that is not our fault now."

Dubois wondered whether she really wanted to go, or if she only said so because she thought it was what Charles wanted. He decided he would never know.

CHAPTER TEN

I never was able to escape the reach of my brother's minions during his reign. There was never any escape attempt from Stanfield. Different stories of the failed rescue were bandied about by Charles and the English council, each claiming different things and few of them true. Throughout Europe rumors ran wild that the rescue had succeeded and that Charles intended to marry me off to his son, Prince Philip, a story I didn't hear until much later. The watch on me grew closer and the harassment of my householders more severe, until it was nearly unbearable. The Act of Uniformity meant the end of the traditional Mass, even for myself in private. By then I was welcoming neighboring gentry to my chapel, who supported me in my use of the Mass. We continued to worship, knowing the danger. Each day I reconciled myself to the possibility of death and prayed to be able to do the right thing if it came to giving my

life. Only the peace of my chapel and daily prayer saved me from madness.

Ultimately, I was called to London to answer for my disobedience.

Niccolò Delarosa rode at the rear of the procession to Westminster, pleased and proud to be part of this entourage. Dozens of knights, gentlemen, and ladies made up the parade, and Mary in the midst of them all, sitting her horse as well as any woman Niccolò had ever witnessed, greeting well-wishers who poured from dwellings and thronged the road for a glimpse of her. Some had come as far as five miles from town to meet them, and joined the train behind Mary's household so that it stretched and wound through the countryside like an enormous, multicolored ribbon at a May Day festival. Some children brought flowers to present, early yellow and white wildflowers they held aloft with eager joy, and she bent to accept them as a gracious, loving princess. It made the musician smile to watch her and see how loved she was by her people. The English were often fools, but he couldn't fault them today for their love of Mary.

Even more joyful than the welcome from the common Londoners was that each member of Mary's household wore their rosaries where they could be seen, as necklaces, the crucifixes resting on their chests. All were large, and many were of ornate design: intricate carvings of wood and metal, of finely wrought corpora, beads of precious and semiprecious stones. The crucifixes were a bright display of God's glory and the love held by the faithful, who today were all around and eager to be seen and counted.

It was a heady feeling for him to wear such a badge of non-conformity in public, for though he was Italian and considered himself inherently different from the English folk around him, he'd spent enough years here to understand how seriously the English Protestants took their break from the pope. Men had been murdered for less than this.

He himself had once been beaten by a gang of ruffians for his religion. He should have known better than to dally too long in town alone, for his accented English gave him away as Italian and a papist. Three men had assaulted him, beaten him unconscious with sticks of firewood, and left him bleeding in a mud hole behind the public house. Years later, he bore a scar on his upper lip and a slightly bent nose from that night. The irony of that beating was that, rather than convincing him to hate the pope, those English heretics had caused him to take pride in that small martyrdom for his faith. Now he smiled at the sea of happy faces as he passed, and it did his heart good to know he was not alone.

The train moved slowly through the streets, hampered by the very throngs that encouraged their mission of confrontation with the king. But when they arrived at the palace, they found no greeting from Edward or his council. Nobody but the royal controller came, and only after being summoned when the queen and her escort had dismounted and entered the great hall. The wait to proceed into the palace was interminable, clearly an insulting tactic designed to teach Mary her place.

The unapologetic controller guided Mary and her immediate household through the building to a gallery, where awaited Edward and the others. The entire council was present, with an overall air of impatience. By their faces Niccolò realized the seriousness of this meeting. The ugly business at hand could mean Mary's life and possibly the lives or freedom of everyone in her service.

Niccolò slipped his lute strap from his shoulder, let the instrument rest on the floor at his heel, and looked around to see where they would have him sit with the rest of the extraneous servants. Ordinarily, most of them would have been directed to another room before Mary proceeded to this gallery, but she'd insisted they stay with her while in the palace. As a musician, Niccolò often was admitted to highly privileged meetings and other gatherings, but this didn't appear casual enough for a lute in the background, no matter how softly played.

Mary made her obeisance to her brother, and formalities were dispensed with in a quick, perfunctory manner. Then Edward informed her she was to follow him and the council, and that her entourage was to remain in the gallery.

"I'll have an escort, I think, Your Majesty." Mary's tone was matter-of-fact, not shocked nor angry but simply a matter of course, as if she'd just been politely asked her preference.

"Alone, Lady Mary. You're to bring nobody."

"I'll have my guard." By her voice she might have added, "Don't be silly."

Edward was equally determined, and at least as blunt. "You've come to make your case to us. We'll hear you or not as suits us."

Niccolò didn't have to see Mary's face to know this frightened her. He himself might have been just as alarmed to be separated from supporters and taken to a room filled with deadly enemies and their heavily armed guards. She turned to survey her escort, and her eye lit on Niccolò. A glance at his belt to check for his dagger, she turned to her brother. "I would have a bit of soft music to accompany me, to ease the soul and the tension. Surely I can be granted that."

Edward's expression told of his distaste for the idea. "These are sensitive issues to be discussed." He looked Niccolò over as if he were a swaybacked mare for sale.

"Dear Niccolò is experienced and loyal, and he served our father faithfully for years. He surely can be trusted with whatever might be said in this meeting, for he's never been known to breathe a word of anything he's heard to anyone in all the time he's been with us.

A thrill of apprehension fluttered in Niccolò's gut, and he wondered whether he might have preferred to be a little less trustworthy and kept out of the thick of these things. However, she was right in that he was experienced in the way of the royal court, and he remained as expressionless as the pillars in the gallery.

"Besides," she added with a rather unskilled attempt at a light tone, "a musician is ever deaf to all but his own noise."

That brought a chuckle from the council members, and even Niccolò had to smile, for it was often true. But not today. Today he would gladly defend his mistress with his life.

"I don't think—"

"I'll have the music, my brother." The moment of lightness was over. Mary would not be moved from this. Everyone in the room understood that she would take her household and return home immediately rather than go into that meeting room alone, even if it came to armed conflict between her guard and Edward's.

Dudley's eyes narrowed at Niccolò, who moved not a hair under the scrutiny, then finally whispered to Edward. After a moment of consideration, he said, "Very well," and waved them all on toward the small meeting room.

The chamber held a long table that nearly filled it. Niccolò was told to take a seat at the far end near the window. There he sat with his lute on his knee and began noodling on the strings gently and quietly, making minute adjustments to the tuning pegs to make up for the variances in temperature and humidity after the long ride with the instrument slung across his back.

He adjusted his belt to make his dagger easily reached, then bent to play a soft love song, one he knew was a favorite of his mistress. He looked up to catch a slight smile from her as she moved to the end of the table nearest him. Her cheeks were pale with recent illness and her brow tense, and he knew she was in a misery of fright. But she smiled nevertheless. From beneath lowered eyelids he watched the council and their guard as he played.

Mary stood at the end of the table, and began with a formal appeal to the council that they lift the ban on her traditional Mass and allow her to celebrate her religion as she'd done her entire life.

Edward, sitting imperiously at his end of the room, a pale, frail mockery of his father with tubercular roses in his cheeks, spoke in response. Though he was nearly a man, it was nevertheless plain his words were nothing more than what had been told to him by his council. "You defy us."

"I only ask for what was promised to me by our father who was king."

"But we are king now. We decide what is best."

"Have you no respect for your sire? Do you despise him for

being old, or for being dead? He made his wishes known when he was alive, and those wishes cannot have changed."

Edward blushed, and his eyes flashed with unseemly anger, but his voice remained calm. "We cannot persist in a time that is not ours. We must press on and make our own laws, which are for the betterment of our people. We must build on our father's work, not wallow in it." He pointed a chastising finger at his sister. "And you must obey his will, which states that you are to submit to the council's instructions." There was a short pause, then he blinked and added, "And mine."

She raised her chin in bold defiance she probably did not feel, and her voice took a sharp, critical tone. "I've read the will and studied it in detail. It states only that I am to submit to the council regarding my marriage. On this point I've given no offense. Indeed, there has been no occasion for me to do so, since the council has not seen fit to seek a suitor for me, nor even entertain the possibility of one, should one ever appear as magic from the ether."

At that last, Niccolò detected a slight quavering of her voice. He'd heard her speak to her ladies on the subject of marriage, and though she insisted she had no need for the carnal aspects of it, he could tell she was desperate for children. It stood to reason, for he'd never known a woman who felt otherwise. All the world knew it was unnatural for a woman not to bear children. He knew Mary feared the possibility she might never marry. The thought always made his heart go soft, for he wished he could step in and fulfill that for her.

His gaze went to the floor for a moment, lest anyone in the room guess his thoughts. Worst of all, that Mary herself should ever know of his longing and think him a fool.

Edward opened his mouth to speak, but Paget said over him,

"The council has done what it considers best for the kingdom and His Majesty's people. By your resistance, you demonstrate your disrespect for the will of your father."

"On the contrary, it is all of you who lack respect. You have never obeyed his stated wishes on any point. You have changed his laws. His orders were that two Masses be said daily for his soul, and four obsequies annually. By all accounts you've never done so in any fashion, particularly not in the manner he wished, which is the rite in place at the time of his death, a rite that cannot by any estimation be called 'popish.' Were he to hear such a thing, it would certainly bring down his wrath. Indeed, according to the promise made to Ambassador Van der Delft, I am entitled to my own rites as practiced in the traditional way."

Edward blurted, "We're aware of no promise to His Excellency. We've only partaken of governmental affairs during the past year and can't have promised such a thing." He was sulky and irritable, his speech punctuated by coughs he struggled to suppress.

"Are you not the king, my brother? Did you not draw up the ordinances regarding the new religion? Well, then, I therefore cannot be bound by them and do not need to obey them."

Niccolò's jaw dropped, and he flicked glances at her then looked to the floor to hide his intense interest in what she'd just said. Might the Catholic rite be legal after all? He was no lawyer, and many fine points often escaped him.

But Paget answered, his voice supple and insistent, very much as Niccolò had always imagined the voice of the serpent in the garden. The man ever made Niccolò want to wash his ears after hearing him speak. "His king's majesty holds the reins of government as firmly as is practicable. His laws are valid, and he expects his sister to respect the law as faithfully as she respects her guardian."

Niccolò nearly grunted. Paget was slippery. Even Niccolò knew that "practicable" meant whatever the council wanted it to mean.

"I have utmost respect and love for my brother, exactly as I did my father. It is only the council I doubt. My father, for all his difficulty with the pope, cared more for the good of his kingdom than all the members of this council can claim."

Dudley finally spoke. "How now, my lady?" His voice carried the derisive tone so common when Henry had been alive and she was not part of the succession. "It seems Your Grace wishes to show us in a hateful light, without cause."

"That is certainly not my intention. You press me hard on the issue of my father's will; I must answer." Suddenly she was on the defensive, and Niccolò knew the argument could be lost.

Dudley played his trump. "Edward is king. You are bound by more than mere filial duty to obey him; you must obey because it is the law."

It was exactly that simple, for flaunting the law sufficiently would turn even her supporters against her, and explaining complexities to commoners was impossible. The masses liked simple ideas and had no patience for fine points. If the single, simple conception that Mary was disobedient and therefore a bad woman were to gain ground with her supporters, she would lose them. Without them she would be at the mercy of Dudley and the council and come to the same end as so many before her. But she continued nevertheless.

"Ultimately," she said to Edward, ignoring Dudley now, "there are only body and soul. My soul is entirely within the purview of God, and that I cannot change. Indeed, I would never be willing to change. It is his alone and was always thus. I could no more give it to someone else than I might flap my arms and fly to heaven whole. My body I offer to Your Majesty's service. Might it please you to take my life from me rather than my religion, I could not object, and indeed would not care to. In my faith I desire to live and die. Anything less, I cannot compass."

Edward, child that he was, seemed moved by that. The men of the council sat with faces of stone, and some even fidgeted impatiently. None looked at Mary but rather eyed Edward to gauge his reaction. The king said, "We have no wish to ask for your life." Paget opened his mouth to speak, but Edward said quickly, "This interview is over, Sister. We charge you, however, to observe our laws. Should you not, we would hear of it. There are those in your household who do not share your views."

"There are many who do." Her gaze flickered to Niccolò, who struggled to concentrate on his playing, lest he falter. "A great many."

"Nevertheless, we would hate to make our sister an example to prove we will not tolerate support of the corrupt Church."

A flush came to Mary's cheeks, but she said nothing further in that vein. Niccolò knew she would not lie and so would not promise compliance with that request. Better to say nothing at all.

What she did say in parting was, "Brother, I implore you to give no credence to those who might believe evil of me. I am Your Majesty's humble, obedient, and unworthy sister."

"God go with you."

"And also with you, Brother." With that, she curtsied, looked to Niccolò for him to accompany her, and the two exited the chamber, leaving the council to discuss what had just passed.

In the presence chamber Dudley stood to the right of Edward's throne as the imperial ambassador, Jehan Scheyfve, was granted audience. Scheyfve strode smartly to stand before the king and bowed in exactly the prescribed, formal manner called for by his office. His diplomatic demeanor so stiffly and precisely held gave away his distaste for the task at hand, which must have been extreme to be so poorly disguised. Dudley wondered what mischief was afoot.

Scheyfve straightened and drew a folded and sealed letter from his tunic. "I have a message from His Highness, the emperor Charles V."

Dudley already knew the message was from Charles, or Scheyfve would never have seen the king that day. A messenger on horseback, the animal lathered in the rider's hurry, had galloped into the yard not an hour before. Edward had made short his dinner in order to receive this message immediately, at the encouragement of Paget, who knew only that it was deemed "most urgent" by the man bringing it for Scheyfve to present to Edward. The thing had been in transit by horse and ship for about a week; the messenger had hurried.

Without delay, Edward broke open the imperial seal and unfolded the page. Dudley peered over the king's shoulder, but at that distance could only tell the missive contained but few sentences. Edward read in silence, then made a choking noise.

"This can't be genuine."

Scheyfve sputtered, and Dudley held up a conciliatory hand. Then Dudley addressed the king sotto voce. "Certainly it is genuine; we cannot doubt that." Then at full voice he added, "What has the emperor to say that is so very shocking?"

Edward handed the paper off to his protector. "See for yourself."

Dudley took the page and held it up to the light of a nearby brazier. As abrupt as its short length suggested, the letter from Charles laid out his point in economical and no uncertain words that eschewed diplomacy completely.

"Good God!" said Dudley. He looked to Scheyfve. "Is he serious?"

The ambassador's eyes widened, and he tilted his head as if to say he was shocked he might need to answer that question. Dudley gathered the matter was most serious. He turned to Paget, who took the letter to read as Edward slouched in his chair to glare at them all. Dudley whispered to Paget as he read, "Charles says that if Mary is denied her Mass, he will declare war on England."

It came to that. Were it not for the intervention of my dear cousin, I might have been arrested and sent to the Tower. God knows what might have happened to me there. I recall what happened to my mother when she held to her conviction regarding her marriage, how miserably she lived and how terribly she missed her life as queen and mother. Only the threat of war kept the council from depriving me of everything, including my religion. When that message came, the day after I arrived in London, I was given permission to leave court. Though before my departure Secretary Petre struggled to convince me to abandon my faith, I knew his admonishment was without teeth. For the moment, I'd won. I returned to Beaulieu shortly after.

During this time, members of Edward's council increased their own rank, awarding themselves new titles and lands and garnering more power and wealth for themselves. They ignored their duty to teach the king how to rule and instead taught him only to obey them. The kingdom lay in a sorry state, all but the very richest unable to feed themselves or live in any way suitable to their stations, however low. The council plundered the king's treasury to have men-at-arms sufficient to keep order, an expense made necessary by rampant unrest. Coinage became nearly worthless. I was ashamed to learn some people of my household had begun to pray for the death of my brother, so that I might ascend the throne and save them all from irresponsible rule.

It was a dark time for all of us, particularly those with concern for the welfare of the English people, for they suffered as deeply.

Jack the Rabbit was hungry. Oh, but he was hungry! He'd been walking for days. Nigh on a week, he thought. He wasn't entirely certain of the date, for he ate seldom and hid from everyone he saw. Travelers weren't welcome anywhere much anymore. Everyone distrustful. Everyone with a firm hand on his own property and a sharp eye on his neighbor's. Jack had been chased away from every town he'd attempted to enter and now only moved through them at night and with a light foot. He stole what he could, but there was precious little to be had.

Staying around London or anywhere near the place had proved too dodgy of late. Besides the mobs that could form and turn ugly at a whim, that summer had brought the sweating sickness again. A portent of bad tidings, that always was. If ever there was folks dropping dead of the sweat, a man could be sure other things would go just as bad. It was enough to make a man truly believe in God, it was.

He'd come to a coast town. Must be. It might have been Tynemouth, he wasn't entirely certain. But he could smell the ocean, briny and cold. A storm in the offing as well. He could smell the snow coming. The wind bit, and he pulled his stitches about him as best as he could. His boots had worn through, and the ball of his right foot was kept from the rocky ground by naught but a handful of dead leaves. The sun had been up for half an hour. He would need to find a place to sleep soon. Something to eat would be nice. The water he'd gulped at the river would only take him so far.

There were docks down on the river, he saw, and a ship stood with men unloading cargo onto that dock, an enormous Dutch merchant, squatting flat on the water like a great, fat duck. Its rigging swung against itself as the ship shifted in the roughening water. The cargo stood in enormous, sprawling stacks in preparation for loading onto wagons. But no wagons yet. Too early in the morning for the teamsters to be at work. Perhaps there would be something to beg there. Or a purse to be snatched, though it had been months since he could pass through a crowd unnoticed, with his clothing beyond ragged and his cheeks aflame with illness. But he picked his way down the hill toward the water. God grant that there be edibles there!

A stiff wind blew off the ocean and up the river, whipping Jack's long hair against his face so that he had to shake his head to see where he was going. He wished for a hat, but his had been stolen from him months before. Men in heavy coats manhandled boxes and barrels from the ship's hold and onto the dock. Jack crept as casually as he could, bringing to bear everything he knew of going unnoticed, keeping to the shrinking shadows as he looked around. He tested lids of crates and found them well nailed. It was to be expected, but there was always a chance of one being secured sloppily, and he would be happy to snatch anything he could eat or sell.

The men from the ship sounded German. Or French, maybe, he couldn't hear well enough to tell. In any case, none of them sounded English. Foreigners. He hated foreigners. They took away English jobs, which made for empty pockets to pick, and foreign merchants charged too much money for everything. Nobody could afford to live, what with prices being so high.

Voices rose farther down the dock, and Jack stepped behind a stack of crates to listen. He was happy enough to stay where he was hidden, for he was out of the wind and could hear everything. The shouters were English, townsmen come to the docks with bludgeons, pitchforks, and axes. The dockworkers quit their labor and stood by their cargo as if to guard it. Even if they didn't speak English, there was no mistaking the tone of those swarming the dock. Someone or something had set the locals out for blood.

"Back off, we're taking this cargo!"

That set off a murmur of German, or French, or maybe a little Spanish, and the foreigners formed up a solid gathering to confront the townsmen. One man called out in German, then in English heavily accented as he strode down the gangplank to the dock. "*Ich bin der Kapitän.* Have you your papers here?" In one hand he carried a belaying pin and twirled it like a sword. His real sword he carried in a scabbard on his belt.

"No papers, we're just taking it."

The German laughed, and Jack flinched. Heinous mistake, taunting these angry, hungry Englishmen. One man carrying an iron pry bar hauled off and swung it at the *Kapitän* who, never having the chance to swing his belaying pin, went down with a single thud.

That set off an outraged wail from his crew, but the English mob wasted no time in charging the sailors. Caught off guard, the foreigners fell back under the onslaught of weapons. They drew daggers, and some managed to pick up cargo hooks, but they were outnumbered and at a weapons disadvantage. Jack decided it was time to disappear into the woods again, and he slipped away from his cover.

"Hey!"

Jack turned to see one of the crowd had spotted him. "Get him!" shouted the Englishman as he came after Jack with a pitchfork raised over his head.

Jack muttered an oath and set to running, but he was weary, sick, and underfed. Several of the mob behind came after him with shouts of outrage. None of them heard his plea that he was English. Nobody seemed to hear him at all. They ran up on him and caught him long before he could reach the trees. Not that the woods could have saved him. There was no hiding anymore; they were too close.

The man with the pitchfork thrust it into his back.

All the breath blew from Jack, and he knew he was as good as dead, but he staggered toward the forest regardless. Another stab, and he fell to the ground, struggling for breath and too weak to even try to rise. He hoped the end would come quickly now. The rest of the mob ran up on him and began beating him. Once more the pitchfork was run into him. Jack died, wishing he'd just kept to himself that morning.

* * *

Thinking myself under the protection of my cousin, I was less than discreet in my use of the traditional Mass, though I doubt I could have been terribly secretive, even had Charles not threatened war. It seemed cowardly in the extreme to do in secret for myself what should be for all believers. I would have been ashamed to deny publicly my actions.

My own household was set against me, to rail against my worship. It was useless to attempt to convince me or cow me through my servants, for many in my household protected me from the pressure for the sake of being allowed to attend Mass themselves. All attempts to move me were taken no more seriously than childish whining.

Finally my brother's council sent men directly to me. Lord Chancellor Sir Richard Rich, Secretary Petre, and a fellow named Wingfield came to Beaulieu to pressure me to do the one thing I could not ever do. I received them with a calmness rare for me, for I knew before I saw them I could not be moved. Indeed, there was a species of peace in knowing there was no decision to be made. I knew without the least doubt where my course lay, and the interview at hand would be naught more than an exercise in debate. No more than an afternoon's diversion.

Mary sat in the presence chamber as Rich, Petre, and Wingfield entered and removed their hats. She refrained from smiling, for it would have been unseemly and unladylike, but she was in a high mood that day. These men could challenge her all they wished, and she would treat it a lark, for the worst they could do to her was to her nothing at all. In fact, it might even have pleased her to be hauled off to London and the Tower in a loud, adamant demonstration of her determination and faith. Then Dudley and the rest might finally understand the hopelessness of their cause and let her be. Her mind was made up. She knew what was right, and she knew there was nothing that lay before her today she could not withstand.

Rich produced a letter bearing the king's seal. "I have a message from his king's majesty."

Mary slipped from her chair, descended the dais, and knelt before the chancellor to receive the letter in both hands. She kissed the seal and said, "I kiss this letter because my brother has signed it, and not the matter contained herein, which is only the mere action of the council." She gave these men a sharp glance and observed their reactions. Rich and Petre didn't flinch, but Wingfield's cheeks flushed pink. He, at least, seemed to know their mission was an evil one and they would fail.

She stood and turned her back on the three without dismissing them as she broke the seal and read the letter on her way back to the dais. As she read, she perched on the edge of the seat and held the paper up to the light of the diamond-paned window nearby. The day was overcast, and the window let in precious little light.

The missive was, as she'd expected, an exhortation from Edward's council—meaning Dudley—that she desist in practicing the traditional religion. Wry amusement took her as she recognized the writing style of Dudley's secretary. "Ah!" she said under her breath but loudly enough for the benefit of the trio before her. "I see Mr. Cecil has taken great pains here." She nodded as if she admired the handiwork of language and didn't care much what the words meant. She didn't, really, for they were not her brother's.

Once finished with the letter, she folded it away to her lap and turned her attention to her visitors. "Very well, I think brevity is in order here. State your mission, if you please." She had no patience with this attempt at coercion, for it was a waste of time all around, and there were things she'd rather be doing just then. Namely, attending Mass. It was time for her to meet her chaplains, and she was impatient for these men to leave so she could go and not think of them anymore.

"We come to implore you to cease employment of the papist rite and take up the Anglican service instead."

"I've told my brother I cannot obey him on that. I don't know why the council persists in annoying me with their demands. I am supported in this. A great many of the English people would also like to be so privileged and would take up arms for relief."

"There are also many who would prefer you quit the illegal practice. They are many and powerful, by name—"

"I care not for the rehearsal of their names, for I know who they are, and they are all of one mind. And rather than use any other service than that ordained during the life of my father, I will lay my head on the block." She knew her brother had nothing to do with this. He was not and never had been the one making the decisions in London. She suspected something nasty was going to happen here today, but even so, she was at peace with whatever these men might do. Truly, she would have relinquished her life rather than continue the struggle to find a course between what they wanted and what she knew was right. "You may have silenced the priests of this kingdom, but you cannot alter my spirit. By no means will I allow heresy in my household."

Rich's eyes narrowed, and she readied herself for bad news. "You would do well to know that Rochester, Walgrave, and

Englefield have been imprisoned for their failure to convince you of your folly."

She raised her chin, for this was not bad news at all. They were being punished, as was proper for those who had tried to steer her from her proper course. Her reply to these councilors was tart. "How foolish of the council to send my own servants to control me. They are, after all, my servants, and I am not in the habit of obeying them." Surely Dudley couldn't expect her to feel guilt for this, as it was entirely his own device, and she wanted none of it.

Rich seemed flustered as he realized she wasn't reacting as expected. "As a result, you've another controller appointed to your household."

This tactic did affect Mary badly. Her temper rose, and control quite left her. "I shall appoint my own officers, for my years are sufficient for it. When your controller comes, I shall leave forthwith. Depend on that." Her eyes narrowed at Rich, and she leaned forward to emphasize her words. "Understand, Lord Chancellor, that I have been sickly of late and occasionally throughout my life. If I chance to die, before I do I will protest openly that you and the council are the cause of my death."

Then she rose from the chair, stepped down from the dais, and knelt at the councilors' feet. She removed a ring from her finger and offered it to him. "Do give this to my brother as a token that I would die his true subject and sister and obey him in all things except matters of spirit." He took the ring. She stood, stared hard into Rich's face, and added, "But this will never be told His Majesty, I am certain."

With that, having lost her composure, she turned and left the room.

In her privy chamber, she vomited into her basin, and several of her ladies hurried to clean her up. Tears tried to rise, but she swallowed them. She was deadly tired of the fear. She hated the constant confrontation, and hated always having to pretend a strength she did not feel. Once more she thought she would throw up, but took deep breaths and was able to calm herself. She longed for the peace of worship.

She ordered her ladies to help her ready herself for the chapel, and they hurried to gather her shawl and prayer book. A maid hurried in from the antechamber, breathless. "The lord chancellor has gathered the household. He's told us all no Mass is to be held. They say we would all be accused of treason if we attended. Is that true, Your Grace? Treason? Would they kill us all?"

Mary sighed. "Nonsense. Not even Dudley would attempt such a thing."

Her maid said, "They've arrested three of the priests."

Mary realized just how bad that was. Dudley had punished her controller and others in an attempt to influence her. His next attempt might be much worse. He might make an example of the chaplains. They had ever been targets of Dudley's evil. The thought of her dear, brave priests receiving a bloody and agonizing traitor's death made her shiver. "I'll have to dismiss them, to relieve them of their dilemma." It would seem the council had succeeded in controlling the makeup of her staff after all.

Then she went to the private door to the passage that led from her privy chamber to the rear of the chapel. There she found her fourth priest awaiting her, dressed in vestments and Bible in hand. He had a white-eyed look that told her he knew what was going on in the rest of the palace. She thought it brave of him to have retained his robe and not stripped to his linens in his fear.

"Come!" she ordered. "Come inside, lest they find you!" She took the surprised man by an arm and pulled him into the room. "Under the bed!"

The poor fellow sputtered an objection, but she wouldn't hear it. "Go! In haste!"

He obeyed his mistress and crawled beneath the heavy wooden bed hung with silk, velvet, and woolen tapestry. Mary smoothed the coverlet and shook out the wrinkles created by his passing, then sat on the bed just in time to face Wingfield, who entered without invitation.

He looked around and said, "We seek your chaplain."

"Which one? There are four, you know."

"Any. I understand there is one loose in the palace."

"Only one?"

His eyes narrowed at her. "Where is he?"

"For what could you possibly need a Catholic priest?"

He continued looking around and declined to reply to her jibe. The ladies stood in the middle of the room, silent and wide-eyed.

Mary said, "Seek him elsewhere and leave my private chamber." It was an order from a princess, and he obeyed as with habit. The women sat after he left, silent and listening for sounds outside the door. They were thankful to hear none.

But now there were voices outdoors in the courtyard below, and Mary went to the window. She leaned out over the deep sill to see Rich, Petre, and Wingfield awaiting their horses. In a fit of anger and not a little relief that her priest had gone undiscovered, she shouted to them, "I pray you! Ask the lords of the council that my controller may shortly return, for since his departure, I figure the accounts myself. To be plain with you, I weary of my office, as anyone must. If my officer is sent to prison, beshrew me if he go not merrily and with a good-will, to lie idle while I do his work."

Her ladies gawked at her impudence and giggled behind their hands. So encouraged, she added, "I pray God to send you well in your souls, and in your bodies, for some of you have but weak ones!"

She turned to find her ladies with hands clapped to their mouths, eyes wide with fearful amusement. Mary went to the bed and lifted the coverlet to address her chaplain. "Be still until they leave. We will hide you here and protect you from this madness."

His muffled voice came from beneath. "Thank you, Your Grace. I thank you most humbly."

"Shh," she said, then dropped the cover and sat on the bed. With sinking heart, she realized there was nothing left to her but to take her worship into secrecy and end her public Mass. Tears rose, and she struggled to swallow them.

CHAPTER ELEVEN

The condition of the English economy worsened throughout my brother's reign. Inflation and debasement of the coinage made English money nearly worthless. Prices soared. Beggars swarmed the streets of London. While Dudley and his cohorts made much of themselves, styling themselves in unheard-of ways and gathering about themselves the wealth denied everyone else in the kingdom, the angry subjects of my brother loudly complained of their misery. Rebellions rose and were thwarted. Men went to the scaffold. We all feared war with Charles, and for me that would have been an incomparable disaster. By God's grace it was avoided.

Edward lost his second uncle to the axe as Dudley grasped at straws to secure his own position and power. Somerset was charged with high treason, having plotted a coup that would have ended in the assassinations of the entire council. Like his brother, he'd earned his execution.

Then, when my poor brother lay dying of the wasting disease, Dudley made haste to wrest the throne from the proper succession and secure it for his own son. A strategic error that would soon cost him his life.

Dudley went to the king's privy chamber first thing after rising, as was his habit every morning. But these days it was less a privilege than a worrisome duty. He had business elsewhere that was far more pressing than attendance on Edward. The king was dying, and that fact needed to be kept quiet. Not that it could be entirely secret, but Dudley wouldn't have it bandied about irresponsibly. Too much talk could bring too much support for Mary in a coup. Even now she might be readying an army to take over London. There was writing on the wall, big and bold, that told Dudley he would not live much past the king if that papist witch Mary were to ascend the throne. Something needed to be done, and in a hurry. If Edward died before Mary could be taken out of the succession, all would be lost.

The privy chamber stank of fear as well as disease. Edward lay in his bed, thin and racked with cough, his skin translucent and his lips nearly white. Bandages covered much of his body, where lesions ate away at him and left large pink spots of bloody seepage on the bleached linen. One of Edward's physicians was occupied winding a fresh dressing over one arm, and the discarded cloth lay in a loose pile on the floor, edges frayed, and limp with various humors. Several council members, including Paget, stood about, most with lips pressed together and deep creases of worry in their foreheads.

"How does the king this morning?" Dudley addressed Paget in a low voice.

"The only good I can say is that he lives. For how long, I cannot tell."

Of course not. Still breathing was the best one could ask for anymore, and soon even that would be impossible. Dudley received this information with a measure of relief. He said to Paget, "Something must be done, and soon."

Paget looked at him as if he'd just brought breathless news that the sun was yellow.

But Dudley continued. "I have a plan."

The others of the council standing in the room turned their attention to Dudley, and he included them in his private conference with Paget. "Obviously we cannot allow Mary to take the throne. Nor Elizabeth, for we cannot find cause to exclude Mary without also excluding the other illegitimate princess."

Though Dudley sensed a hesitation in Paget that perhaps this wasn't entirely true, Paget nevertheless kept the thought to himself. God knew what Elizabeth might do were she to become queen, and nobody wanted to find out. The others nodded in agreement and looked to Dudley for him to go on.

He obliged, pleased to see he had their full attention and Paget's tacit—and probably provisional—cooperation. "The only course open to us is through the female line and Henry's sisters." He added in a rather snide aside, "I've never known a man to have so many female relatives." There was something vaguely unsettling about all those women so close in blood to Henry.

Paget said, "You speak as if the succession were only a matter of choice."

Dudley shrugged. "Old King Henry set the order we so ab-hor and yet never made his daughters legitimate. Is there cause to suppose Edward might not make his own will and choose his own successor?"

"Making a will and having the king's subjects honor his choice are not the same thing. Mary's supporters are enough in number to make a stiff fight for anyone attempting to take her place."

Dudley held up one finger. "I think I can offer a plan satis-factory to all."

Paget nodded that he should continue.

"We can all agree that sister Margaret's issue is out of the question, yes?"

They all nodded again. Henry's sister Margaret had married James IV of Scotland. Her son, James V, had died a decade ago, and his daughter Mary was a ten-year-old foreign mon-arch in France while her mother ruled as regent in Scotland. Putting Mary Stuart in the succession would be as handing En-gland over to Marie de Guise, her mad Scottish allies, and her unholy French relatives. Not to mention that the little Scot-tish queen was Catholic and completely unsuitable for En-gland's needs just then.

"Therefore we must have Edward decide the succession in favor of the progeny of Henry's other sister." Mary Tudor, the younger daughter of Henry VII.

"How terribly unfortunate she had no sons."

Dudley didn't think it unfortunate at all, for a son would have inherited without question, and he himself would have been left out in the cold as surely as if one of Edward's sisters ascended. "Be that as it may, we do have recourse. Mary's grand-daughter, Jane."

He paused a moment to let that sink in, then hurried to

speak as Paget opened his mouth to respond. "She's young, but no younger than Edward."

The men looked over at the king, who was mercifully asleep. They returned their attention to the discussion, voices lowering. Paget said, "Even if the king signs a device to fix the succession, how do you think the nobility will accept this girl? Her claim is tenuous, and she's female in the bargain."

"He'll settle the succession not on Jane herself but on her eldest son."

"She's unmarried."

"She's to marry Guilford."

There was a stunned silence. Dudley held his breath as he gauged their reaction. Guilford was his own son, and now his intention was out in the open. Because a husband was by law and nature the ruler of his wife, any female monarch in England would be subject to that. Were Jane to marry Guilford Dudley and inherit the throne of England, even without the crown matrimonial bestowed by parliament, he would effectively become the king of England. All would look to him for rule rather than his wife. Furthermore, were the marriage to take place before the announcement of the king's will, there would be no treaty—or even discussion—regarding his powers in government. By the time anyone knew Jane was heir apparent, the marriage would be fait accompli, and Guilford would become king without Parliament or the commons having the slightest opportunity to object.

The look in Paget's eyes told Dudley he understood all the implications of this plan. The subtleties weren't lost on many of the others, either. Before one could speak, he said, "Jane is a devout Protestant, and so is Guilford." Dudley may have been stretching the point about Guilford, but at least the young man wasn't a devout Catholic as Mary was.

Paget finally spoke. "You've approached her father? You're certain he's amenable to the match?"

Dudley shrugged. "We've spoken. He'd be a fool to marry her to anyone else." Paget nodded in agreement. They all knew Dudley had enough influence over the king to convince him to settle the succession on whomever he chose, and Jane had cousins with equal claim to royal blood. Declining this marriage offer would be no smarter for Jane's father than shooting himself in the foot.

"There will be rebellion."

"The ascension of Mary would mean civil war, without a doubt. There will be a fight regardless. We should approach the coming troubles from a position of strength rather than weakness."

"Have we the resources to withstand it? Can we prevail?"

Dudley hesitated to tell too much, but needed to convince Paget this not only could be accomplished, but that it was the best benefit for them all, not just himself. "I have amassed arms and provisions and have men ready to control enough castles and strongholds to quell any unrest."

Paget nodded.

The king awoke with an outburst of wet coughing, and all attention in the room turned to him. The physician on duty and his assistants burst into action like a disturbed nest of roaches and hurried to prepare a drink to aid the cough. One of the assistants took a basin from under the bed and thrust it under Edward's chin just in time to catch a dribble of bright red blood. The young man spat and moaned, his eyes dull with pain and a desire to sleep again.

Paget whispered to his companions, "We must move quickly."

* * *

We all knew Edward was dying, but of course nobody knew exactly when, for that is the way of things. John Dudley would surely make an attempt to maintain his power, but my supporters were kept ignorant of exactly how. Indeed, the death of His King's Majesty was kept secret for days after. They summoned Elizabeth and myself to the deathbed, ostensibly for a final visit with our brother, but Dudley's true motive in demanding our presence was that we might be more easily arrested if we stepped voluntarily into the palace. But the protector hadn't counted on the prescience of Henry's daughters. Elizabeth ignored the summons, no more obedient to authority than her mother. I obeyed in word if not spirit, for the true spirit was evil and ulterior. I could hardly have been expected to present myself on the authority of an order so given. I began a slow progress to London, expecting at any moment the approach of armed men.

Simon Renard and his fellow imperial diplomats, Jacque de Marnix and Jean de Montmorency, stood in the presence chamber at Greenwich, awaiting entry to the privy chamber to see the king, but as the day wore on, it appeared less and less likely they would be admitted. The guard stood silent in their blood-red livery, as straight and stern as the iron pikes they held, ignoring the imperial envoy, and there was no traffic through the chamber door to speak of. Not even of the sort one might expect of a sickroom, where there would be a need for caretakers, food, and medicines. How odd.

Montmorency drifted over to a window while Renard settled onto an upholstered bench near an empty candelabra to rest his feet, sore from too much standing in new shoes that didn't quite fit. The day was warm and unusually sunny, the summer well along now. One could smell the river, dark and dirty below the window, and sounds of the streets on the other side drifted in with the faint breeze. Renard idly considered the commons scurrying about below, going about their lives, unaware their king lay dying. Many might not care if they did know. He looked over at the door to the privy chamber again, a sour feeling in his gut. His sense was that something was terribly wrong. Nothing about this place was right, but he wasn't entirely certain what it could be.

Montmorency gazed out the window, then leaned over the deep sill to take a longer look out to the side. Then the other side. He looked over at the privy chamber door, then back out the window. He grunted.

"Excellency," he said. Something like alarm in his voice caught Renard's attention. Marnix and Renard looked over at him. Montmorency said nothing but made a small gesture to them both that they should come look. Renard reluctantly hauled himself to his sore feet and strolled over to the window. The landscape across the river lay before him. Montmorency didn't need to tell him what he was looking at.

Men-at-arms. A mass of pikemen had gathered in a field on the other side of the river. Armor and helmets flashed in the sunshine, and a forest of iron pikes waved as the men milled about. Then Montmorency pointed wordlessly off in the distance. There Renard saw a line of wagons making its way along a road toward the west. The train was at least a mile long, and though many of the wagons were covered and seemed loaded with foodstuffs, many were not and appeared burdened with cannon and shot. At a whisper, Montmorency said to his associates, "Where do you reckon they're headed?"

Renard looked upstream toward Westminster. There wasn't much to see from here in that direction, but he knew what lay beyond the trees and around the bend. "The Tower."

"Right. That's where they are going." He nodded toward the pikemen, who had not yet begun their march but seemed likely to head in the same direction as the supply wagons. He continued. "Have you noticed the heavy guard on the palace today?" He turned for a glance back at the guards before the door to the privy chamber. They gave no indication of interest in the envoys' quiet conversation, which was in German and probably would not have been understood by these common soldiers in any case.

Renard grunted and realized that was what bothered him. The guard on the king's chamber was twice what one might expect. Montmorency was right. The palace guard had an unusually strong presence today. And yesterday as well. The air of emergency seemed a bit more intense than one might expect from a household in the grip of a deathwatch that had been going on for months. He said, "The king is too ill to receive us, and I believe them. If he is dead, he is certainly too ill by far for an audience."

I did not yet know of the device naming Jane Grey as heir apparent, but there was ample reason to distrust the council even without it.

At Hoddesdon, a clandestine messenger from friends arrived with the news that Edward had died and that John Dudley's son

Robert was on his way to us with several hundred knights to take us prisoner. Though the letter was unsigned, we understood it had come from Charles's envoy in London. It contained a great deal of information regarding Dudley's preparations for war and the news of Guilford Dudley's marriage to Jane Grey. Though we did not yet know of Edward's will, plainly the council had no intention of relinquishing the Crown to me. There was no choice of action and no time to lose. Nine of us departed immediately to the southwest, toward Yarmouth. There we would escape across the channel to Flanders and plan our recourse from there. With only two maids and six gentlemen to escort me, I fled for my life.

Renard, his two associates, and their attendants were on their way to the Tower to meet with John Dudley and some select members of the council on this night. A few days ago the regent had finally admitted the king was dead, which came as no surprise to the imperial envoys. Indeed, Dudley had been rather insulting to present the news so breathlessly, as if they were too stupid to have worked the fact out for themselves. Renard wondered whether the English all assumed the rest of the world was as backward as themselves. Now he and his companions rode through the narrow streets, hurrying to arrive at the Tower before dark, which was almost upon them. Renard disliked London, where even the nobility seemed rather grubby and unstylish. And rude. Englishmen—even those among the ruling class—had no manners.

The men jumped and their horses shied at the boom of cannon fire from the White Tower just within sight. A thin bit of smoke rose into the air, then another shot echoed across the press of houses on this side of the Thames. Off in the distance voices rose here and there. Heralds spreading news, and the three diplomats perked their ears to hear.

"Long live the queen!" came a cry.

The three looked to each other in question. Queen? Certainly not Mary. Not Elizabeth, either, for they knew she was nowhere near London. Who had been coronated, then?

Then the name of Jane Grey was shouted by a herald near enough for them to hear. Of course. Renard should have guessed it. They all knew of the recent marriage of Jane Grey and Dudley's son. He should have anticipated this. Perhaps he was as stupid as an Englishman after all.

In stunned silence the imperial envoy listened to the heralds in the streets, who were alone in their enthusiasm for the new queen, their voices lonely, interspersed with bits of silence. Folks who had paused in their business to listen began to talk, but nobody joined in with their own cries of joy. Indeed, in some quarters there were shouts in support of Mary. A fistfight broke out nearby, and others came to put a stop to it. The atmosphere in the London streets was eerie. Such a subdued reaction to the announcement of a new monarch was nearly unheard of. It did not bode well for the reign of Queen Jane.

Renard spurred his horse forward, now in a hurry to get to the Tower, and his companions followed.

They found Dudley in the great hall of the White Tower. The stronghold swarmed with men-at-arms, and every door, inside and out, was heavily guarded. All the various apartments were abuzz with men preparing for war. Renard made mental notes of things he saw, the number of cannon ranged along the battlements, the number and types of men at hand, the stacks of supplies and ordnance everywhere he looked. Later, once he was tucked away in sleeping quarters, he would write it all down for dispatch to Charles.

Renard, Marnix, and Montmorency all bowed in diplomatic greeting and made formal congratulations to Dudley as an Englishman on the coronation of his new monarch. It made Renard want to spit, but the situation called for great discretion, and this was not a moment to invoke the name of Mary. Dudley nodded his appreciation of the sentiment, though he must have guessed the extent of Renard's doubt and distaste. Imperial support of Mary had never been a secret.

Just then a shout at the door announced the entrance of the new queen.

Queen Jane was not quite sixteen years old, born within days of Edward, and she appeared much younger. More pale than even an average Englishwoman, she was thin and moved with a frail, ethereal presence, nearly as if her feet did not actually touch the floor but rather floated an inch or two above it. She held her chin high, and though Renard saw an intelligent light in her eye, he also noted she never looked directly at anyone. Not in the face, at any rate. Her gaze settled on the chest, shoulder, or even the hands of those she addressed. An irritating enough trait in any woman, but fatal in a monarch. Renard took heart there might be a chance for Mary to wrest her rightful throne from this usurper after all. The men all bowed their obeisance to the young queen.

Jane addressed Dudley. "Northumberland, I wish to have a word with you in private." Why she hadn't sent a messenger to summon Dudley to her privy chamber, Renard had to wonder. Not that he minded this opportunity to see her personally and assess her. From this visit he would have quite a bit of valuable information to pass along to His Highness the emperor. She continued. "I've summoned you twice, but I go ignored. I must insist you come with me immediately."

Dudley bowed again. "Certainly, Your Grace." He turned his attention to Renard, but before he could speak, Jane interrupted.

"Now, if you please." He turned to her again, and she continued, "It concerns the crown matrimonial. I shan't give it, and I wish to have this matter settled without delay or confusion."

Dudley actually paled, and he went a bit walleyed. Renard attended to what was said next, with great interest.

Jane went on as if she couldn't see she'd struck a nerve, and Renard wondered whether she even realized it. "I shan't offer my husband the Crown, and now I understand it's expected. I really don't know how anyone can expect me to simply hand over the throne to—"

Dudley took the queen by the arm and drew her away from the imperial envoy. In a low, tense voice he bent to admonish Jane in a way that seemed very much against protocol, even in uncivilized England. Renard and the others couldn't hear what was said, but could guess that Jane was being told she would bloody well do as she was told.

She objected and said quite clearly for the room to hear, "I should be content to make him a duke but would never consent to make him king."

Dudley looked up and spotted his son entering the room. "Guilford! What sort of husband are you? Come retrieve your wife and educate her on the value of discretion, if you please!" Aside from Jane's appalling indiscretion, Dudley's behavior was a shocking lack of respect for a monarch, which left Renard with his mouth agape.

Jane tried to object, but again Dudley grasped her by her upper arm, and though everyone in the room was held at stunned attention, nobody came to her rescue, least of all Guilford, who came to claim her by also taking her by the arm. He drew her toward the door and from the room, all the while lecturing her in a low voice as if he were admonishing a child. She argued in response, but her words had no discernible effect on her husband.

The scene left Renard speechless, but Dudley didn't let him stand there very long. "Come," he said, and guided them toward the outer door. "My man will show you to your quarters." He made a gesture to one of his attendants, who smiled and bowed to them all. Then he quickly herded the three diplomats from the room and toward less sensitive areas of the Tower. Renard, Marnix, and Montmorency found themselves shunted far enough away from the royal household to make Renard less than sanguine about the treatment. The empire's diplomatic relations with England certainly were suffering this evening.

The three changed from their traveling clothes, and their servants had been dismissed for the time being. Marnix and Montmorency lounged in chairs by the fire, sipping mulled wine in preparation to retire. Renard looked to the door of their suite. After some consideration, he said to his fellows, "Stay here. I feel the need to stretch my legs."

Marnix gave him an exhausted look that said he was content to let Renard wander about all he wished and that he himself was in for the night. Montmorency leaned back in his chair and warmed his hands on the cup held between his palms. "Enjoy your stroll," he said, then took a sip. "Do not be seen."

Renard only nodded, then slipped from the apartments to

test how far the English would let him wander before he was escorted back to his bedchamber and a sentry set on his door.

Though the guard was heavy throughout the Tower, this far into the sanctum they were less alert than they might be at the gate, and anyone wandering about was more or less assumed to belong there. Renard donned an insouciant air of authority along with a bit of irritable attitude, and everyone he encountered treated him as an honored guest. He moved through the great hall, greeting courtiers as a diplomat and wishing well their new queen.

To his advantage, tonight the household was in a tizzy of uncontrolled apprehension over the coronation. Nobody wanted to ignite an incident. He went barely noticed.

Renard made his way toward the council chamber off the king's gallery, in hopes of learning or guessing the council's plans regarding Mary. Once past the great hall, he went yet unchallenged through the great chamber and through to the queen's watching chamber. About to step into the king's gallery, he heard angry voices and halted. They were coming his way. Too deep into the system of private chambers to want to be caught by anyone on the council, Renard instantly stepped behind a large tapestry hung nearby. There was barely enough room behind it for him to hide without an obvious bulge in the fabric, and he hoped his feet wouldn't show much. He stood as still as possible. Then he mentally cursed himself for his too hasty response, for there would be no explaining this if he were caught hiding behind a tapestry. But there was nothing for it now but to be very, very still and hope for the best.

The voices came near enough for him to discern the conversation. Then they entered the watching chamber and paused in their progress. Renard's fear of being found evaporated as the words being said loomed large in his concern. The voices were Dudley, Paget, and a third man whose voice was less familiar and not quite identifiable.

"The letter is a statement of right to the throne. Mary thinks she will wrest it from us."

"You mean, from Jane," said the third voice.

"Of course, Henry."

Ah, now Renard knew the voice. It was Henry Grey, the duke of Suffolk. Jane's father. Dudley continued. "She's evaded Robert and his army. If she succeeds in crossing the channel, surely Charles will support her and give her men to return for a revolt."

Relief filled Renard. Mary was alive and aware of her danger. She would escape Dudley's clutches and return to claim her throne. He closed his eyes and mouthed silently a quick prayer of thanks.

The air behind this tapestry grew stuffy, and Renard found breathing an effort. He wished the men would move on so he could step out and take a deep, cool, dust-free breath.

But Dudley continued, rooted to his spot. "Further, we've word that Bath, Sussex, Wharton, Mordant, and Bedingfield are all with her at Kenninghall. They've brought horsemen for her, and a number of commons bearing pitchforks and sickles. It appears a very rebellion."

"That much support?" Paget sounded doubtful rather than fearful.

"The report comes from Robert. I trust it."

Paget made a neutral humming sound in an expedient and rather noncommittal concession of the point.

Dudley said, "We must send a force. Immediately. We can't let her reach Flanders."

"Who would command?"

"Why, you, of course, Henry."

There was a bit of sputtering and hawing. "I'm afraid not, Your Grace. Not unless you intend to keep watch over my daughter every moment." It crossed Renard's mind that Dudley would be happy to keep his thumb on the puppet queen with her father off to war. But Dudley said nothing, and Suffolk continued. "She's not so strong a girl as we might have her, though in the end that might be to the good. At any rate, God knows what she might do with her newfound authority without me here to calm her. In her current status, there might be inordinate and irreparable damage."

Dudley gave that a thought, then said, "Right."

Paget suggested, "What about yourself, John? As a commander you bring terror to men's hearts. A force with you at the lead couldn't help but prevail."

Again Dudley considered, then said, "You may be right." His words agreed, but his voice betrayed doubt. Perhaps he was reluctant to make himself absent from court just then, with so much at stake and so little surety of the outcome.

"Of course, he's right," said Suffolk. "There's really nothing for it but for you to lead the resistance to this revolt. Show the world you're the defender of your queen. How many men have we ready?"

"Thousands. Three thousand men-at-arms, all the cannon here in the Tower, and a great many wagons of shot. I've seven ships guarding the coast at Yarmouth. She won't get away and will have to stand and fight here in England."

Paget said, "Good. You'll leave immediately, then."

The three men found chairs nearby and settled in to discuss the minutiae of the military action. Renard continued to stand behind the tapestry, feet aching and legs stiffening. Nevertheless, he attended closely and carefully memorized every detail he heard.

Peter Barnacle arrived at Framlingham Castle just in time, it seemed. The place was a-bustle with men and arms, knights and their attendants, and swarms of commoners such as himself wanting to fight for the right of the true princess to ascend to her throne as queen. It had rained, and the ground was spongy wet and slick in places. The force had been there long enough for horses to trample the sod to mud. It squished through the holes in Peter's shoes so that he longed mightily for dry feet.

The scene leaving his home in London had been a teary one. Ruth was pregnant again, but only three of their children had lived past their first year, and there had been some miscarriages. Not an excessive number, but she fussed at the decision to join Mary's forces, though she was as much in support of Mary as he was. But she rather felt he should stay at home and only fight if the battle came to him. Sarah was twelve now and somewhat unruly. She turned sulky when she learned of his plan to leave. Richard and Margaret were yet small and knew little of what was going on.

Peter's fear was that the fight might never reach London if Mary lacked support at the start. So he'd taken a sack of as much bread as could be spared from the household and a waterskin, slung his hunting bow and a quiver of arrows over his shoulder, and set off down the road to the coast.

He'd ridden part of the way from London on the back of a passing wagon but had walked most of it and would be happy to present himself at the castle today, just for the sake of a meal and a place to sleep. He had but a small supply of arrows, but he figured there might be more to be had in exchange for his offer of service to Mary. And always there were some to pick up after an engagement. Even a small hunt left arrows lying about on the ground; Peter could imagine the supply to be had after a battle.

He made his way toward a cluster of men around a fire where meat was roasting. It smelled like heaven. "Any chance of claiming a ration this evening?"

The men looked up at him, and one said, "You ain't from around these parts, is ye?"

Peter shook his head. "Down from London, thereabouts."

The speaker waggled his black, beetled eyebrows. "Ohhh, he's from *London*, then," he said to his companions with good humor, but humor nevertheless. Then to Peter, "Not a spy, is ye?"

Again Peter shook his head. It was a reasonable suspicion, but it just happened to be wrong. "A Catholic. Come to set things right." He nodded to affirm his words.

That brought chuckling and nodding, for they all were there for that. Suddenly Peter was no longer such a stranger. The local said, "Ye haven't a care about her sex?"

Peter shook his head once more. "The one they've crowned isn't any more a man than the princess, and with less right to the throne, to my mind. And anyone at all has got to be an improvement over that tyrant who has been ruling in the king's stead these past years." Oh, but it felt wonderful to be able to say that aloud! "I wouldn't mind a bit more bread on my table of an evening, and a pair of shoes that ain't worn through." He lifted one soggy shoe from the ground to show the spot where his toe could be seen through the leather.

The group by the fire all muttered their anger-tinged agreement and nodded vigorously as they displayed their own thin soles. The speaker said, "I say 'tis God's judgment against the heretics. 'Tis the spiritual corruption of the Lutherans on the council what's made things so hard. As soon as we've got our Catholic queen, she'll make things right between us and him."

Peter thought that might be true, though he was one to wait and see what God wanted. In all his time on earth, he'd never known the Lord to shout things. Always he had to be still and listen to know what to believe.

Another one of the locals pointed toward a wagon nearby, where a man was picking mud from the hooves of horses tethered to the back end. "Ask that fellow over there for yer bread ration, and perhaps there'll be some meat for ye as well."

"Thank you much," said Peter, and he tipped his floppy hat in imitation of the gentlemen who so irritated him. More loudly and with greater cheer he declared, "Long live Queen Mary!"

"Oh, aye!" said the local. The others joined him as he shouted, "Long live Queen Mary!"

The cry was taken up by some farther away, then men even farther off, spreading across the field and into the distance. "Long live Queen Mary! Long live Queen Mary!" Wordless hurrahs rippled across the army after that until the noise settled into a widespread good cheer.

Peter looked up at the castle and saw a figure at a window, gazing out across the expanse of armed men. He thought it might have been Mary herself and liked the idea enough to decide it must be so. He couldn't help but smile that Mary would soon be on the throne, and all would be well.

CHAPTER TWELVE

The struggle was a short one and near bloodless. Dudley may have once been a formidable commander, but over the previous years had made himself so well hated he could no longer trust his own men. The countrymen hated him as well, and all the support they gave anyone in this time of confusion was mere lip service. When my commander entered a town to declare me, the people cheered. Then when my army left and Dudley appeared, they cheered Jane. Nobody knew who would be queen, and so nobody truly supported either of us. There was no telling who could prevail.

Dudley hoped for aid from France but waited in vain. And most disheartening for Dudley was the mutiny of several of his ships in Yarmouth Harbour. Hundreds of seamen rose against their captains in favor of me and my cause. That, in the end, turned the tide, for when the council heard of it they revolted against Dudley and issued a warrant for his arrest. When I heard that bit of news, it was as if the heavens had opened up to reveal a bright, shiny new day. I knew I was meant to prevail. I'd long felt I would one day be queen, and it appeared that day finally had come.

In London, Renard rode out to join the procession for the sake of witnessing this great moment. With royal mace-bearers at the van, the council members who had defected from Dudley's oppressive leadership rode into the public square. All those about them went silent at their approach, and not a few commoners slipped away down other streets to go unseen. The riders surrounded the cross at the center of the square and came to a halt. All was quiet, save for the occasional snort of a horse or clop of hoof on cobble. Paget sat his mount with utter dignity, as if this weren't a defeat of all he held holy. Indeed, he put on the appearance that this was a most joyous occasion for himself and his fellow councilors, the better to convince onlookers of his sincerity, Renard was certain.

"All ye men of England, draw near and attend!" He paused, then repeated the call and looked around to see he had the full attention of everyone in the street. After another short pause, he proceeded. "By virtue of the settlement of succession by our late king Henry VIII, which designates the heir presumptive to Edward VI as his daughter Lady Mary Tudor, and by declaration of the regency council of King Edward VI, on this day I proclaim Lady Mary Tudor queen of England, Ireland, and Wales!" He rolled the paper bearing its heavy seal and held it in both hands across the pommel of his saddle as he looked around at his audience. For a moment, there was no sound in the square.

Then he shouted, "Long live Queen Mary!"

That seeped into the consciousness of the stunned onlookers, and finally the crowd believed him. A shout went up. Men and women in the streets began to holler, "The Lady Mary is proclaimed queen!" The shout rang out across the city, through the streets and from the highest windows. Whistling and joyous laughter rose. The relief was palpable, and Renard well understood their joy that war had been averted. Some folks danced and sang. Old men, even, and some threw off garments in their delirious celebration. Renard laughed, as happy about the news as the English commons, and looked forward to writing the letter he would send to Charles in the morning.

For two days bells rang, and the celebration continued. Bonfires at night lit the city, and all the people rejoiced.

Dudley watched the royal standard-bearers riding ahead, flags swaying with the rhythm of walking horses, and reflected how only a week ago he would have been master of these men rather than prisoner. Surrounded now by horsemen who protected him from angry mobs, he removed the cap from his head and held it in his fists in a gesture of begging for mercy. He was as good as dead, and he knew it. There would be no forgiveness for him, and the shouted epithets of these massed Londoners gave him also to understand that any charity in Mary's heart would be overruled by the demands of her subjects. He thought of his sons and hoped they at least would be spared the axe.

* * *

A fortnight after the proclamation, Mary made a triumphant procession into London that contained nearly a thousand mounted men, and ladies by the hundreds. Her raiment glittered so well as to set her apart from the others, even among the wealthiest nobility and even seen from a great distance. Renard, who was accustomed to displays of the enormous wealth of his master and several other princes on the Continent, was impressed by the rich, stylish purple velvet of Mary's gown, her satin sleeves laden with finely wrought gold, and a boggling display of jewels. She wore a gold baldric that shone so brightly in the sun as to flash and blind the eye. Trumpets and heralds preceded her. Crowds raised a shout even more joyous than on her proclamation, for today they were calling to her personally. They let her know she was their queen come to save them from the darkness that had cloaked their land, and they loved her for it.

When the procession drew near, Renard saw Mary's face lit with that joy. Her eyes sparkled as brightly as the gold across her breast, and the slight dimples in her cheeks deepened in a genuine smile. The rosy glow in her spoke of a life that had been denied her and now surged forth in confidence. She appeared ten years younger than when he'd last seen her, and it warmed his heart to see her so.

Montmorency sat his horse to Renard's left as they watched the parade together. Once the bulk of it had passed, leaving only lesser nobility and some commoners on foot, Montmorency leaned over to say in a voice just audible above the ruckus, "She'll bring back our religion."

Renard nodded. "I think we all welcome it."

"Not the Protestants."

"Of course not. They're heretics, and God doesn't love them."

"They would have us believe she is the Antichrist."

Renard chuckled at the idea. Mary the Antichrist. It would horrify her to know anyone thought that. Even her enemies. "But see ..." He gestured to the cheering crowds. "The English people want her. They don't want the old rule. They don't want to live in error, either. They want what Mary can give them, which is a return to the days when a man could live and be happily right with God." A banner was unfurled from a window across the way, and it struck Renard as utterly appropriate. *Vox populi, vox Dei*, it read. "The voice of the people is the voice of God."

Renard believed it was the destiny of Mary and themselves, and he thought Mary believed it as well.

At the time of my coronation, my kingdom was rife with poverty and had been so for half my life. The changes my father and brother had made in the spiritual and economic life of the people had made existence hard and the people angry. The only bright spot for all of us was the hope of setting things as they had been before. To return to the days when every man had food in his belly and clothes on his back. The time when God was not angry with us. It seemed so very simple. But alas, nothing is ever that simple.

Mary took her seat at the council table in her privy chamber, and those attending also took theirs. High-ranking servants stood or sat behind their masters. This was to be an informal talk and rather more public than a true privy council meeting. The group was large—more than forty, not counting their servants—and included the imperial ambassador Simon Renard. Mary liked him and wanted someone she could trust to keep her in touch with her cousin Charles. He was a tall, slender, genteel man, calm of demeanor and visibly filled with grace. He had the look of someone who knew what he was about and gave Mary the comfort of a competent advisor. Most of her council was made up of the members of Edward's council who had gone against Dudley in the end. Though they deserved reward for their actions, and she did understand the need for men on the council to represent views of those in England who disagreed with her, she nevertheless could not trust these radical Protestants to see things as she would have them. She needed a strong Catholic presence among her advisors. Renard was a welcome aid.

Dudley was dead. His son Guilford and Jane Grey were imprisoned in the Tower. Though Mary disliked the execution of so close a relative as her cousin, it might be unavoidable, for Mary had learned well from her father to beware of those with blood ties too close to the Crown. To leave the girl alive would invite another attempt on the throne by the next man who might see a likely tool, regardless of Jane's own desire to be queen or lack of it. She'd been used once and could be used again by any ambitious man. Her very existence made her dangerous. But Mary hesitated.

It wasn't far into the session that Renard brought up the subject of the kingdom's return to Catholicism. "Of course, it is assumed," he said, "that you will restore the faith to your realm." Renard stated the obvious, to Mary's mind, but his tone suggested he didn't think so.

"We would be remiss in our duty if we did not."

He hesitated before continuing, touching a finger to his lips in deep thought, then spoke slowly as if choosing his words more carefully than usual, even for a diplomat. "I've been instructed by your cousin His Highness the emperor to caution Your Grace on moving too quickly. Quite naturally Charles wishes to see England return to the fold, but his many years of experience in rule tell him that to expect an immediate reversion would be hoping too much."

Mary's hands rested in her lap, folded and quite still, in spite of their impulse to flutter. Her mother had instructed her well in royal decorum. "Of course, it cannot be immediate. It would hardly be reasonable to begin taking action against the heresy while the laws and policies of the past two decades are still in force. We must wait until Parliament can return the law to its former and proper state. Then we will see a change among the heretics."

Paget spoke up, his insinuating voice cutting through the room with a clarity and force that made Mary listen well. "There have been incidents already. Those who practice the new religion are terrified of that change."

"They should be terrified of the wrath of God." They'd all certainly seen enough of God's wrath in the economic hardship of this kingdom since her father's break with the Church.

"A dagger was thrown at your chaplain Bourne as he preached at St. Paul's. He might have been killed."

Mary had heard of the incident. "We abhor violence, and it has no place in church. Nor anywhere else if avoidable, for that matter. The man who threw that dagger has been dealt with."

"With all due respect, Your Grace, the entire congregation rose against your priest, he angered them so with his attacks on their faith. I feel Your Grace may be underestimating the determination of Protestants to remain on their chosen path."

"Their heresy, you mean."

Paget gave a slow nod to indicate that he thought it a matter of semantics and not important what it might be called.

She gave a similar nod of acknowledgment, and said, "We have no desire to force anyone to go to Mass. But those who wish to go should be free to do so."

"And those who wish to worship with the new service should also be free to do so."

Mary's lips pressed together. It was one thing to allow non-attendance but another entirely to encourage active participation in heresy. The souls of the English people were at stake, and she hadn't the heart to look through her fingers at their error. But to say so would invite the sort of violent resistance that had been rampant in London since her arrival. She side-stepped the issue for the moment. "The heretics shall not be encouraged. Already they go too far in their resistance."

"They are afraid."

"What could they possibly fear?"

"That you will take from them their faith."

"Rather, we would return it to them."

"That's not how they see it."

Mary brought herself even more erect in her seat. "We shall tell you how we see it, Your Grace. We see small enclaves of malcontents making great noise and bringing harm to people and property in a singularly unchristian manner. We see those who persist in their error while our world comes crashing down around our ears. No good has come of England's break with Rome. Our goal now is to help those in error to see the path that will lead to light, prosperity, and spiritual well-being."

Paget's voice remained utterly patient. "Of course, Your Queen's Majesty. Our goal here is peace. I only hope Your Grace might entirely grasp the determination of the people and their willingness to resort to ugly means to maintain their faith."

"We cannot call it faith."

Paget coughed, refolded his hands, then said, "Their understanding, then."

Mary's temper, much akin to her father's, rose and sharpened to become like a dagger in her heart. Her face warmed. "We are well aware of the Protestant tendency to unchristian riot and murder."

Paget's face flushed at the insult.

She continued. "We don't need to be told how dangerous heretics can be. We understand things cannot be set right in an instant. One thing our faith teaches us is patience. My mother taught me that, as well as perseverance. However long it takes, we will persist in pursuing our goal of bringing our people back to the light."

As if changing the subject, though Mary saw they remained on the theme, he said, "Our late king has not yet been laid to rest. What will the service be?"

A thorny question, for the entire kingdom watched to see what she would do. "We cannot in good conscience allow our brother to be buried improperly."

"Edward's wishes, of course, were for a Protestant service."

"His King's Majesty deserves better than to have his soul in hell."

"Indeed, that is true." Paget left it at that, as if to suggest a Catholic service might send him there.

Mary fell silent for a moment, to let her rage settle. Why couldn't these men see what was so obvious to her? How could she explain to them how wrong they were, and how well she knew the danger of their error?

Once calmed, she said, "We will authorize two services. At Westminster a Protestant service, and then a requiem Mass elsewhere. But mark me, all of you. We must return our kingdom to the old faith. To neglect that duty would be death for us all."

The statement was met with frustrating silence. Finally Paget referred to some notes scribbled on a piece of paper before him and said, "There's the matter of marriage prospects. We've a number of suggestions Your Grace might wish to entertain. Shall I enumerate them?"

Mary's heart leapt to her throat. By no means did she wish to have this conversation in so large a meeting, for she was nearly forty years old, and her advanced age was a deep shame, but she was loath to make her apprehension public. She swallowed the embarrassment and told Paget to continue. She was curious what he considered a marriage prospect for her and eager to leave behind discussion of policies she considered a matter of course.

Feeling light-headed, she listened carefully to what he had to say.

Chapter Thirteen

The prospect of marriage, particularly the marriage bed, was fraught with tangled emotions that gripped me so terribly I often found it hard to breathe. Since childhood I'd been taught to expect to be married, and indeed had spent most of that time betrothed to or in negotiation with one prince or another. Of course I would marry. It was my duty. My highest purpose. I was taught womanly skills to make me attractive as a wife and knew that pleasing my husband would be as basic to my existence as breathing. At the very least I was expected to respect and obey whatever man I received as my master and guardian. It was the natural way of things, and now that I was sovereign, marriage was absolutely necessary for the sake of ongoing peace in the land. To provide the kingdom with an heir, to ensure my grandfather's dynasty would endure, to bring stability, peace, and prosperity to my kingdom, was my greatest goal.

My father had kept me from it for fear a husband might attempt a coup. My brother's council had the same fear, and so also kept suitors from me. Now that I was queen, the need was great, but the time seemed to have slipped away. It was nearly too late.

Plainly the only advisor I could trust in this matter was Charles. Since the death of my mother he'd been my only truly faithful ally, and so I turned to him for his help in finding a suitable husband. When he offered his widowed son who was eleven years my junior, it seemed my perfect destiny.

Simon Renard hurried along the gallery that led to Mary's presence chamber as quickly as possible and maintain his dignity. His attendants scurried and hopped to keep up without losing theirs. The imperial ambassador to Mary's court carried with him a message he knew she would receive with pleasure, and he was eager to present it. The woman seemed ever unhappy and so rarely smiled. It lifted his heart to see her smile, for she was a handsome woman when she did. Today he was certain this news would not only brighten her demeanor but bring her heart joy for days or perhaps years to come. His step lightened even more at the thought, and he gave a jaunty toss of one side of his cloak over his shoulder to show off its shiny blue lining.

The wait to see the queen wasn't long. Nearly as soon as he arrived, he was allowed into the presence chamber, where Mary sat under the canopy of estate, perched in a most ladylike manner at the fore of her seat, one elbow set lightly on its arm. The posture was too uncharacteristic to be as casual as it was meant to appear, and he surmised she'd guessed at the purpose of his visit. Indeed, he thought he detected a slight curve of the corners of her mouth in anticipation of hearing what he would say.

He began speaking even as he rose from his bow. "Your Majesty, I bring tidings just arrived from your cousin, His Highness the emperor Charles."

Her face broke into the genuine smile he'd seen lurking. "Do tell me, how is my cousin? I pray he is well and happy."

"He is as well as can be expected for a man of his years, Your Majesty, but perhaps not as happy as he might be, for he's instructed me to tell you that which might disappoint you."

The smile faded, and her expression turned apprehensive. "Proceed, Excellency."

Renard felt small guilt for his teasing and proceeded as instructed. He knew she would be smiling again in a moment. "His Highness writes in regard to a proposal of marriage. He says he would be honored to marry you but is old and ill."

A slight frown of puzzlement creased Mary's brow, and the smile ventured onto her lips once more. Tentatively, for that was her way. He knew she'd once been betrothed to the emperor and held him as dear to her as her father. More so, perhaps, given the way her father had treated her for so long. What Charles was proposing now might fly in the face of that, and so Renard's diplomatic mission was to make a tip of his cap to that former relationship.

He continued. "As he is no longer a suitable bridegroom, he must offer his son in his stead."

Now Mary's brow cleared entirely, and her true smile came to her. "Philip."

"Yes, Your Majesty. He proposes a marriage between yourself and his son, Philip."

Mary placed her fingers over her mouth, as if to contain her joy. Her eyes lit like coronation fireworks, and her cheeks blushed as if the prospective bridegroom were in the room and demanding his conjugal rights on the spot. As much as Mary had always publicly denied interest in marriage, Renard could see her reserve was more for the sake of form than honesty. No woman wanted to be thought a whore, but neither did spinsterhood ever hold much appeal.

She laid her hands demurely in her lap and said, "'Tis a most interesting proposal, Excellency. But I ask, how does Philip view it? I must say, most of my suitors are so young that I might be their mother. Philip is, I believe, only twenty-six?"

Renard nodded.

Her voice took on a slight edge of doubt. "If he might be disposed to be amorous, that would not be my desire."

Obviously she wasn't talking about the marriage bed but rather of the likelihood of mistresses. It was a probability Renard regarded as inevitable, given Philip's taste for vice and his several illegitimate children born during his first marriage. The prince was personally not well-liked among the nobility in his father's lands, nor among his mother's people for that, and part of their distaste was the fault of drink, gambling, and sluts. Renard had no idea how much Mary knew of it, but surely she had heard something. In a heartbeat he weighed his reply, then said, "Your Majesty may be overestimating Philip's amorous nature. Though there may be some truth to reports of it, I can assure you the matter is not so grave as one might fear."

Mary appeared to accept that, but nodded with an air of "We shall see." At least she hadn't rejected the proposal for it. Then she said, "I'm told Philip is making a journey to Flanders from Spain in the near future. Might there be a chance he would come to England while on his way?"

Renard's mind flew in search of an adequate reply that would not offend the queen. In reality there was no chance of Philip making the dangerous crossing for the sake of being examined and to have judgment passed on him like livestock at auction. As quickly as he could cobble his answer, he replied, "Your Majesty, I couldn't say whether such a journey would be possible. Or proper." Yes! That was it! Not proper! His speech gained energy as his theme took hold. "Indeed, Your Majesty, having heard of your virtues, he has taken it to himself to approach you himself. He wishes to come to you in proper order." A lie, but one that would flatter this woman inexperienced in the ways of courtship.

Mary held out her hand to the ambassador, who relinquished his. She put it between the two of hers and squeezed. "Tell me in all honesty, Excellency. Have you told me truthfully of his virtues? Is he of even temper? Good judgment?"

"He has qualities as virtuous as any prince in the world." Not such a lie, for Philip had his moments, and every nobleman Renard had ever met had his peccadilloes.

"Do not speak to me as a servant, wanting only to ease my mind. Tell me as a friend, in all assurance I wish only the truth and nothing more."

Renard knew the truth would ruin any chance of this proposal coming to fruition, so he swore on his life to the honesty of his words. He would have to beg a priest for absolution later, but he was confident God would understand. God surely knew what was at stake. On hearing his oath, Mary smiled and squeezed his hand again before letting it go.

"Well, then," she said, as if something important had been settled in her mind. "As my friend and a favorite advisor, how do you see the English people accepting Philip as their king?"

Here Renard needed more truth, and therefore more care, in his reply. This was an overwhelmingly important issue, far more pertinent than the question of Philip's potential for marital fidelity, and for this Renard was prepared. He would make plain what Mary needed to know. "It will not be easy to convince your subjects that Philip has no intention of plundering their country. They hate the Spanish, as you well know."

A shadow crossed Mary's eyes. Her mother having been Spanish, and her grandparents the monarchs of Castile and Aragon, she knew well the sharp edge of hatred the English people had for Philip's countrymen. They held distaste for all foreigners, truth be told, but most particularly the Spanish, who were perceived as cowardly, unprincipled, lazy, and untrustworthy. Though Catherine had been well-loved by her husband's subjects, she'd had to earn that love in the course of nearly two decades of marriage to the king. "Philip will need patience with our people."

Prince Philip of Spain was not known for his patience. But neither was he stupid, and the throne of England dangled as a pretty pearl before him. He would more than likely do anything reasonably required to gain it and hold it.

She continued. "We shall need him to live in England, in order to assure our subjects of his good intention."

"I believe that should not be an obstacle. Particularly when His Highness sees for himself your great virtues."

That brought the smile again and a bit of blush. "At first, to be sure. But what about when he's inherited his father's lands? How can he possibly rule them from here?"

"I'm certain there will be no obstacle." The empire was vast, and after Charles's death, Philip stood to rule territories on the Continent and in the New World so bogglingly wide-spread that he could not be expected to stay in one place long. In short, though Renard would never say so aloud to anyone, England was but a dot on the map for Philip, Europe's backwater, unsophisticated of culture and not particularly wealthy. Renard hoped the English people would take as little notice of Philip as he did of them.

Peter Barnacle sat with David Wheeler in the Three Angels public house deep in the heart of London, having a drink with some of the cash Peter had earned carrying wood that day. His wife would go all over in a snit at the expense, but Peter figured he'd earned a chance to rest his feet and have a taste of ale. And he reckoned it was his prerogative to spend the coppers on a cup for his friend if he so chose. He was, after all, the master of his household. Naught else, but his household, in any case.

The room was close, dark and warm, and smelling of a venison haunch on a spit over the fire. He rather liked venison, the more because it was such a rare treat for him. The richer, bloodier taste than mutton or poultry appealed to him. Even boar, which came to him more rarely than deer, wasn't as tasty. Peter's mouth watered at scent of this haunch, and he weighed his purse in his palm under the table, but he knew the limitations of his finances and couldn't spare what it would take for a portion. Nor even a piece of bread, for that, and he would prefer Ruth's bread at home in any case. He made himself happy with the cup between his hands and ignored the thick scent of burning fat.

"So what do ye think of Her Majesty's betrothed?"

Peter grunted. He hadn't the slightest care who the queen married, so long as he was Catholic. The last king had been an ineffectual child controlled by a corrupt Protestant council. The king before him had been a tyrant even to surpass the evil of that council, whose self-interest plunged the country into a morass of religious dissent and economic disaster. For most of Peter's life, his country had been in the grip of hardship of one cause or another; so long as Philip remained Catholic, he was as good in Peter's eyes as the next man. "I try not to think about it much." They would get by. They always just got by, with the grace of God.

"You've got to, man! How can ye not have a thought for what is sure to happen, should the marriage take place? Ye know what them Spanish is like!"

Peter didn't know, for he'd never actually spoken to a Spaniard, but he'd certainly heard. Everyone knew what the Spanish were like, for the stories were numerous. And David was sure to tell him again. His friend had a tongue that wagged faster the more ale there was to lubricate it.

"They're vile drunkards, they are!" David took another deep draught of his ale and continued. "They're whoremongers and thieves! Every last one of them!"

"And what of our late queen Catherine?"

"Oh, she was a saint, that one! And more English than Spanish for it, I say. But no, them Spanish is all filthy, low-living swine." That from a man who actually kept pigs, and stank of them even now. Peter said nothing and let David continue. "I tell you—"

The door of the room banged open, and in staggered three well-dressed men. They were in loud conversation, and their tone indicated they had already drunk quite a bit elsewhere.

"Beggars!" shouted one of them, and fell against an open barrel that nearly toppled. One of his friends caught it as a slosh of brine dribbled over the side and onto the floor. "Thieves, they are!"

Everyone in the room fell silent. This was not a place frequented by such fine blood, and the common folk went still to fade into the woodwork with the expertise of those accustomed to avoiding the attention of men more powerful and dangerous than themselves. Nobody except the proprietor liked it when the nobility wandered in where they didn't belong. Peter kept his head low, but watched the scene from under his eyelashes as he pretended to peer into his cup.

Of the three of them, one wore a suit so rich Peter found it hard to not stare openly. The man was tall, in blue brocade and wearing a heavy collar of enameled gold roses linked with gold chains bearing dozens of large pearls. His slashed sleeves revealed a shirt of snowy white silk. He was the loudest of the three. The others wore less showy and formal hunting tunics and leggings, but all carried ornate swords that bespoke knighthood.

The man in blue continued the tirade he'd begun in the street outside. "Mark me, my friends! Jack Spaniard will be the end of us all!"

His friends were perhaps a little less drunk than he, and they drew him to a table where they sat and tried to calm his excitement. But he continued to rant. "They're a lousy lot. And monstrous. Westminster will be crawling with loiterers and merchants. And drunks. They carry their open bottles around their necks, you know. Never without their bottle of wine. And livestock everywhere. The courtyard will be filled with cattle and goats. And chickens. Chickens everywhere! They'll have the queen picking her way among the dung, soiling her slippers just to walk to her chapel of a morning."

"Now, James, it won't be so bad as that." One of the more sober gentlemen took a soothing tone as he gestured to the proprietor of the establishment to bring them some meat. Peter agreed it might be good for that James fellow to have something on his stomach other than ale.

He thought about swallowing the last of his own ale and making for the door but thought better of it. Attracting any attention at all might bring the ire of that already angry drunken knight down on his head. Better to be still, become a shadow, and wait until these rich men were on their way again.

James plopped down in a rickety chair beside the table and leaned back in it while his more sober friend and the third gentleman took their own seats. He said, now sounding less sloppy than he had before, "You know he'll be the one ruling the country, not her."

"He won't."

"He'll be her husband, will he not?"

The other two nodded.

"Then even if she *appears* to rule, he'll be the one telling her how. He'll be the one telling her what to do and what to say. He'll be dictating policy and law. And manners. Good English manners will be a thing of the past, I vow."

"You exaggerate, I think, James."

"And how can any woman refuse her husband what he requests? Those Spanish are hard, you know. Spanish governors are more cruel than any others in Europe. Corrupt. Worse, even, than the French, and I hate the French as much as the next man. But the Spanish are to be feared by even their own people. Those Spanish are worse than any Frenchman ever was."

"Nonsense, James," said the more sober one. "They're no worse than our own rulers."

"They are, Richard. I assure you they are terrible, terrible evil. And you know what I hear?"

"No, what do you hear?" Richard seemed deeply unimpressed by whatever James might have heard, but he humored his friend.

"I hear that in Plymouth they're declining to go along with the entire proposal. They say the gentry of Plymouth have appealed to France for protection from the Spanish threat."

Even Peter, who had little thought of what went on outside the kingdom, knew that was serious business, if true, and he looked for Richard's reaction. His gut fluttered when the sober Richard seemed to believe his friend. "Protection? They would surrender English territory to France for the sake of refusing to accept our queen's choice of husband?"

"Our queen's choice of *king*. She's not the only one Philip will be fucking if someone doesn't do something. And quick."

"And what do you suggest we do?"

At that James fell silent. He appeared to be thinking hard, as if there actually were something anyone could do. After a very long moment, he seemed to come to the conclusion there was nothing to be done, and he sighed. "You know that Prince Philip is a lascivious fiend."

The others nodded, and Peter took note. Philip an adventurer? That did not bode well for anyone, especially the queen. What sort of life would there be under a king with no moral integrity? They all remembered what had happened when that heretic Henry and his whore had been on the throne. Peter began to wonder if David was right in rejecting the idea of Spaniards at Westminster. It could change the entire country, were such things accepted by the English people. Life was hard enough without having to relinquish their Englishness to a swarm of foreigners.

"Those of us with gentle sensibilities should live in fear of what those people would do to our kingdom. We cannot allow it. We must give the queen to know she shall not foist her low Spaniard on us."

"Very well, then, James, you march right up to the palace this very instant and tell the queen how wrong she is and how you simply won't allow her to make this terrible mistake. I'm certain she'll be ever so pleased to have her error revealed to her, and she'll send off a letter to her cousin the emperor to let him know the whole thing is called off. And then surely she must make you a duke for your trouble. I don't doubt it a bit, my friend. Do not tarry here. Go to her now."

"I could."

"But you won't. Even you have more sense than that."

"I should do it. I should go there now."

"No, you will not. You'll stay here, eat some meat, and then we'll return you to your wife so she can tuck you safely into your own bed. And when you awake in the morning, you'll not likely remember the things you said to us, and that will be your salvation, because we'll forget them as well." Richard glanced around the room as if to warn the onlookers that they would do well to develop amnesia themselves.

Peter bent his head to his cup, his nose nearly touching the rim. He would never forget what he'd heard, but also he would never speak of it, and neither would his friends.

Chapter Fourteen

The musician Niccolò Delarosa sat with his fellows in the gallery where Mary passed some quiet time sewing with her ladies. The long day of meetings with her council was behind her, as were Mass and supper, and now she engaged in idle talk with women. Among her ladies she could let down her guard some, and Niccolò could see she liked these evenings when there was little pressure and nobody around to berate or attempt to manipulate her. The women chatted about their embroidery, or sometimes it was the marriage prospects of one or another of their number. Some gossip arose occasionally, but Mary discouraged unchristian wagging tongues, so the talk was rarely of other people.

Gentle, nondescript background music was the order of the

moment, and Niccolò plucked chords without much thought behind a line of flute melodies well familiar to them both. Little creativity was required of him at the moment, and the less obtrusive he was, the better, so he let his mind wander and observed Her Majesty from under his eyelashes.

The announcement of her betrothal had hit him well between the eyes, and his heart clenched to think of it. Not that he'd ever believed she would cast her favor on him in that way, but so long as she remained unmarried, it was possible to dream. But no longer. That Spanish boy with entirely too much wealth and power for one man had won her hand, and it appeared the prince had also won her heart. The queen was aflutter with the prospect of meeting him, and though the glow in her was a beautiful thing to see, it nevertheless wrenched Niccolò's carefully hidden places.

Particularly it tore him when she asked after word from her betrothed. Each day the ambassador came to meet with her, and each day she inquired whether there was message from Philip. But he sent nothing. Not letter, not gift . . . nothing. Mary went about her duties as queen, meeting with her council, setting forth policies and designing laws to return her realm to prosperity and light. Some days she worked well into the night, discussing at length the serious matters of relations with other monarchs and the state of commerce within her possessions and between the English and other countries. Listening to those conferences made him glad he had talents that allowed him to ignore such mercantile and political matters. Music was his bread, and bringing the queen joy and pleasure his drink. He had no desire for anything else, even though he never complained that his dress was as rich and stylish as could be had for his station and he ate well every day.

Today his mistress seemed especially wan and sighing. Her needle moved slowly, and though her ladies chattered most cheerfully, they never noticed the queen was not as enthusiastic about the discussion as they. Niccolò hated that Spanish dog Philip for making her so melancholy. Would that there be dimples in her face, for they never appeared when she only pretended to smile.

Mary's chamberlain announced Renard at the door, just as he often did this time of an evening. The imperial ambassador made his entrance, this time with a bustling and air of high pleasure. A liveried servant scurried along behind him, carrying a rather large item wrapped in a thick wool blanket and tied with a great deal of sturdy hemp twine. The servant staggered under his awkward burden, for it was flat and oblong and large enough to prevent him from seeing where he was going. Renard seemed oblivious to the difficulty of his man and hurried to bow to the queen.

Mary laid her sewing in her lap, as did each of her women. The cluster of ladies stared at the gift, obviously a painting. The shape of the frame could be discerned under the nondescript brown blanket.

"How now, Excellency? What have you there?" Hope tinged her voice, and the wide smile on Renard's face encouraged it.

"A gift from your future husband, Majesty."

Mary's face lit up, and there finally came the dimples. She set her sewing aside in the basket at her feet. "A portrait? He's sent me a portrait?"

"Indeed he has. I've not seen it yet, but I have it on authority that the likeness is a good one. Your cousin the emperor relays that it's not perfect but will do well enough until the prince can come himself."

Mary waved a hand toward the gift. "Do open it. Let me see it, then, if it is so true to my betrothed."

The servant set the thing on the floor so as to have his hands free to untie the twine and loosen the blanket. The brown wool fell away to the floor, revealing a fine painting: Philip of Spain, against a dark background, wearing a black tunic and carrying a sword with gold hilt. His sleeves were cloth of gold, and the buttons on his tunic intricately wrought gold. His head seemed to rest lightly atop a discreet linen ruffle at his jaw. Also around his neck, on a delicate chain, hung a jewel so dark it seemed black.

Niccolò looked to Mary for her reaction and found her eyes wide and her lips slightly parted, the smile fallen from her face. She seemed to not breathe at all. Then she blinked, realized the spectacle she was making, and clamped her mouth shut.

"His features are regular," she said, though the tightness of her voice betrayed that she was understating his beauty.

"Indeed they are, Your Majesty," said Renard.

Niccolò looked at the portrait once more and saw Philip's cheeks were ruddy and his skin pale. The young man had a straight nose and full, red lips. The hair and beard were nearly black, and his brow was clean and serious. Given the prince's reputation, Niccolò guessed this was the area in which the portrait failed in accuracy. The man in the picture seemed sensible, but most who knew him considered him to be otherwise.

"He seems dashing."

Dashing! There was a word! Niccolò's disappointment in the queen's judgment tried to rise to his face, but he kept his expression carefully bland.

Mary's fingers entwined with each other in her lap, as if she were struggling to keep them still. All the royal family seemed to have that trait—the difficulty containing themselves. Henry had always seemed filled with preternatural energy, ready to leap across the room over one thing or another, or sometimes even just to show he could. Elizabeth in private was as nervous as a cat, forever nibbling a fingernail or twisting a handkerchief into a knot. Edward had been a fidgety boy and even as a young man rarely could attend to one thing for very long. By the white line around Mary's bright red mouth, Niccolò knew she was far more excited about this gift than she would ever let on. No dimples, and there would be none until Renard had gone; Niccolò was sure of it.

For a long time Mary stared at the painting, as the liveried servant held it up to her for better vantage. He shifted the weight of it in his arms as it grew heavy for him.

"You can see he has fine royal lineage," offered Renard for lack of conversation from Mary.

"He is my cousin, after all."

Renard nodded and blushed. Then he recovered with, "Exactly, Your Majesty. It is no wonder he bears a comely visage."

She graced him with a brief smile, then returned to her perusal of the gift. "His father is less handsome, I fear. Philip seems to have been graced with a chin less . . . obtrusive."

"Your Majesty makes a good point." Renard then fell silent, the better to keep his foot out of his mouth for the rest of this interview.

Finally Mary took a deep breath and let it out slowly. Niccolò heard it as a sigh, and probably it was an attempt to avoid sighing. She gestured to the servant holding the gift and said, "Take it to my privy chamber, and set it where I can see it until it might be properly hung in the presence chamber."

ulianne Lee

The servant gave a soft assent, bowed, and carried the painting from the room. Renard watched him go, then said to the queen, "May I relay your approval to His Highness your cousin?"

Not too quickly, Mary said with an air of thoughtfulness, "You may tell him I find Philip agreeable. I pray him good health until we may meet face-to-face."

Niccolò wondered whether Mary realized the double entendre, but then decided she could not possibly. Of all people, Mary would be the one to say such a thing and be perfectly innocent in it.

She dismissed the ambassador with compliments, then picked up her sewing from the basket again. She returned to her pastime as before, but now there was an air of excitement and pleasure in the room and dimples in her rosy cheeks.

It was after supper one evening when many of Mary's household first realized she was somewhat more sanguine about her impending marriage than she let on. Simon Renard lounged in his chair, unobtrusive as he observed those around him. Though he thought of himself as a servant of Mary, his first loyalty was necessarily to His Highness the emperor, and so his sharp eye was ever to the fore, and his evenings just before retiring he spent writing those observations for dispatch to his master.

Some others sitting about the high hearth were in low, soft conversation, but Mary didn't attend well. She stared into the fire, her gaze seemed to focus at a distance of miles. The admiral William Howard wandered over with a reckless grin on his face and a sparkle of mischief in his eye. The man was a bit of a hearty fool, ever with a joke on his lips or a flip word to say that was not always appreciated by its target. His tongue made more trouble for himself than for anyone, and it was only by his reputation for harmless buffoonery that he was tolerated by those around him. Tonight Renard looked sharp for a chuckle to be had as Howard leaned down to whisper in the queen's ear.

A sudden blush rushed to Mary's cheeks, and though she turned to give the admiral a disdainful look, it was plain a smile struggled to her face. Suddenly she appeared a young girl, unable to refrain from giggling. "Shame on you, William!"

Howard chuckled and returned to his seat next to Renard.

Renard leaned close and asked in a low murmur as Mary struck up new conversation with others in the room, "What did you say?"

Howard shrugged and grinned. "I live to serve Her Queen's Majesty. I merely informed her that I wish her Philip were here to drive thought and care away."

"You overstep, Lord Admiral," said Mary, but she yet struggled with the smile that wanted to come.

"Oh, Your Majesty, I vow you cannot be angry. I daresay you like my suggestion well enough that care has been banished even at the mere thought of the prince."

Mary laughed. The sound was so strange to Renard, it almost didn't seem like Mary at all. As if someone had stepped into her place who only looked like the English queen but was a changeling, a younger, prettier queen. It surprised them all into laughter themselves, bringing a rare moment of honest pleasure to each courtier in the room.

Of course I wanted to love my husband. I cannot imagine any wife preferring not to. When I first saw the portrait of Philip, my soul leapt for joy to see him so comely and filled with grace. Indeed, fear touched my heart that he might find me too old. A man such as he could win any woman who caught his eye, and so powerful a prince, any princess. I understood it was his father who wished us married, and so I approached our first meeting with deep apprehension. I prayed every day that he would find me as agreeable as I did him. If so, then it would surely be a happy and fruitful marriage.

Alas, many of my subjects found him far less agreeable, and some few nobles—led by Sir Thomas Wyatt of Kent—leapt upon the opportunity to rouse the malcontents to revolt and take power. They saw me as weak, even expected me to simply leave the country and turn my crown over to them without resistance. In this they were deeply and fatally mistaken, for I am my parents' daughter. Neither Catherine nor Henry would have been thought so cowardly, and in my determination to maintain the stability of England, I was even less likely to submit.

Sir Thomas realized his mistake far too late, lost the fight, and was duly executed. Those who followed him to their ruin were hung, as custom decreed, at the city gates, on London Bridge, at Tower Hill . . . often before their own houses. Nearly a hundred rebels lost their lives for their treachery. Nearly as many were pardoned, en masse, and were grateful enough for their salvation to become loyal subjects. My sister Elizabeth, who knew of the revolt though she refrained from participating, was imprisoned in the Tower for three months. And finally, I was forced to order the executions of Guilford Dudley and Jane Grey. I hated to do away with such a close relative, but there was nothing for it. I am, after all, my father's daughter, and I have learned by his example. As his father before him, he was ever wary of ambitious men with blood ties too close to the Crown. I ordered cousin Jane beheaded that February.

As weddings were forbidden during Lent, and I could hardly set the example by disobeying Church law, mine was put off until after Easter. The wait was interminable to me, the more so for having so little word from my betrothed. Philip sent no word nor token, though his father Charles sent a wondrous large diamond and a charming letter in response to the signing of the marriage articles. Philip wrote to other people, sometimes he wrote of me, but the months passed and I had no letter for myself. I began to wonder why. Indeed, I began to wonder if I should consider myself insulted.

Then, shortly before Philip was due to arrive, came word and gifts to calm my mind, lift my heart, and ease my soul.

Mary made her best effort to appear unruffled and unhurried as she and her ladies made their way to her privy chamber from the chapel after Mass. Word had come an envoy from Philip, the Marquis de Las Navas, had arrived scant weeks before Philip himself was expected in England. Her heart tripped along uncomfortably. What would she read in his letter? What messages would come through his servants? She dashed through the small private door from the chapel passage and immediately snatched at her veil to have it off the quicker. Her ladies hurried to help and had her ready to receive the Spanish envoy in only a few moments. She sat in a large, heavy chair at one end of the meeting table and took a deep, silent breath. The blood high in her cheeks, she smoothed her gown and nodded for the Spaniards to be admitted.

Five men entered, four of them bearing several wooden caskets. The marquis, standing to the fore, held a wallet of papers. They all bowed to her. De Las Navas straightened and absently flipped his traveling cloak back to reveal its bloodred lining. They were emissaries from Philip, and spoke directly to her in Spanish, with no need of an interpreter.

"Your Majesty," said the marquis, "I come in advance of my master, your betrothed, Prince Philip of Spain. I bear word from His Highness and gifts to grace Your Queen's Majesty and your ladies, tokens of his regard for his future bride."

At last! All those months of silence must have been nothing but an oversight. Perhaps Philip simply hadn't realized so much time had passed without word. Perhaps he'd assumed oral communication through intermediaries would be enough. One never knew with foreigners whether they were being insulting or simply unaware of English custom. Mary was perfectly happy to forgive, and was overwhelmed with relief.

Mary greeted de Las Navas with heartfelt warmth. She hadn't the words to express her genuine pleasure at this visit. The marquis handed over the wallet with Philip's letter, which she skimmed quickly to see that it was filled with soothing words of regard and anticipation. Satisfied of Philip's good intentions, she folded the letter again to be savored later in private.

The marquis proceeded directly with his presentation. He gestured to one of his men, who stepped forward with an armload of glistening silk fabrics of deep purple, blue, and red. "I bring gifts from His Highness for your ladies. Velvet and brocade; this is but a sample for you to see." The man with the silk draped over his arm stepped back, and another two took his place, bearing a rather large casket they set on the table before her. Inside the ironbound box, which they tipped forward for her to see, was a large earthenware pot containing a baked boar preserved in fat. Other caskets contained jewels for Mary's ladies. Pearls, diamonds, and rubies brought exclamations of joy and pleasure from the women in Mary's service.

More boxes were brought from the anteroom, and the presentation became a parade of gifts. Mary found herself agog at the display of regard for herself. Not since she was a child had she been showered so lavishly.

Then finally the last casket was presented, one smaller than the rest, laid on the council table before her and opened with reverent ceremony. "These are especial gifts to Your Majesty: jewels of incomparable value and great significance." He lifted trays from the casket.

The first held a necklace of eighteen brilliant diamonds that seemed to fire sparks into the air above them, the setting so finely wrought its gold seemed at first glance almost like a fluff of carded wool.

The second was an enormous diamond, nearly large enough to cover the palm of her hand, on a long gold chain, with a large pearl dangling below it.

The third touched Mary's heart in a way she'd never thought possible. The final gift from Philip was a table diamond mounted in an ornate gold rose setting. De Las Navas held the velvet-covered tray with special reverence for the queen to see, and explained, "This jewel, worth eighty thousand crowns, was first given to the mother of your betrothed by his father, the emperor."

Mary lifted the gem from its velvet nest and held it with the fingertips of both hands. Aside from its beauty and extreme value, her joy in receiving this gift came from the knowledge of what it meant to Philip's family and her mother's family.

Slowly, she sat in the chair behind her and gazed at this token. For so long she'd relied on Charles as the caring family she'd lacked. To have this heirloom was a more weighty token of regard from Philip than any letters he could have sent in the past six months. It rendered her speechless. The room waited in respectful silence as she assessed this wondrous thing.

Finally she tried to speak, but her voice was gone. She coughed to clear her throat and tried again. "Please send word to your master we are deeply honored by these gifts. We await his arrival with great longing to be joined with our bride-groom and our true destiny."

The desire to meet Philip was as keen as a Toledo sword that cut to her very core.

Those final weeks before the arrival of my intended were torture. Each day I rose from my bed and counted off another day to bring me closer to seeing him. The difference in our ages loomed large in my troubled mind. My heart fluttered at the thought that he might find me appealing, and it stood still at the moments when I became certain he could not possibly. I was, after all, nearly forty years old and he but twenty-six.

Mary wandered back and forth in the master's gallery in the palace of the bishop, unable to sit and be still. She gazed at a painting, then wandered to a window, but when there was nothing to see in the darkness outside, she turned toward the hearth that contained a low fire. There were chairs beneath the canopy of estate that had been set up near the hearth, but sitting just wasn't possible for her at the moment.

Those around her chatted amiably and, she thought, somewhat inanely. Admiral Howard was, of course, struggling to lighten the mood with his coarse jokes. Mary liked humor as well as the next woman and usually appreciated the lord admiral's wit, but tonight he merely irritated. How could anyone engage in small talk on so momentous an occasion as this? They should all be sitting in dead silence, in reverent anticipation of the thing that was about to happen. All their lives were about to change, and Mary could only guess how hers would turn. Her heart thudded in her chest, her pulse nearly choking her, at the thought Philip might regard her with distaste. She wore plain black velvet and had no doubt it made her appear deathly pale. Now she fretted over whether there might be time to return to her chamber and change into a brighter color, something a little more youthful. More flattering. What a shame she'd listened to Renard, who had suggested the black! Her ladies had tried to talk her out of it, but the long, sleepless nights of late had her in a fog, and she wasn't thinking clearly. Surely she needed to go back and change.

But, no, there were voices now coming from the windows overlooking the garden. Mary burned to rush to the balcony to see the approaching men, but held herself in restraint and stayed rooted to the floor. There was nothing for it now but to stay where she was and brave this through, even though she knew she must appear a cadaver in this gown.

The voices neared, and she struggled to discern which one, if any of those speaking, might be Philip. Was he a talkative sort? Might he be the loud voice that carried so far? Or was he the laughter in response? Or perhaps he was entirely silent and listening to his attendants' chatter?

The voices dimmed for a moment as the group entered the building, then sounded again in the narrow stairwell at the rear of the gallery, away from the windows. Footsteps on stone reached her ears, and she now had to stop herself from retreating from the stairwell. She gazed at the doorway for her first glimpse of her future husband.

Then he stepped through, followed by the other men. Mary held herself back from gasping, though she couldn't help taking a long, deep breath.

Young Philip was a vision in his white kid doublet and trunks. His surcoat was of the French style, embroidered in breathtakingly intricate silver and gold. A long plume descended from his cap, which was also worked in the thread of precious metals.

He resembled his portrait well enough, and it struck Mary that to see him living and breathing before her made him even more attractive than the painting, for now there was a soul within the visage. His brow was broad and clear, and his chin narrow enough that his beard came to a remarkably delicate and genteel point. His complexion was as fine and ruddy-cheeked as the portrait, and the artist had not lied about his well-proportioned and healthy limbs. He was formed as beautifully as her father, though far more gracefully. He looked strong, and Mary felt a surge of joy that he also seemed in good health.

But even more important than his outward appearance was that revealed in his eyes. His gray eyes that lit as he looked at her and his red mouth that smiled in greeting made her feel beautiful. For the first time in ever so long, Mary felt beautiful under the gaze of a young man. A handsome young man, who could have nearly any woman he cared to approach. And now he approached Mary with an outstretched hand.

"Good evening, Your Grace," he said in Spanish as finely wrought as the embroidery on his surcoat and a voice so deep and gentle as to seem edible. Mary nearly giggled, she was so pleased by it.

She went to him also with her hand out in greeting, and he took it to bow over it. Then he straightened and kissed her on the mouth in the English manner. His lips were warm and gentle. Soft. He looked directly into her eyes once more. A shiver took her, and it felt as if he were seeing into her soul. There was a bit of a tickle at her core, and it moved her to give him a genuine smile of the sort she rarely made on first meeting. This vulnerability astonished her. Never in her life had anyone dared to peer so boldly into her heart. What he saw there even she couldn't guess entirely, for it was a confusion of pleasure and fear and blossoming affection and terror of rejection. She smiled as brightly as she could and hoped he couldn't tell how awkward she felt.

"Welcome to England, Your Highness," she said in the formal Spanish she'd been taught by her mother, her voice far more wobbly than she would have had it. But if he noticed, he never let it show. "How do you find our country?"

A flicker passed through his eyes. One of his men opened his mouth to speak, but Philip glanced at him, and the attendant remained silent. Philip said, as charming as when he'd first stepped into the room, "Your country is lovely. I look forward to making it my home."

Mary could tell he was putting a good face on something he liked little. The marriage contract, drawn up and signed months ago, provided that Philip would live in England. He had no choice in the matter. It was the only arrangement that would ease concerns of those who were against England having a Spanish king. But though it was too much to ask Philip to truly like England, he was at least polite about the matter, and that would go a long way toward making a pleasant life for them both.

She gestured to the pair of chairs beneath the canopy of estate and suggested they sit to visit. Philip gave a small bow, little more than a nod of his head, then threw his attendants a look that said they should amuse themselves elsewhere in the room while he chatted with his future wife. Mary sat, and Philip followed.

The furious blush that warmed her cheeks embarrassed her, but Philip never seemed to notice it. If he did, he never let on. Indeed, though he was one of the most charming men she'd ever met, and certainly the most lovely she'd ever expected to marry, there were moments in their talk when he struck her as focused more on himself than might be proper. Many men were self-centered. It seemed a male trait particularly common to royalty, and self-centered wasn't necessarily the same thing as self-serving. Philip's conversation always seemed to circle back onto himself, and though it wasn't appealing, Mary rather expected it.

Admiral Howard's voice carried from the cluster of attendants near the stairwell. "Don't sit too close, Your Highness. She's pretty, but you'll have to be patient and wait another few days." He spoke English, so most of those in the room didn't understand him, including the prince.

Philip looked over at Howard, a slight frown creasing his forehead. "What did he say?"

Mary was mortified to have to repeat Howard's words. A furious blush heated her face to a fever, and she stammered a little before finally saying, "He wishes to remind you that the wedding is not long in coming."

Philip smiled. "Indeed." He spoke to Mary, ignoring the lord admiral. "I count the days and know well the date."

It was a flattering thing to say, and Mary hoped it was truth.

CHAPTER FIFTEEN

Our wedding was, of course, a traditional Mass. There could be no question but that the entire affair would hold true to strict Catholic practice. All was proper. The banns were said, candles and crowns offered, Communion served, and I received a plain gold ring. Because England was still excommunicated, a dispensation was obtained from Rome, and Philip's priest was brought from Spain to ensure the validity of the ceremony. I would not have my honor compromised and doubt cast on my marriage as on my mother's. There could be nothing untoward about this ceremony. I'd learned well that lesson.

Winchester Cathedral was a glory beyond compare, decorated more richly than anyone had seen in generations. Enormous, finely woven tapestries and cloth of gold hung everywhere, damping all echoes and warming the air. It brought a comfort to the proceedings—a *gentility and elegance I found calming and proper. The dais was covered in purple. My gown glittered with jewels, some given to me by my betrothed, and Philip was resplendent in white silk, cloth of gold, and a jeweled collar. When I entered the church and saw him there at the altar, he quite took my breath away. He was my knight. My prince. Nay, I'd just had word he'd been made king of Naples. So I was to wed a king that day, a thing I knew must be a good omen for our future. Together we became the rulers of England, France, Naples, Jerusalem, Ireland, princes of Spain, archdukes of Austria, dukes of Milan, Burgundy, and Brabant, and counts of Hapsburg, Flanders, and Tyrol.*

Though the wedding Mass lasted several hours, it never seemed so long, because it was blissful, peaceful communion with God. Worship was never tedious for me; I always enjoyed the calm it brought, even during the nuptials that changed my life.

But the wedding feast was ever so lengthy. Banqueting amongst courtiers who loved to outdo each other in ribald wedding night commentary nearly moved me to cut short the festivities. And wouldn't that have made for some lovely gossip, to proceed to the conjugal chamber prematurely! My reputation would have disintegrated to a shambles in an instant! So there was nothing for it but to have patience and wait for the evening to play itself out with eating and drinking and accepting felicitations from the hundreds of guests and well-wishers. And every time I thought of what was to come that night, my heart skipped a beat, and I quite lost my breath for the moment.

The air was a bit stuffy in the privy chamber where the newlyweds were to spend the night, what with so many present to witness the occasion. "Privy" was certainly an overstatement, and some jostled for position and sidled into pockets of space between and behind furnishings to make room for all who pressed in. Tucked into the space between the bed and the far wall, Mary's chancellor blessed the marriage bed, to the approval of all present. The queen and her husband stood patiently at the foot of the bed for the rite to be finished, then there was applause and a hesitant moment of expectation. Several of the party looked around at each other, then at the couple, who gazed back, equally expectant. Then the onlookers finally realized it was time to leave the room, and the crowd began to move toward the door. Mary's pulse picked up as the moment approached when she would finally be entirely alone with Philip. She'd spent her life anticipating this moment. She could hardly believe it was here.

But she would never let her feelings be known. She was deeply ashamed of them, for though she was no wanton, her body betrayed her. Particularly, her belly distracted her with sensations she hadn't felt in nearly twenty years, though she'd thought she'd brought them under control so they could not lead her astray.

But now there was no denying them, and no opportunity to splash cold water on her face or go for a long walk to exhaust her energy. The room had emptied of courtiers, the door closed with a thud of wood, a clank of iron latch, the royal guard posted, and now Mary was alone with her husband still dressed in his wedding finery and with a kind smile on his face. More than anything just then, she wanted confidence in what she should do next, but it wouldn't come. She was locked, immobile, unable to decide where to go or even whether to move. All she could do was stand with her hands clasped before her, gazing at her new husband like cornered prey, her chin drawn in and her eyes wide, alert to the smallest expression in him.

Mary's husband didn't make her decide anything. It wasn't really her place to choose that night, for there were no choices to be made by either of them. Tonight was about tradition and duty above all else. All of Europe knew what would take place in this room.

Philip closed the distance between them with a couple of steps and gently pressed his lips to hers. Then, in a gesture completely alien to her experience, he laid his palms against her cheeks and kissed her again, but now more insistent. Demanding. She'd never been kissed like this before, nor touched at all in the manner his hands made their way down her neck to her throat. His smile widened, though his lips remained on hers. His beard tickled her chin, and she resisted the urge to reach up and scratch.

"I feel your heart beating so hard. You are excited," he said.

"I am not."

He gave her a slightly hurt look that brought her a tinge of guilt, and at the same time had an odd effect of putting her a bit more at ease.

She clarified. Though she wanted to sound stern and a proper lady, she found her own voice terribly weak and non-committal. "I am . . . nervous. You frighten me a little."

"There is no need for fear. I am your husband." It was difficult to tell whether he meant to reassure her or remind her of his authority over her. But then he said, "And you know they say for a woman to conceive she must also have the pleasure."

"I don't know whether I believe that."

"Oh, do! I assure you 'tis true. In my first marriage my wife was a proper, pious lady. But she did not conceive our son until she learned to be . . . a little less so." He laid a finger on her lips, and his smile turned a bit sly. "Besides, Your Grace, I like it best when my wife enjoys her time with me. It is proper for a wife to be joyful in the company of her husband. I would not like to think my charms are lost on you."

A knot in Mary's gut loosened, and suddenly it was easier to breathe. Of course. The better to please him, she could trust him and be pleased herself. A genuine smile lit her face, and she was able to raise her chin and look straight into his eyes.

He took her clasped hands in both of his and separated them. Then he pressed a kiss to each cheek and again to her mouth. This time he encouraged her to part her lips. The sensation was so heady to her she found it necessary to grasp the front of his doublet to steady herself. She glanced at the bed, but it seemed more of a danger than sanctuary. At once she wanted both to flee like a child and to pull him onto the bed like a whore. Instead she did neither but clung to him so that she might not sink to the floor.

Philip removed the pins that held her headdress in place and dropped them to the stones at their feet. The ornate piece followed and made a hollow noise when it landed. Then he removed the pins in her hair holding it in place, and they dropped to the folds of silk that preceded them. Mary felt lighter now, and certainly lighter-headed. A quiver took her, and she couldn't stop shaking. The room felt cold, as if the headdress were the only thing that had kept her warm. Philip took her in an embrace and kissed her even more deeply as he ran a hand into her hair.

It felt like chaos. Like being stirred with a spoon. So terribly undone and unrestrained! In a moment of high glee she knew must be wickedness in spite of Philip's permission to enjoy him, she kissed him in return the way he'd done her. A small hum came from the back of his throat, and he sighed. This pleased him, she could tell, and knowing that he could find pleasure in her felt wonderful. Her excitement rose, and wicked or not, she couldn't resist it. She told herself it was good and proper to feel this way about one's husband, and finally allowed herself to experience the wonderful things his kisses were doing to her.

She allowed him to undress her, then himself. As quickly as he could without assistance to untie and unbutton all the fine garments, he deposited their clothing on the floor at their feet. She couldn't help staring at his nakedness, for his male organ was much, much larger than she'd been given to believe was even possible. She'd seen paintings and statues of men and boys without clothing, and they'd sported members no larger than a finger or toe. Philip's resembled a rather large sausage, in both size and color, and it pointed at his chin. Mary was doubtful it would fit where he intended it to go.

He drew her by the hand to the bed, where the coverlet had been strewn with wildflowers and rose petals. The gentle perfume of flowers filled her head. Mary reminded herself the bed had been blessed. It had been consecrated to their union and the creation of children. There must be joy in that, and no denying it. So it was with deep faith in the rightness of this that Mary lay atop the silk comforter and down mattress with Philip.

"Relax," he said, a nearly absent murmur as he pressed his mouth to places never touched by any man before, and particularly not in this way. His tongue and lips on her skin nearly made her gasp, and his fingers in moist places made her too weak to move. Her knees parted unbidden, and she lay back where he guided her. He knew exactly where to touch her to make her helpless in his hands. Every move sure. Never did he give her a moment of doubt that this was how it was done. His very breaths, heavy and warm against her skin, pleased her and moved her to press her own mouth to his shoulder. His skin was smooth and his muscles hard. Tense. She felt a quiver there like her own trembling. Her effect on him pleased her as much as it seemed to please him. A moan escaped her, and she barely noticed it.

Philip shifted himself to lie between her thighs, and before she realized the moment had come, he was there. Filling her, his hips pressed hard against her, his arms holding her so she could barely breathe. The pain was enormous and sharp. It filled her as he did, and she cried out once. But it didn't seem to matter. Suddenly she could no longer tell pleasure from pain, nor his body from hers. Blood surged through every part of her, and some of it from her onto him and onto the bed. As he moved, faster now, she wanted to move with him. Like part of him, helping him in this effort. God would give them a baby. Joy grew in her until there was no room for anything else. Philip's trembling also grew, and his excitement moved him to ram himself against her hard, gasping, moaning, and uttering things in Spanish under his breath, words she didn't understand.

Finally, with a low growl and an oath she did understand, Philip jerked twice and then went still. He lay atop her, breathing hard, his weight heavy on his elbows and his damp brow pressed against her shoulder. The scent of him was something she'd never before known, and though she didn't find it un-pleasant, it was nevertheless dark and filled with mystery. Something like sweat, a little like blood, but more than either and more private than anything she could imagine.

Philip lay to the side and rolled to his back, his chest heaving for breath and his member still erect but shrinking quickly. She watched his face for clues of his opinion of what had just happened, but his eyes stayed closed and his mouth agape for air. Slowly his breathing returned to normal, and only when he was able to take a deep breath and let it out slowly in a deep, long, sigh of satisfaction did he turn his gaze on her. He brushed her hair from her face, and she realized she must look terribly out of sorts. She hurried to organize her locks in something resembling proper order, but it was hopeless to attempt it without assistance. He kissed her, and a smile lifted the corners of his mouth.

"Are you happy, my husband?"

"I believe discharging my duties will be an easy enough chore to accomplish."

She didn't know what to make of that, and her puzzlement must have shown on her face, for he hurried to add, "That is, of course, my wife, our marriage bed will be happy and fruitful." He took her hand and kissed her palm.

"My age causes you no trouble?"

"Ay, I am a virile and enthusiastic man with a sharp appetite. It would take an ugly woman indeed to put me off, and you are far from that. I assure you we will have an heir for England in short course." He said it with a jaunty smile, then kissed her damp forehead. "Come," he said. "Let us hurry beneath the bedclothes before a chill takes us and brings us our deaths."

Mary slipped beneath the comforter and silk sheets with her new husband, and for hours lay awake while he slept, turning over and over in her mind the marvelous news that she was not ugly.

Niccolò Delarosa stood in the anteroom to the queen's privy chamber with his lute slung across his back. He was to provide breakfast music for Her Majesty, and, he supposed, His Royal Highness the Spanish prince. But a cluster of men and women blocked his entrance, and he stood at a discreet distance to hear the ruckus.

Four of the Spaniards brought by Philip were insisting they be allowed into the chamber to visit their prince. The ladies, horrified by the invasion, were adamant they leave their mistress to her privacy. Since the ladies present did not speak Spanish, and the gentlemen did not speak English, the discussion was a morass of irritated demands that went unheeded, punctuated by stray vocabulary spoken by tongues unfamiliar with the words. The only word understood by both parties— the most useful one common to both languages—was the ladies' repeated, "No!" It was the only thing that kept the men from pushing their way past the women and through the door.

"You!" Niccolò said to the men in his passable Castilian. "What do you mean by this?"

They all turned to see the musician with his instrument, and one of the Spaniards looked Niccolò up and down with a hauteur not really necessary for the occasion. Niccolò returned a bland gaze and waited for a reply. He knew there would be one, because he was this man's only hope for being understood.

The Spaniard said, "We wish to see our prince."

"For what? He is on his marriage bed and should not be

disturbed." Not that Niccolò would have cared a fig if Philip were disturbed just then. It was Mary he wished to protect.

The Spanish courtier shook his head with a frown that suggested Niccolò was a capital rube for not knowing proper custom. "No, no, no! He must be congratulated on consummating his marriage! We must see him in his bed, where he has accomplished the task! He is our prince, and we cannot be remiss in this." The man seemed genuinely distressed by the prospect of failing this tradition.

Ah. Niccolò now understood. This was certainly not the custom in England, where a queen was expected to hide away for a day or two after her wedding. He sucked a bit of air between his teeth as he considered what to tell these gentlefolk. He then turned to the women and said in English, "They wish to congratulate their prince. It is Spanish custom."

The ladies' eyes all went wide. The one at the fore said, "No! No, she cannot be disturbed! It is dishonest!" She was an older woman, rather matronly and stiff, definitely of the old tradition. "They would cast doubt on the virtue of our queen, were they to go marching in there. You cannot imagine the scandal. The insult! And how upset she would be! She is so pious, and so innocent, she would be utterly mortified, were a troupe of men to barge into her privy chamber the day after her most trying night. We cannot allow it! It simply cannot be done!"

Niccolò translated to the men, who exploded in angry, slang-filled Spanish he couldn't quite follow. Their leader took it upon himself to attempt to enter against the will of the women, but they came together with a cry to block his way. Niccolò himself grabbed the Spaniard by his doublet and hauled him back. The man shrugged him off in irritation and turned belligerent.

"I must see Philip!"

"You cannot. This is England. We behave as Englishmen here." Niccolò lowered his voice and said to the men, "I understand how you feel. I've been in this country for many years, and sometimes still I long for the customs of my home. But heed me when I say you must learn to understand their ways. And particularly today you must acquiesce to the customs of the queen. She is your queen now. Treat her as such, or you will be sorry."

The man in Niccolò's grasp opened his mouth to speak again in protest, but a page hurrying past stopped to take in the scene. He quickly assessed the situation and said with bright, oblivious cheer, "If it's the prince you're wanting, he's not in there. Rather he's been at his desk all morning and now has gone to Mass. You'll find him in the chapel, at prayer."

All fell silent at this. The men looked at each other for a moment, then as one they hurried away in search of their master.

With a smile, Niccolò turned to the ladies who were left gawking, bowed, and inquired whether Her Majesty would care for some breakfast music.

Those first few months of marriage were easily the happiest within memory. I was certain my destiny was at hand, that all the suffering that had gone before would be vindicated in the restoration of the old faith to the realm, that I would bring forth a son to ensure the stability of rule, that I would live the rest of my days in piety and peace as would all of England.

Of course, no life is perfect, for why else are we put on the earth but to learn? Though the English are a wonderful people, hardworking and earnest, pious, and filled with an energy and curiosity that sets them apart from much of the world, my subjects were terribly enamored of their own Englishness. Though my marriage was accepted as necessary for the security of the kingdom, my husband's Spanish court and household were not well received. Philip had brought with him hundreds of courtiers and servants and millions of crowns in gold. The treatment of Spaniards in England was scandalous. Fights became common, robberies even more so than fights. Bold English highwaymen found easy targets in Spaniards, who were more accustomed to sneak thieves than those who would accost their victims in the open. Philip himself was a victim of thieves who robbed a party of his servants bearing four large chests. It was useless to demand action against these highwaymen, for there was hardly anyone in the realm who would treat the Spanish with respect. They expected Philip to go home the very instant an heir was conceived and so were hard put to make his men feel welcome. Fights broke out in the palace nearly every day. One terrible brawl necessitated the hanging of four men.

One by one the Spaniards asked permission to return to Spain. I watched my husband's court diminish and saw how it made him feel stranded far from home. I feared he would wish to follow his courtiers.

But rather than that, my dear husband stayed with me. He treated me with a gentleness I'd never known and attended to me as well as if I were a great beauty and a young woman. Would that I could have made him as happy.

Mary found herself more nervous than she might have expected for her first meeting with the Duchess of Alva. She wanted very much to make the woman feel welcome, as she hoped to do for all the wives of Philip's courtiers. The duchess was the only one she hadn't yet met, having missed the wedding for a delay in her arrival from Spain. Relations between the English and Spanish courtiers were not off to a smooth start, and Mary deemed it essential to her future marital happiness that the situation settle at least into nonviolence. Today she dressed in the Spanish manner, wearing black damask and velvet embroidered in gold. Not wishing to appear too stern and unapproachable, she awaited the duchess in the anteroom rather than in the presence chamber. They were two women today, visiting for the sakes of their husbands. Mary stood in the anteroom with a small group of her favorite courtiers, and the Duchess of Alva was escorted into her presence.

The duchess wore black velvet also, with lace and black embroidery. Mary took that as a sign of a kindred spirit and was happy to approach her with outstretched hand. The duchess, taken by surprise with the informality, dropped to her knees before the queen.

Mary slowed to a stop before her, not quite certain what to do with her hand now. The duchess reached for it to kiss it, but Mary would have none of that. It wasn't for nothing she'd forsaken the throne today. With cheerful words of greeting, she leaned down to hug Alva's wife and urge her to stand. She kissed the duchess like a sister, causing the duchess to go stiff and once she was released to back off a step. Mary realized she'd shocked the woman and tried to set her at her ease by guiding her to a chair near the hearth.

"So lovely to finally meet you, Your Grace." Mary spoke English and depended on an interpreter, for it was one thing to expect Philip to understand her in private and another entirely to have a meeting such as this subject to the differences between Aragonese and Castilian Spanish. "Do tell me all about your voyage. I hope the weather wasn't troublesome." There was only the one chair, and next to it a large cushion on the floor. Mary took the cushion, leaving the duchess to the chair.

The duchess's eyebrows went up, and she stared at the chair with the same horror she might have regarded a large spider. Then she looked at Mary as if to plead to have the cushion. "Your Majesty," she said, "I cannot possibly take the chair. It is not proper for me to take a seat higher than Your Queen's Majesty."

"Nonsense, Your Grace. You're my guest, and you'll have a seat of honor." Mary gestured as gracefully as possible to the chair.

"But, Your Majesty, it is not right."

"Well, Your Grace, I daresay what I wish is what is right, for I am sovereign. And I wish for you to have the chair."

The woman fell speechless and merely shook her head.

At an impasse, Mary called to her chamberlain for the two stools kept next to her bed in the privy chamber. They were matching brocade and the same height. But when the stools arrived, the duchess refused to sit on either of them. When Mary moved to one, her Spanish guest promptly sat on the cushion on the floor. That simply wouldn't do. Mary moved from the stool to a cushion as well. The duchess then stood, distressed. "Your Majesty," she said, and her voice betrayed she was nearly in tears. "I beg you, please do not place me so high. It is not proper. Perhaps both of us could sit on the stools."

Mary agreed, for that was why she'd requested both of them to begin with. "Excellent idea, Your Grace." She moved to a stool, and the duchess settled onto the other one with a smile of great relief.

"So, Your Grace," said Mary, "how went your voyage?"

* * *

*It was good to laugh. In spite of the everyday frustrations, all was
well. Philip himself was liked well enough by those who mattered,
and his courtiers seemed to accept me. And when I found myself
pregnant, my joy was boundless. Indeed, the entire kingdom rejoiced.*

Niccolò Delarosa watched his mistress and her husband from
under heavily hooded eyes. He hated the king. With every
fiber of his being, he hated Philip for the way he treated Mary,
the way he deceived her. It was plain the Spanish dog did not
love her. He only toyed with her, making her think he cared
for her as a woman. Philip only wanted the crown. He bided
his time until the day Parliament would bestow the crown
matrimonial on him. Then he would be king in his own right,
and Mary's regard would no longer matter to him. He would
dash her heart to the ground, and the poor queen would be as
eviscerated as a condemned traitor.

Tonight the king and queen chatted among some favored
courtiers in the privy chamber. The lord admiral was, as usual,
the loudest of the lot, laughing at his own jokes and taking
little very seriously. The others enjoyed him for entertainment
value, but nobody seemed to think him particularly competent
at his post, and his value to Mary seemed to stem from the
fact that he probably was not in league with pirates. That
much had improved since Edward's death. Paget was present,
an intense figure in the midst of the discussion at hand. Paget's
rehabilitation was already well along. Despite his years on

Edward's council, he was now proving himself an honored addition to Mary's. And as a Protestant, he gave keen insight on the thoughts of Mary's enemies. Mary frequently queried him on the subject and seemed to take his answers to heart.

Some others of the council also were there, and they talked with Philip of the process of restoring Catholicism to England. The Protestant advisors warned against too much change too quickly, and though Philip's feelings were strong on the matter, he seemed to understand that he risked triggering a rising among the Protestant minority. Mary said little, for it was her way to listen to the men talk then make her decisions based on what she'd heard. In any case, she was rarely addressed in these discussions. The men talked amongst themselves, and Mary said little beyond a question here and there.

The talk was casual, and nothing would be decided tonight. The hour was late. Soon they would all retire, for both Philip and Mary were conscientious rulers and there was always much to attend to of a morning.

Niccolò watched the pair. They sat near each other in chairs that nearly touched. Philip kept leaning over to speak privately to Mary, and whatever he said to her made her smile. Niccolò thought he also made her blush, but it was difficult to tell in the flickering firelight. It went like that for a while, with Mary and Philip carrying on a sub-rosa conversation of their own while others maintained the discussion at large amongst themselves.

Ambassador Renard commented once or twice in a teasing yet pointed tone that the king and queen didn't seem to have much interest in their courtiers, but Mary assured him he was mistaken. Still, she seemed to pay more attention to her husband than to anyone else in the room, and Philip's attention was fixed on his wife. Niccolò's heart clenched, and so did his teeth. He thought he might like to vomit from the unseemly, sentimental behavior.

Then Mary leaned close to her husband to whisper something behind her hand. Philip sat back in his chair to regard her with pleased surprise. He said, "Is it certain?"

Mary nodded.

He tilted his head to regard her midriff. "I cannot see it."

"It's there. Perhaps you'll notice tonight."

Philip's smile widened, then he said to the rest of the gathering, "Well, it appears my good wife enjoys her marriage bed well enough to have conceived in it!"

A round of exclamations rose among those in the room. Niccolò kept his face utterly blank, though he wanted to leave. It was too much for him to tolerate. The king was so smug! Niccolò hated all the Spanish. He wished this one would go . . .

Then the musician smiled. Ah, yes, of course. He would go. Now that Mary was pregnant, perhaps this Spanish pig would return from whence he came. Back to Spain with him, or off to Flanders, or some other place under his father's influence, now that England would have an heir! Niccolò drew a deep, relieved breath and renewed his enthusiasm for his playing with so much energy the others in the room looked to see what had him so excited. He ignored them and continued his joyful music as if he were the only person in the room.

Mary laughed, a bright, tinkling sound, and clapped her hands. "Indeed, there should be happy tunes this evening!"

Mary pregnant. And Philip might leave. Though the day was late, for Niccolò it had improved mightily.

CHAPTER SIXTEEN

All of England rejoiced at news of an heir. Church bells rang. Cheers echoed in the streets and the squares. Plays were written and performed in my honor. It even seemed the hatred of Spaniards lessened for a time, and brief but oh-so-sweet peace descended on England. However, the respite turned out to be nothing but a breath before even worse unrest took hold.

Protestants were a very small minority in England, but an extremely noisy and obnoxious one. They had never liked the idea of a Catholic king, and even less wanted a Catholic heir. To be sure, they'd never wanted me to be queen, and would much rather have had Elizabeth, or Jane, for that matter, though it was more Dudley who had liked Jane and Guilford on the throne. In any case, I did my best to make the return to the traditional religion a smooth one. I never asked that the property stolen from the Church be returned

to it. I showed mercy and allowed Protestant leaders to escape pun-
ishment and flee the country. For a time I had even been willing to
allow young Jane and Guilford to live.

I and my advisors preferred to make the transition slowly, to
help my subjects accept the change and know it was the right thing
to do. They would see, for a certainty, that it was what God wanted.
They were good, well-meaning people but misguided by decades of
irresponsible rule. I would make things right again. In November
of that year, England was reconciled with Rome, and Parliament
began passing legislation to bring our laws back to what they had
been before my father's terribly selfish and destructive reign.

The Protestant minority took exception and let their dissatisfac-
tion be known in ways so horrible they could only have been in-
spired by the devil.

Peter Barnacle made his way to church with his family on a
cold December morning. His wife had stayed at home, being
so sick with a bad cold she could barely breathe. Peter only
agreed to leave her for church in order to pray for her recovery.
He had all four of his children with him, and they made a fine
parade of good Christians making their way down the lane
toward the low, wooden building bearing a large cross on its
front.

The old stone church that had dated from the time of Edward III had been torn down years before and its accoutre-
ments plundered by King Henry. For a long time there had
been no church at all nearby, and only those who accepted the
new faith were allowed to worship in any case, so the poor
appearance of the new building was easily forgiven. Peter was
happy to have any church at all near his house.

This church had been a stable at one time, abandoned for lack of need. On the ascension of Mary, the man who owned it gave the property to the Church in thanks for the return of the old faith to England. The locals went to work to convert it to a usable sanctuary, and it would do until a better place could be built. These past months with Mary on the throne made it possible for most of Peter's neighbors to return to their worship.

Peter's daughter Sarah carried her baby brother while Peter held the hands of four-year-old Richard and five-year-old Margaret. Richard skipped along, filled with energy and, Peter knew, also with mischief. If he hadn't a firm hold on the boy, he would be off wandering in the weeds just out of curiosity. Margaret, on the other hand, walked daintily beside him, a proper lady and done up as prettily as her father's finances would provide. Though her clothes were cut from woolen dresses and linen shifts that had once belonged to her older sister, she wore them as if they were the finest velvet and brocade. Her perpetual smile shone pink on her face, and her blue eyes sparkled in anticipation of the Mass.

The air nipped them as they walked, and Peter could smell snow in the air. He would be glad to reach the church, where a hearth would be lit and the press of fellows would warm them body and soul.

They came upon David Wheeler, alone now since his wife had died and his son had gone north to make his fortune. "Ho, Davey!" Peter called out. David turned to see the Barnacle family and broke into a wide grin.

"Ho, to you, Peter! And your little Barnacles as well!" Though he spoke to Peter, his gaze clung to Sarah. The girl was only a year from marriageable age, and Peter knew how David hated the loneliness of widowhood. David had been hinting at his hope to marry Sarah next year. The match might have had its good points, but Peter was rather hoping for a more advantageous husband for Sarah, and Sarah was rather hoping for a younger one. David was discouraged from making suit, but it was still in his eyes that he held faith that she would find him her best prospect. He fell in with the Barnacle family as they approached the church.

Though the outside was still weathered, and the plaster ragged with cracks and holes, the interior of the sanctuary had been recently plastered and whitewashed, and a rough pine floor built. There wasn't enough money to restore all of the furnishings stolen from the old church, so the altar seemed bare, and seating was no better than plank benches and mismatched chairs, but the room was as neat as a pin. The new floor was well-scrubbed of the mud tracked in by the congregation of farmers, and the rafters were swept regularly. A dim smell of livestock lingered a bit, but the scent of beeswax candles and incense had made inroads. Soon there would be none but church smells, and the conversion from stable to sanctuary would be complete. The cluster of Barnacles made their way inside and moved toward their usual seats near the rear.

David said by way of conversation, more to Sarah than Peter, "Did you hear about the priest they killed last week?" Sarah thought David a lump and paid no attention. "Shot him dead e'en as he preached, they did."

The news dismayed Peter. "Who did?"

David shrugged. "Protestants, I vow, though I couldn't tell you names. Nobody found the culprit. And then there was the stabbing. I expect you heard about that."

"Aye, I did." Only two days before in London the servant of

a Protestant man stabbed a man preaching on the street in support of the Mass. All the countryside was in an uproar over that. It seemed nobody was safe from the evil of renegade heretics.

Sarah spoke quietly as they found their appropriate seats on wooden stools near the rear of the sanctuary. "They've no sense of right or wrong, them Protestants. They think they can do what they like, and there's no answering for it. They've no true service; they make it up as they will and can't even agree amongst themselves what is correct and what is heresy. They're like a boat adrift, without anchor nor even a star to guide them."

"'Tis a shame, it is. They would unmake the world and return it to chaos." David had maneuvered himself to sit next to Sarah, and Peter didn't see it in time to get the seat himself. She shot him a hard glance, and he looked away as if oblivious. He'd apologize to her later, and for now it wouldn't hurt her so much to have to sit next to David. It was only for a couple of hours that were supposed to be for worship in any case. Besides, the baby would probably fuss at some point, and she would then have an excuse to leave the room. The sanctuary filled with neighbors, the air abuzz with people visiting and catching up with news of the past day or so.

Sitting at Sarah's other side and letting Richard and Margaret sit next to the aisle, Peter leaned over toward Sarah to speak to David. "It's nearly impossible to walk the streets anymore, with them Lutherans always on the lookout to prove their faith in Jesus by murder and mayhem." That brought a wry smile from David. It would have been funny, had it been less true.

The congregation went silent as the priest came into the room and the service began.

Sunday Mass was a long affair, for there were those who came only the one day of the week. Communion alone took a great deal of time, and the sermon tended to be longer the more people there were to hear it, as if the priest wanted to provide as much of his message as possible to as many people as possible on the one day they could spare from work to listen to him.

It was about an hour into the service when the smell of smoke caught the attention of those inside the church. Not smoke from the hearth, which smelled only of wood and per- haps a bit of moss, nor the sweet scent of the candles, but of burnt dirt and paint. And a bit of sharpness that reminded Peter of burning dried manure patties from the pasture. It stung his nose a mite, and the overall smell grew stronger.

The rest of the congregation noticed it, too. They raised their heads and looked around. The priest fell silent. He was looking at the floor before his pulpit, and Peter saw a thin line of smoke rise from it.

A shout rose from outside. "Fire! Fire in the church!"

A murmur of query gathered within. People rose from their seats and looked around. What was happening? There were no windows. Nobody could tell what might be burning.

Then a holler came dimly from outside the church. "Let them know the fires of hell for their idolatry!"

Now the congregation's hubbub became that of alarm. Some rushed to the door to fling it open, and the man who grabbed the iron latch found it too hot to touch. He yanked his hand back from the pain and shook it, tried again, but couldn't lay hand on the latch.

Peter reached for Richard and Margaret and held each by an arm.

"Open it!" Several behind the man at the door shoved him aside to attempt escape, but they were burned as well. One of them wrapped his hand in his coat and tried to move the latch, but it was stuck and wouldn't budge. He banged it hard but with no result.

"Knock it down!" The crowd pressed forward. Smoke began to pour through cracks in the floorboards, and it came in around the edges of the door. People tried to back away from it, but the press from the rear stopped them. Those behind the Barnacles knocked over stools to get away, but nobody knew where there might be another exit. In panic, the people inside the sanctuary began to climb over each other to get out.

Peter was knocked to the floor from behind. His grip on his children failed. Feet stepped on him and kept him from rising. "Richard! Margaret! Sarah!" He struggled to grab the little ones again but couldn't find them in the press. When he tried to rise, others knocked him down. Smoke now filled the room, and Peter couldn't breathe. Coughing took him. He kept close to the floor, where there was still air to breathe, and crawled along it in search of the little ones.

"Richard! Margaret!" Nobody could hear him over the screams of congregants struggling to escape and other parents calling for their own children and men shouting for their wives. Surely there was a way out. Black smoke darkened the room. If he raised his head, he couldn't breathe. "Richard! Margaret!" Panicky tears stung his eyes more than the smoke, and ran down his face. "Richard!" A space opened up before him, and he began to crawl toward it. There was a door to the rectory somewhere. If he could find the right direction, perhaps there would be a way out.

Then he found Richard, coughing and retching on the floor before him. Peter reached out to scoop the boy into his arms. "Where's Margaret?"

But Richard couldn't speak. He could barely breathe. Peter kept crawling and dragged his son with him. Someone was pounding on something somewhere. Then there was a crash and a rush of air. Smoke swirled, and the air cleared some. Peter saw daylight through the thick, black air and moved toward it.

There were flames ahead. It was the doorway, but the way was blocked by high, orange flame. Some fell back, screaming. Some rushed the breach. Without stopping to think about what he was doing, Peter rose from the floor, picked Richard up in his arms, and ran toward the fire.

It burned. For what seemed miles he ran through the flame. It seared his nose and caught his clothes. For a moment he thought he would fall and die there in the doorway. But then he broke through to the clean, cold outside. Someone slapped his clothing to put out the flames. Another man lifted his coughing son from his arms. Richard would be all right.

Peter turned back toward the church. Flames engulfed it. Screams came from within.

"Margaret!" He looked around and saw Sarah with the baby and David. Tears ran down her face, making black streaks in the soot there. "Where's Margaret?"

Sarah shook her head, unable to speak for her sobbing. The baby screamed in her arms. David stared at the burning building, aghast and uncomprehending.

"Sarah, where's Margaret?"

But Sarah still only shook her head.

Peter ran back toward the church, but several men caught him before he could run into the flames. "No!" they cried, and they hauled him away.

"Margaret!" The scream tore his throat. *Margaret!* He wrenched at the grip on him, but the three men held him tight. He struggled against them. "No! She's still in there! I can't leave her in there! No!"

The rafters of the church gave way in a shower of sparks and fresh flame. No more screams came from inside the inferno. Peter collapsed with an incoherent scream and began to sob, begging to be let go. He sank to his knees and wailed his agony along with all the others in his congregation still living.

Mary and Philip sat on their thrones in the palace presence chamber. It was an ordinary day at ordinary state business, hearing suits and giving audience. There was still much to accomplish in bringing England back from the brink whence Dudley and his minions had taken it. Still much work to do. Paget was escorted into the room. He carried a booklet and wore a look of apology. This was quite unlike him, and Mary looked closely to see what his true intent might be. He made his obeisance, his bow lower and more ingratiating than usual, then he spoke.

Through the royal interpreter he addressed the king, as most people did, for everyone knew it was impolite to directly address another man's wife in his presence. Not to mention, in spite of the carefully constructed marriage treaty, there was no denying that at the heart of it the nature of a man was to rule his wife. The way men and women were made was not subject to legal manipulation. Mary listened, knowing she would nevertheless have the final say in whatever issue was at hand, for that was her own nature as she'd inherited it from her mother, and there was also no denying that. "Your Majesty, I bring a piece of writing that I fear must distress you."

"Then perhaps we could do without it," said Philip with a bit of a smile. Mary was glad to see him in a good mood today.

"It comes from John Knox, the exiled preacher."

Philip frowned, and Mary nearly groaned. "Knox," she said, "is a rouser of rabble, an intellectual flea, and a man who takes no joy in life or God. We're well rid of him."

Paget looked over at the queen as if just realizing she was in the room. To his credit, he did finally address her. "Ah, Your Majesty, but now he makes his attacks by pamphlet, from Scotland. I have one here to present to Your Majesties." He handed the printed matter to Philip, who glanced at it, saw it was in English, and handed it off to Mary, who read the cover.

Faithful Admonition to the Professors of God's Truth in England, it read. She translated for Philip, who grunted, unimpressed. Then she opened to a random page, and what she found there made her comment, "Oh, dear."

"What is it?"

She translated as she read, "Mary is an open traitress to the Imperial Crown of England, contrary to the just laws of the realm, to bring in a stranger and make a proud Spaniard king—to the destruction of the nobility . . ."

"Ay," said Philip. "Destruction, he says?" His face bore the sour look he habitually had for all Protestant nonsense. He had little patience for English tolerance of heresy.

Mary read further. "He calls for the assassination of some of my advisors. My 'associates in treason,' as he calls them."

Paget said, "Many voices abroad voice such things. Men you allowed to escape when you ascended the throne, Your Majesty." There was an edge of criticism in his tone for Mary's weakness in dealing with her enemies. Though Paget himself had been a recipient of exactly that same mercy, he often pressed for the destruction of his fellow Protestants in his struggle to show himself a valuable and loyal supporter of the current monarchs. Mary thought he sometimes went too far with that and took him with reservations.

"Who prints these traitorous tracts?"

Paget shrugged. "They are untraceable, I'm afraid. Printed on the Continent, by men who do not speak English. One man sets the type, another prints, a third transports, and they do not know each other. Additionally, many come from the strongholds of Lutheranism, where rulers are pleased to support attacks on a Catholic queen." Again, his tone struck Mary as critical, as if he thought she was at fault for her staunch Catholicism. She bristled at it.

"Add to this the unrest here in England. Priests are being murdered. Crime is rampant. A church in the country was burned last month."

Mary's gut turned at this news. "No! Was anyone hurt?"

"A number of people died in the fire, some of them children."

"Who set fire to this church? Have they been found?" They would be executed; she would make sure of it.

"The men responsible have been imprisoned."

"Where?"

"They are in The Fleet Prison, Your Majesty. They are Protestants who claim they do God's work in burning idol worshippers."

"They should be burned themselves." Blinding rage clenched her. Her fingers twisted together until her knuckles turned white.

"It is my considered opinion, Your Majesties, that something should be done." Paget glanced over at Philip, lest the king think he was being dismissed. He appeared a little distressed over not knowing where to speak, for though it was common for a queen to be present during this sort of discussion, there had never before been any question of whom to address. Paget glanced from one to another and settled on Mary when she spoke.

"They should be burned." Mary's ire tore at her at the thought of what those heretics were doing to the people under her rule. The minds led astray, the evil brought down on the realm. Everyone suffered for the transgressions of but a few. "Evil must be burned away. The rot cleansed and the loss cauterized. We must put to death at the stake those who would poison the minds of our people." She'd long thought the greatest danger facing the English was moral decline. It had begun when she was young and reached its zenith with her brother's reign. She knew it must end.

Paget opened his mouth to speak, but Philip said, "I hesitate to do this thing." Slightly raised eyebrows were Paget's only reaction, but in him that meant great shock.

Mary turned to him, stunned to hear him call for mercy toward Protestants. "You would let heretics go unpunished?"

Philip was a bit defensive at this challenge to his piety and shifted in his seat to cross his legs and laugh lightly. "Oh, but I have every enthusiasm for the burning of Protestant pigs. My father has ordered the execution of thousands of Lutherans and Anabaptists in Flanders. I myself have ordered many burnings and relish the sight of a heretic having his first taste of the fires of hell."

Mary opened her mouth to speak, but Philip continued over her.

"However, my wife, I also think mercy might be shown here in England, for such punishment might be resented by our subjects who hate Spaniards. Even those who are true to the faith might take exception to such a thing if only for the opportunity to blame us. We are in a delicate position."

Mary saw no logic and rather resented the idea that such evil could be better tolerated in her country than on the Continent. "That makes no sense. How can punishing heretics be right in Flanders but wrong in England? We must make clear what is right and not be weak in punishing that which is wrong. How can our people know how to behave if we don't show them by example?"

Now it was Philip's turn to bristle at insult. "Certainly we hold the safety of our courtiers in high estimation. Attacks on my Spanish by your English have been rampant. They fear to walk about, even in the palace halls, where there have been three brawls already this week."

"And I remind you I have only just lately pardoned two of your household for the murder of one of mine." The incident had left a particularly bad taste, though she'd made the pardon as graciously as she could manage.

"I remind you, my wife, that we have already discussed that matter, and it has been settled." His tone stressed the words *my wife*, and Mary knew she'd overstepped.

She backpedaled a little, for fear of being accused of disobedience. Of all things, she did not wish to be a bad wife. Nevertheless, she pressed her case as much as she felt she could within her purview. "We must consider all of our people, not only your courtiers. I'll not have the least man suggest we are remiss in our duty to maintain a high moral standard among our people. Anything less invites chaos. We've had quite enough of that over the past twenty years, don't you agree? Our people need us to restore what once was."

Since Philip was not so old as to remember much further back than twenty years, and in any case had only known England for six months, after a brief show of furrowed brow to save his pride, he acquiesced to her statement with a curt nod.

Mary turned to Paget with an air of urgency. "We must burn the leading heretics. Then their followers will see their error. We will purge our realm of the evil and return our people to peace and the grace of God."

Peter Barnacle walked several miles for the sake of watching a bishop die. He'd had word the day before that John Hooper, the bishop of Worcester, was condemned to die at the stake today. That morning he'd awakened in the dark and cold and dressed without lighting a candle and waking his wife or any of the children. He'd eaten a piece of bread left over from supper the night before, then tied another piece along with a bit of salt pork into a rag, which he stuffed inside his tunic before setting out on the road to London. The weather was cold, and the wind buffeted, shaking bare trees and sounding like faeries off in the woods, whispering and tittering as he passed. He held his cap to his head with one hand as his purposeful stride took him onward. There was no business for him in the city today other than witnessing the execution, but he needed to make this journey.

Since Margaret's death, his heart had blackened and hardened until he felt very little at all but only hatred for the people responsible. All of them. The entire lot of Protestants and their lack of moral compass. His poor wife, though recovered from her illness, pined every day for her murdered girl. To lose a child was terrible enough, as most people knew, but to lose her to the evil of men was a tragedy beyond comprehension. Sarah had married David a week ago. It was plain she'd fled the household and its pall of grief.

It was Protestants who had done this thing, and Hooper was a leader who taught the heresy that had made the murder of his child acceptable in the eyes of those who had done it.

When he reached London at midday, he made his way to The Fleet, where there was a crowd to watch the day's execution. More were coming, gathering and blocking the street, shifting and jockeying for the best places to see the proceedings. The assembly was a mix of Catholic and Protestant, the former attending for vindication and the latter for the sake of supporting a martyr. Peter veered from coming too close to the heretics spouting prayers for the heretic, for he feared losing his temper and assaulting one of them. Then he would be arrested and made a resident of the prison, these aberrant creatures bringing yet more evil to his life.

The day was cold, windy, and heavily overcast. A darkness had descended on the earth and was manifest in the weather. Peter moved into the press of people, and as he pulled his coat around himself for warmth, it crossed his mind he would be happy to warm himself on the fire of this execution.

It was not a long wait to gawk at the condemned. The Protestant bishop was brought out to the yard, wearing nothing but a gray shift and a skullcap tied over his shaven head. He was dirty and thin, and by the look of his hollow, blackened eyes, he may not have slept for days. He appeared crazed, as if his mind had slipped away during his imprisonment. Peter considered the possibility the man's mind had gone long before he reached the Fleet. Hooper looked out over the crowd, chin raised and chest out like a knight in the lists, and a great wailing began among his followers. Now Peter could see where they all were, scattered throughout the assemblage, but with a cluster of them very near the stake. He and his fellow Catholics watched in silence the display of zealotry as Hooper dropped to his knees to pray.

For a great long time, he prayed. Peter tried to ignore his heretical ramblings, much of which made no sense to him spiritually—or even in a practical way—and some of which was gibberish on any account. He didn't want it to make sense, for that way lay madness. As the prayer went on, Peter began to wish they would get on with this thing. He shifted his weight impatiently, felt in his tunic for his dinner, and idly considered eating it while waiting for the fire to be lit.

Finally the executioner interrupted the incoherent prayer, asking to be forgiven. Hooper peered up at him for a moment, as if struggling to understand the man's meaning. Then he said, "I know of nothing to forgive."

"O sir!" said the executioner, in a tone that suggested he was pleased to explain the proceedings to the bishop. "I am appointed to make the fire." He pointed with his chin toward the stack of faggots laid on the ground near the thick stake sunk deep into the ground.

"Therein thou dost nothing to offend me. God forgive thee thy sins, and do thine office, I pray thee."

Though this exchange was customary, and extremely risky

for the condemned not to profess forgiveness lest he find himself shortly in hell for it, most times it was perfunctory and
not entirely sincere. At every execution Peter had witnessed,
the prisoner had spoken through his teeth or with an edge of
anger or hatred. But Hooper was blithe in his forgiveness of
this man and utterly genuine. His every nuance bespoke a sincere happiness he was being made a martyr, fairly pathetic for
his ragged, unhealthy state. Had Peter not already been convinced of Hooper's insanity, he would have known it now.

The executioner hurried to comply, his conscience clear. As
others guided Hooper to the stake and tied him there at the
waist—and Peter could see the ropes were unnecessary, that
Hooper would have merely stood there without restraint—the
executioner began laying the wood about Hooper's feet. The
faggots were green, as Peter could see even where he stood.
Criminally green. Cruelly green, for there was no chance they
would burn properly. A dark thrill of vengeance shot through
Peter's gut. This was likely to be an ugly proceeding indeed.

Hooper, in his zeal to be remembered and to demonstrate
his extreme piety, took some of the reeds from the stack,
hugged them to himself like a small child or a well-loved pet,
and kissed them. Then he stuffed one bundle under an arm.
That brought a scattered, hesitant chuckle from the crowd, and
when Hooper pointed to a spot the executioner had missed to
make a complete circle of wood around the stake, several
onlookers laughed out loud. Forgiven though he was, it quite
disconcerted the executioner to receive such assistance from
his victim, and he hurried to fill the inadvertent gap.

Then the torch was put to the wood at Hooper's feet. As
Peter had expected, it didn't kindle well. It threw small billows
of smoke and hissed as it heated, but there was very little fire.

Nor did the dried reeds burn well. The damp, windy day kept the fire from Hooper, and only his feet burned. In spite of his earlier enthusiasm for martyrdom, the pain at his extremities showed well on his face. His brow popped out with sweat, and his cheeks went quite gray. His words were few, but his tears betrayed his wish for this to be over.

Though his feet blackened and his shift was singed at the bottom, after only a few minutes the fire went out, leaving nothing but a thin trail of smoke carried away by the wind. The smell of crisp skin and burnt meat and hair made Peter think of the church fire. Voices of screaming, pleading victims—women and children, old people who had never harmed anyone— echoed in his head and heart. Bile rose to his throat. Tears stood in his eyes, and he wished to shout for the executioner to renew the fire in haste. Others did shout, but Peter only pressed his lips together in silence. Hooper himself, in agony with feet and legs burnt to the bone, called for more fire. His fists gripped his thin, gray garment, perhaps readying to rip it in his distress.

When more wood was brought, stacked, and lit, even then the fire was inadequate. It didn't reach higher than the wood had been stacked, not much higher than his knees, and there was not enough smoke to choke him. He prayed Jesus to take him, but the Lord was heedless and left him to live on. Peter wept and told himself it was for his daughter, that this man in agony deserved his punishment. This fire also went out.

Yet a third time wood was brought, and finally it was sufficient to bring a good flame. Bladders of gunpowder tied around Hooper's waist beneath his shift in order to bring mer- ciful death exploded in a startling puff of smoke and flame, putting a hole in the garment at his crotch and bringing a high, thin scream of agony but no death. The condemned now wailed his pain and hung heavily on the restraints about his middle. He prayed at a feverish pitch and incoherently, panting as he did so. His eyes rolled back in his head. His words were punctuated with incoherent cries and thin, falsetto screams. His fingers fumbled desperately at his ropes until the flames climbed higher, finally reaching his chest, then he let them go. His head wagged back and forth, rocking to and fro then side to side. He continued to move, to pray, to scream, even when his mouth was aflame and his burning lips curled back to expose his blackening teeth. Fat and blood dribbled from them, and from his cheeks, making shiny rivulets down his neck. He pounded his chest in contrition, sending charred and flaming chunks of his own skin and flesh leaping through the air. Only when he was entirely burnt, the meat off his bones, did he finally sag forward and die.

The flames did not die, and continued to consume him.

Peter stared, appalled. Nobody raised a cheer, and perhaps that was good. No, certainly it was good. Catholic and Protestant were motionless and silent, humbled by the terrible thing they'd all witnessed. Peter told himself once more that Hooper had deserved to die but found himself less convincing than he'd been before.

The crowd began to break up and move on, and Peter followed without much mind to anything but going home. His dinner stayed in his tunic, uneaten.

CHAPTER SEVENTEEN

I could not abide the evil of leading astray those impressionable souls who would lose themselves on a path of error. Leaders who encouraged violence and hatred, selfishness and falsehood had brought the kingdom to the brink of ruin. I knew my purpose was to save my people from those who would destroy their very souls. I had no choice but to purge our society of evil.

Simon Renard disliked the French ambassador intensely, though he had to admit the fellow had his uses. Renard's master and the French king had many things in common: political ambition, desire for wealth, and skill at war tactics among them. But the great overriding thing Charles V shared with King Frances was that they were devoutly and adamantly Catholic and wanted all vestiges of the Lutheran heresy purged from neighboring England at the earliest possible moment. Renard was able to stand aside from time to time and let His Excellency Antoine de Noailles promote his agenda at no political cost to himself.

Noailles was not one of the court favorites. In response to rumors of French involvement in the defeated rebellion a few months before, Noailles had been given a house formerly occupied by Renard, minus all its doors and windows. Also, Renard had generously provided a servant, whose loyalty to himself was unquestioned and who reported back everything seen and heard in the Noailles household. All the better for France and Spain being at odds with each other, for any hint of support of Noailles by Renard was seen as grudging truth.

For the moment, Renard let Noailles speak to the queen on the subject of the burnings. Most of Mary's courtiers were of the opinion that she risked overthrow if the executions continued, and though Renard thought there might be some truth to the idea, he also hoped she might nevertheless succeed in purging the heretics from England, and that would please Charles mightily. Particularly it would please Renard if he could claim credit with his master for the queen's success. He watched in silence as the French ambassador addressed Their Majesties in the presence chamber.

It was late in the day, and many others had been heard by the king and queen. Only a small group of lesser courtiers remained, and they were herded into the presence chamber like so many cattle. Renard maneuvered himself to linger in the room, though his business with the sovereigns was finished, and he might have excused himself at that point. He wanted to see what the French ambassador would say to the queen.

Noailles appeared stiff and impatient from waiting for hours to be called. He was an officious, fussy little beast, his Gallic nose sticking out of his face like a pickaxe and his tiny, birdlike hands ever picking at and straightening his robes and decorations. Renard himself was a bit wearied, but his languid interest perked when Noailles spoke in response to an entreaty from Paget that the burnings come to an end. Neither courtier was in particularly good odor with Their Majesties for their resistance at various times to her right to rule, and Renard's interest was keen as to who might prevail here. It was his opinion Paget would have the better luck, for his recent successes in gaining the queen's trust over the past two years.

"I beg Your Majesties to consider the spiritual state of your subjects." Of course, he addressed the king. Mary sat heavily on her throne, puffy about the face and pale in her condition, her robes of state nevertheless draped gracefully and cascading in an artfully arranged sweep to the dais at her feet. In spite of her wan look, she was dressed as splendidly as was her custom, and as richly decorated in jewels as any sovereign. Philip lounged on his throne, as well-dressed as his wife but somewhat weary and impatient, and Renard knew him to be eager to have done with this business so he might retire to his desk to accomplish some correspondence before supper. As late as the day was, there would be little time for it, even if Noailles were succinct, which happened rarely for the self-important Frenchman.

Mary's response to Noailles was sharp enough to make even Renard wince. "Excellency, we assure you, the spiritual state of our realm is ever foremost in our thoughts. Indeed, we take dire exception to the suggestion it is not."

Noailles was quick to bow in apology, then said in his rather stiff Latin, "It is Monsieur Paget's assertion to which I refer,

Majesty. He has suggested Your Majesties might consider mercy for those who would lead your subjects into darkness and sin, and I only wish to say he thinks we punish the heretics too much, that the common folk have no stomach for the burnings. Though I understand that Your Majesties—"

Philip interrupted, though this was addressed to Mary. "There may be some truth to it."

Noailles glanced at Philip, then attended to Mary again, but changed his mind and finally addressed Philip. Mary took the most acceptable course and listened to the men discuss the issue between themselves. Noailles said, "It is naught but Protestant whining. Paget is a heretic himself, warning us to avoid angering him. He means to make us fear him and bow to his wishes, which are the same as those of the heretics."

"Us?" said Mary, in the end unable to be patient and quiet.

Noailles turned to address Mary now, apprehensive. "We Catholics, Majesty. Though the French have had some differences with England in the past," he stressed the word *past*, as if all were settled and forgiven, "on the question of Lutheran heresy we are as one in Christendom that the error must be purged from all of Europe so that we might live in peace as God intended."

Mary nodded, and Renard knew it was a point she could not deny. Philip said nothing, neither agreeing nor disagreeing. Renard knew he was still concerned that too much unhappiness among the people of his wife's country would be risky for himself and his household. There was also that the king considered the realm a backwater among his possessions and was unwilling to risk much for its well-being. Philip yawned and scratched an itch inside one ear with his little finger. Mary tugged her robes a little closer about her.

She said, "Paget tells us of murders committed by Protestants in protest of the new laws."

"All the more reason to protect yourselves from heretics. If enough of them are burned, the rest will think it too risky to continue as they do. The murders will stop, along with the wrong thinking."

Philip said, "But what of the grumblings from Catholics who see their neighbors in terror of the stake? It is something we see much of on the Continent, and even my father has been able to press the punishment only so far."

Noailles again shifted his attention, a bit walleyed at not knowing whom to address. "With all respect, Your Majesty, the emperor has ordered the burning of a great many more heretics than have died in England. In addition, I've heard no such grumblings. I believe whatever risk may exist has been exaggerated by the heretic Paget."

"We have it on better authority than yours, Excellency."

The French ambassador bristled at the insult but drew himself up and asked, "Whose, if I may ask, Your Majesty?"

"Paget and others."

Renard wondered who those "others" were and made a mental note to have his various agents around the household find out.

"Again, I say to you, they are heretics and cannot be trusted. In truth, were one such to tell me the sun has risen, I would need to open a window to look out."

Philip turned to Renard, who wished to be invisible and hated to be drawn into this discussion. "What say you, Excellency? Grumblings or no? How do you assess the minds of our subjects?"

Renard's thoughts flew in search of a diplomatic reply, then he said without too long a hesitation, "The realm has been in terrible turmoil for a great many years, Your Majesty. The English are well-known for their grumbling, and in fact change their minds on every issue according to a given day's wind. It is difficult for me to take to heart every word from a malcontent bent on making himself more important in the eyes of his fellows by criticizing everything he sees and hears."

Philip nodded. Mary leaned forward in her seat and asked, "So you believe there is no danger of a rising if we continue to discourage the Protestant error?"

"In short, Your Majesty, I do believe any danger is exaggerated."

Noailles gazed at Renard with hooded eyes. Renard nearly laughed to see the French ambassador struggling to analyze the statement, looking for the lie and the ulterior agenda in agreeing with him. The more amusing because there was none. Renard meant what he said and meant for the English monarchs to continue the punishments here just as the burnings would continue on the Continent. What he did not say, and would never say, was that he thought Philip a hypocrite for hesitating to burn English heretics while ordering wholesale slaughter in his Continental possessions.

However, Mary also seemed to think it not right to treat England as if her country were different from Philip's, and was not as reticent about saying so as Renard. She said, "I believe my husband may have the right idea about the best way to address the problems caused by religious error. And his father, as well. There is no reason to believe our subjects are so obstinate, nor our heretics so numerous as to make them such an influence over our policies. We will continue our vigilance against this evil, in order that it may be purged from our realm and, God willing, from the earth."

And that was that. Mary was decided, and there was nobody except heretics to suggest she reconsider. Renard's face remained expressionless, but in his heart he knew this was the best path.

Our path was clear before us. Conformity was the way to peace, for it was the splintering of thought that brought dissent, protest, and destruction. It seemed to me there was little to discuss on the matter and far more important issues pressing for our attention. Not to mention the anticipated arrival of our heir.

During that time I gained little weight, though I thought of little else. My health had never been excellent, but I knew I was destined to fulfill the roles of wife and mother as well as queen. Any other outcome was unthinkable. Like my mother, I would let nothing keep me from it. For what else was I if not that which God had made me?

Once Mary was put to bed and her ladies had gone to their own quarters, she sat on the edge of her mattress and felt for a bulge in her belly. There was none, but it was early yet. Soon, though. It wouldn't be long before she would see the baby grow, and she would truly feel like a mother. It warmed her heart to think how it would be when that happened.

A tap came on the door, and Philip entered without waiting for a reply. She looked up, knowing before she did so that it was him, for nobody else would have been allowed into the anteroom and past the guard. He was dressed in nightclothes and a robe of heavy blue brocade, and that meant a conjugal visit. Possibly even that he would spend the night. Mary idly wondered whether she would need to employ the door bolt to discourage him once she was far enough along that it would be unsafe for the baby for him to visit. As young as he was, these nights were more frequent than she would have liked, and though she had no deep objection to the act within marriage, her enjoyment related only to her wish to make him happy. A worthy enough reason, but she nevertheless looked forward to a short respite.

He smiled at her, and a bright glint sparkled in his eyes. Her heart warmed, and seemed to fill her throat to receive his affection. She returned it freely and stood to greet him. He came to kiss her. This was what she loved best, the gentle intimacies. Her husband always treated her with a tenderness she understood to be rare, and Mary thought she might have him sleep in her chamber every night for the sake of being kissed and held. On the nights he stayed to sleep afterward she lay awake to listen to him breathe. The mere sound of breath in him, sometimes even a little snoring, was a delight to her, a warmth she longed for when he was absent. He would lie sprawled across the featherbed, and she would lay her head on his shoulder, where she could breathe him in like the forest after a rain. Often her heart swelled so with her love for him, it ached terribly and even brought tears to the corners of her eyes she had to blink back. Sometimes, were she to admit it to herself, she wished for him to mount her a second time just for the sake of the attention.

Tonight his kisses brought joy, for they reminded her of earlier ones that had led to her condition. He guided her to the bed, and he helped her under the comforter. She slid into the bed and snuggled in. Then he dropped his robe on the floor and slipped in next to her. He took her in his arms and kissed her hard. His passion was plain, and the affection he demonstrated touched her deep in her heart. He loved her, she was sure of it, though he never said it directly. She never said it, either, but she was certain they both knew theirs was a love match. No man could be false in bed—the member was useless unless aroused, and no husband needed to seduce his wife—and Philip in particular had no reason to pretend to love her. As his hands sought the warm, damp places beneath her nightdress that made his breaths shallow and ragged, she shifted her hips for him and sank into a lovely, soft enjoyment.

Tonight she didn't have to ask him to be gentle for the sake of the baby. He went slowly, carefully, pressing himself into her rather than thrusting. The feel of his belly against hers, undulating and hard, tonight made her own breaths go short and ragged. Her thighs lay back against the mattress, and as it went on and on, soon her hips moved of their own accord. A sensation she'd never known rose in her. Philip raised himself on his hands to look into her face, but she couldn't bear it. She turned aside and closed her eyes.

Suddenly the sensation was like a fist in her loins. A tight pull that seemed to draw all her blood from everywhere else. Her mouth gaped, speechless. She gasped for air. Then it all exploded in her, and she cried out without meaning to. Philip ground his hips against her, and it happened again. Unable to stop herself, she bucked against him and pulled him against her.

He chuckled. "You like this."

Without thinking, she nodded. It was undeniable in any case. What she felt in those moments was the finest thing her body had ever done. In a few more moments Philip had finished, but instead of rolling to the side as he always had before, this time he remained where he was, his hips pressed against her and a dashing smile on his lips.

"You finally did it."

Mary had no reply for that, and a blush of deep embarrassment warmed not just her face but her entire body. "I'm sorry."

His smile faded, and he rolled off of her. "Don't be sorry. I only wish for you to do it more. Be less sorry."

"I'm not a whore." The scent of the soiled sheets began to turn her stomach, and she knew she'd made a horrible mistake.

"I never said you were."

"You implied it."

"I did not."

She fell silent, yanked down the hem of her nightdress beneath the comforter, and turned away from him.

He gazed at her for a moment, then grunted and lay back against the pillows. The silence that followed was long enough that Mary began to think he might have fallen asleep. But then he said, "How long must I wait for the crown matrimonial?"

She turned to him and examined his expression by the guttering candle on the night table. "I've told you I don't think it a good idea at this time. The nobles are too fearful of Spanish rule. They won't give it to you until they've been shown you will rule like an Englishman and not a Spaniard."

"I am not English. I will never be English enough for them. And they certainly won't give me the crown until you tell them to."

"We must choose our time wisely."

Philip made an ugly sound of disgust and sat up on the

edge of the bed. Mary held her breath, knowing she'd angered him and hoping he would get over it. She wanted to reach over and lay a hand on his back, to feel his body beneath the fine linen of his nightshirt, but she refrained lest he think her wanton. She willed him to forget his anger and lie back down. But instead of slipping under the comforter and taking her into his arms, he reached for his robe on the floor and stood to pull it on. Her heart sank, and she tried not to watch him. Then, without another word, he left the room.

Mary listened to him go, trembling with regret. She should not have angered him. She should have found a way to soothe him and convince him it would be a short wait for his crown. Tears tried to rise, but she swallowed them, blew out the nearly spent candle, then lay on her side with her back to the door, staring into the darkness.

Ultimately, it would have been impossible to bestow on Philip the crown matrimonial. The English people would never have tolerated the rule of a Spaniard, but even more to the point, the nobility didn't like Philip well and would not have relinquished rule to him. For my part, I saw no reason to forfeit my authority. It was my destiny to return England to grace, and I hadn't yet done that.

Soon I entered my confinement. Only then did I begin to understand that perhaps God's intentions for me were not what I'd thought.

By the time she went to her lying-in, Mary had not gained nearly enough weight to suit her physicians. Her belly was full, but not as big as might be expected. Mary crossed her arms over her middle as she sat quietly while her maids drew heavy curtains over the windows. Darkness descended, and the room enfolded in muffled sounds. The bed was prepared, but she had no interest in it. She sat in a large, cushioned chair and daydreamed of Philip. She wouldn't see him again until the baby was born, and that made the coming weeks loom before her as if they were endless.

The days passed like a heavily laden barge. There was little news from court to mark the time. Though she required reports of all events, it was often like pulling teeth to learn anything of import. Only her maids were allowed into her rooms these days, and they were poor informants, for they often didn't understand the issues they were relaying. Mary began to order interviews with courtiers in order to keep abreast of goings-on. Like her mother and her grandmother before her, she was a queen and could not neglect her responsibilities even for the sake of her health.

As the weeks wore on, Mary's belly did not grow. Her physicians began to tell her she must have been mistaken about the date of conception, but she knew there had been no mistake. Nevertheless, her due date passed, and no baby came. Terror rose that it had died. Even worse, perhaps there had been none at all. She now spent her days sitting, rocking herself, and weeping, holding her middle as if the child were really there, and wishing she didn't have to face the truth. The child, if there ever had been one, was dead. Furthermore, there was something wrong with her that her physicians couldn't comprehend, never mind treat.

Mary rocked and prayed every day, terrified that she would not live and knowing that if she couldn't conceive, she might no longer care to live.

CHAPTER EIGHTEEN

The time came that even my physicians couldn't deny the truth any longer. They each, one after the other, tried to convince me the pregnancy had been false, but I know it was not. I'd felt the baby move. It was no false thing, it was a child. But God chose to take him from me. I cannot fathom the reason, but there are many things we are not meant to know but can only accept. I struggled at acceptance, but it was a hard thing, and I met with little success. Shortly after I returned to my governing duties, the swelling disappeared, and my courses returned. I received this with immeasurable grief and took to my bed with weeping for several days. The mere thought of carrying the weight of my own body, even to stand, became crushing, impossible. To make myself presentable and to pretend to a strength I did not have would have required a miracle. I couldn't ask that, for I had no more prayers to give. I lay in my bed, bereft of all that mattered.

It was only at the insistence of my closest advisors that I rose from my sorrow and pressed onward with the business of restoring my kingdom to its former glory.

Philip returned to my bed but without the enthusiasm he'd shown before. He often asked after the crown matrimonial, and each time he broached the subject, I became less patient with him. Why couldn't he see the impossibility of the situation? How could he believe my English subjects would accept him as their sovereign? He'd accepted the terms of the marriage contract, which severely limited his purview, even as my husband. Did he hope to set aside the contract once he was sanctioned by Parliament? I was loath to believe that was his goal, but his behavior after my failure to bear him a son might lead one to think so.

Simon Renard was enjoying a rare afternoon in private conversation with the king. He'd been invited for an outing of target shooting with pistols, and he was mano a mano with Philip while their attendants stood to the rear, reloading guns and passing them forward to their masters. Renard wasn't terribly fond of the activity itself, for he wasn't much of a shot, he was uncomfortable setting off explosives in his hand, and he disliked the sharp stench of gunpowder and the way it stained his sleeve. But he was intensely interested in anything the king might say casually. Indeed, it was significant that Renard was the only opponent in today's competition, for it meant Philip had something on his mind he wished to discuss without the unwelcome influence of lesser men. Renard waited to hear what the king would say and knew it would be worth his time and effort.

After about an hour's shooting, when Philip's score was a good lead on Renard's poor showing, Philip finally sighed and spoke low enough for those behind them to miss his words, even had they been in English, which of course they were not. "I believe I shall leave for Flanders at the earliest opportunity."

Renard looked sharply at the king, who took less than careful aim and fired off a sloppy shot that nicked the edge of the target. Philip then handed the pistol off to his attendant and crossed his arms to await Renard's shot. Or his reply.

What he got was a reply as Renard ignored the pistol offered to him by his gentleman. "Do you think it wise, Your Majesty?"

Philip's brow furrowed. He was unaccustomed to having his wisdom questioned by an inferior.

Renard amended himself quickly and reached for his pistol. "That is, may I ask what in Flanders is so pressing?" He fired, then handed his weapon off to his gentleman just to get the smelly, smoking thing out of his hand.

"I need to attend to my military efforts there, now that my father has decided to retire and pass his holding to me."

As if this were an ordinary conversation and to smooth any impression of criticism, Renard asked, "How fares the emperor? What do his physicians say of his condition?"

Philip reached for his freshly loaded pistol but then sighed and stared at it rather than firing. "He is an old man and cannot move from room to room, let alone from one holding to the next to rule over them. He has healing waters brought to him, but I'm told it does little good. He forgets things, and there are those who say he suffers some of the mental troubles of his mother." He fired his shot, then let the spent pistol hang at his side. His grandmother was recently deceased and had spent half her life insane.

"Charles, in his time, was a singularly great ruler." Renard could say this in all sincerity, for he believed it heartily, though there were some who disagreed.

Philip was noncommittal on that point and stared down-range at the big, stuffed archery target now tattered with ball holes. There was a heavy pause, then he spoke in a dull, re-signed tone. "I need to make myself visible to him." This was quite the confession from Philip, who was never humble and rarely admitted the slightest inadequacy in himself. His arro-gance was one of the things that made him strongly disliked among most of his father's courtiers and many of Mary's. It was the very thing that kept Renard from liking him as well as he should a countryman so far from home.

"You don't think your father will understand the need for your continued presence in England?"

Philip gave Renard a long, considering gaze, then seemed to make a decision. He handed his pistol back to his gentle-man, took Renard downrange away from the others and out of earshot, then admitted something even more astonishing. "Alas, my business here is finished."

Renard blinked. As far as he could tell, Philip had accom-plished nothing in England. He said, "Her Majesty is preg-nant again, then?"

Philip shook his head, and an edge of disgust entered his voice. "Her Majesty is barren. I think we all knew that when I married her."

"Conceiving an heir for England was the reason for the marriage. At least, that is my understanding."

"An heir for England was *her* reason for the marriage."

"And yours?"

Again Philip looked hard at Renard. "I understood I would

be king. That England needed a strong ruler, not a woman on the throne."

Renard knew the terms of the contract and wondered exactly what was meant by that. "You knew you would have no authority here."

"Don't be silly. I am her husband. I have complete authority. I have expected it to be acknowledged, but Parliament resists bestowing the Crown, and my loving wife imagines herself a sovereign, capable of ruling in her own right." He said this as if it were so ridiculous he could barely utter the sentence, though Renard thought Mary was not so incapable as most women. Perhaps not as strong a ruler as her grandmother had been, but certainly not without a degree of competence. But Philip continued in that vein. "I cannot any longer bear the humiliation of my powerless status here. I must go where I am respected." He thought that over for a moment, then added, "Where I am needed. I am not needed here. Let her rule her country as she will; I am extraneous. Mary herself will tell you that."

Renard knew Mary would never do any such thing. If anyone needed Philip, it was she. If anyone in Christendom other than Charles and Jesus loved Philip, it was his wife. But Renard said nothing.

Philip continued when Renard declined to reply, "As for creating an heir, she is nearly forty years old and far past her days when she might have been a mother. I'm afraid I have come too late to serve that purpose. Furthermore," and here his voice dropped so low as to be nearly inaudible even to Renard, who stood as close as propriety allowed, "I rather dislike the role of stud. As if I were an animal meant only to breed and who would become useless once it were accomplished. Particularly since I expect to meet with no success at it in any aspect. Aside from her infertility, she is not an eager or skilled partner, and though early on there may have been the possibility of satisfaction in one thing or another, it's become clear her interests are far different from mine. In short, Excellency, I can no longer afford to stay here. The cost is too high politically, financially, and emotionally." There was a brief silence between the two men and Philip gave Renard a look filled with meaning, as if to convey that the ambassador might have known this already. Then the king returned to the firing line to accept a loaded pistol from his gentleman and wait for Renard to follow him.

Philip's words saddened the ambassador, for he rather liked Mary and knew how unhappy she would be when she heard this news. He wondered if she knew how Philip perceived her and hoped she didn't.

Renard received a pistol from his attendant, took aim at the target, and put a hole straight through the bull's-eye.

There are no words to describe my devastation when Philip announced he was leaving for the Continent.

Peter Barnacle heard a cry from the direction of the town square. Something about a queen. Mary? Could it really be the queen? Not long ago there had been a terrible rumor she was dead, then another rumor she was not. Nobody knew the truth. Peter's heart leapt, and he hurried from his orchard and around to the front of the house to follow the crowds gathering near the road.

Everyone in the village was there, and it seemed many from farther out in the country, as if word of the queen's presence had gone out to everyone, and they were pulled to this place by a magical force. Off in the distance he could see a knot of people gathered around the head of a column in the road, a procession that stretched into the distance and around the bend in the forest. Onlookers ran and danced around a litter accompanied by a guard of knights, and beside that litter rode a man so resplendent he could only have been the king. Even had it not been Philip, by the sight of him Peter would have wanted him to be the king.

Peter's wife came to look, and shaded her eyes with one hand while she grasped his arm with the other. Ruth's strength had improved in recent months, taking solace in the baby, who was walking now. She stood on tiptoe to see the column, but there would be nothing to see until the procession came closer. "Is it them?"

"I think that's the king near the litter." The dark chestnut horse carrying the splendid figure was enormous, a Spanish breed, and its gait was proud and prancing. It was only by skilled horsemanship that the rider was able to control it. "They say it's Mary inside." The litter swayed a bit, and curtains lifted in the breeze, though the procession moved slowly.

"Mary? That can't be. They say she died."

"Perhaps 'twas aught but rumor. I've heard such things before that have turned out untrue." Many such, for folks were always on about things beyond their ken.

She made a noncommittal humming noise that acknowledged he might be right, but she wasn't yet convinced. She said, her voice distant and sorrowful, "They've said there's no heir."

That much Peter did believe. They'd all waited far too long

for the announcement of a birth for there ever to be one. Many assumed she'd miscarried, but there were dark murmurings that there had never been a baby, even that the entire pregnancy had been a story made up by the queen and her privy council to ease the fears of the commons. Peter didn't like to think it, for he wanted more faith in his queen than that.

The procession came closer, and Peter could make out the astonishing outfit of the king. His sumptuous costume and gear shone in the sun, and his young, handsome face gave faith in the rightness of his rule. Peter wondered at those who said the Spaniard was an ill king for England. From what he could see, Philip was as fine a ruler as any had ever been.

As the litter neared, Peter took his eyes from the rider and vanguard and peered into the cushioned interior. The curtains had been drawn back so all could see, and Peter's heart leapt at sight of the woman he recognized from his service in the south.

"That's her, all right. She's still alive." He waved, and he thought she recognized him, because she waved back, though she was smiling and greeting everyone she saw, and waving to everyone. Surely she would remember him from the days before her coronation, when he marched with the men who supported her right to the throne. She was a queen; she must remember everyone. She continued waving as the litter moved on past the Barnacle house and away from the village.

Someone nearby said he'd heard the king was on his way to leave the country, and Peter gaped. Leaving? Why? How could he rule from the Continent? What would England do without a king? He watched the litter and its guard proceed down the road to be swallowed by the forest, and wondered at his future if the ruling class was going to neglect its responsibility to rule. What would become of them all?

* * *

Mary wasn't sure of the name of this village, though it was near enough to London she should know it. It didn't even seem much like a village, but rather nothing more than a cluster of houses along a road through a forest near London. It was the sort of place that alerted travelers that they were nearing civilization but weren't quite there yet. She'd lost track of exactly where they were, for her mind was in ghastly turmoil over Philip's impending departure for the Continent.

But the masses of people who rushed to pay their respects to their queen gratified her in ways that also mystified her. They reminded her that she was sovereign, she held the authority to rule, and all would be well in Philip's absence. She would keep steady the reins of her country for her husband and king, just as her mother had for her father during the Scottish troubles and the Battle of Flodden. As she waved to the crowds of the thrilled and curious, a pleasant memory surfaced of the similar enthusiasm she'd received on her arrival in Wales three decades before. It made her smile, though a queer, unsettled sensation rose in her belly. There were so few good memories to be had, and they were all frightfully treacherous for being so far distant and no guarantee there would ever be any more in her life. Nostalgia was poison. Trust was risky. Only God knew what lay in her future.

She shook off the feeling and set aside all thoughts but the business of rule while Philip would be gone. She forced herself to ignore the childhood memories and dwell on coming discussions in Parliament of trade issues: what to do about the English economy that had collapsed while Dudley was in power, and what to do about the failed harvests caused by relentlessly wet weather. She turned over in her mind the details and some possible avenues of thought, like tilling the soil of her imagination to plant facts and hope ideas would rise and reach for the light. Her country was desperate, and so was she.

At Greenwich Mary spent the last moments before Philip's departure alone with him in her apartments. Their attendants more than likely thought they would say good-bye in bed, but neither of them was terribly keen on the idea. Instead, Mary sat in a chair near the hearth and watched Philip fuss over his clothing. Though his costume was perfect, he nevertheless found lint to pick and interminable bits to tug here and there.

Mary wanted to talk, but couldn't. There wasn't much to say, for she could only think to argue with him that he shouldn't go, and he seemed reluctant to say anything at all, lest she begin to harp on him. Mary didn't want that any more than he, for she would rather have cut off an arm than to behave as a sharp-tongued fishwife. Her mother had never been that way, though she'd sufficient cause over the many years of her suffering at the hands of Mary's father. Catherine had borne her treatment with dignity, and so Mary would as well.

She watched her dear husband from the far side of the privy chamber, seated on a cushioned chair as he put the finishing touches on his travel costume, then he knelt at her altar for a final prayer before leaving. She lowered her head and her eyes and sat in respectful silence as Philip prayed for a safe journey in a low, mumbling voice. Mary's lips moved silently in a truly heartfelt prayer to the same effect.

Then he rose, and she watched him. He came to her and stood before her. For a long time he gazed on her. She looked no higher than his shoes. Finally he said, "I promise to return."

She shut her eyes and hoped it wasn't a lie. She said, "I wish you all success in your efforts in Flanders." It came out sounding false, though she meant it sincerely.

He paused a moment, considering, then replied, "I expect there will be great victories."

"God keep you safe."

"And you." He held out his hand.

She grasped it and kissed the back of it. He said nothing, but retrieved it.

"It is time to go," he said.

"Yes. Time for you to go." She was afraid to look at his face, lest she break down and lose all the dignity she'd struggled so hard to achieve. She rose and followed him from the rooms.

She accompanied him to the head of the stairs, where his gentlemen awaited their master. Here he insisted he leave her, for it would be unseemly for her to follow him to the boat like a whore at the docks. She nodded, though she would have liked to follow him there, and all the way to Flanders if she could have. Philip nodded to affirm his words, then proceeded down the stairs. Mary watched him go.

Then each of his men took her hand and in turn kissed the back of it. While Philip hurried away, his gentlemen said their good-byes to their master's wife. She wondered whether Philip was as eager to leave as his men all seemed. They each in order of precedence followed him away and down.

Mary felt cold. Dizzy. She barely heard the words of the departing men and struggled to keep her expression neutral as she watched the back of her husband's head recede in the distance. She wondered whether this would be her last sight of him.

Once Philip and his men had gone, Mary went to the window in her privy chamber and sat before it where she could look out and see the river and the barge that would carry Philip away. Now, finally, she could cry. With nobody near, she could let the tears come and weep without shame or loss of dignity. She watched the loading of the barge, the horses and men and trunks swimming in her vision and blurring together incomprehensibly.

Then she saw Philip himself go to the barge and board it. Her heart clenched at sight of his now-familiar figure. The way he walked, the way he moved and held himself, she could tell him easily even from this distance. With one arm she hugged herself with grief, and the other hand she held over her mouth to hold back any sound she might make. Then he disappeared belowdecks, and Mary knew in her heart she would never again lay eyes on him. The sailors cast off, and the barge moved down the river toward the palace. Philip was on his way. Fresh grief made her sob aloud.

But just as she might have succumbed to the urge to run away from the window where she couldn't see him leave, Philip returned topside. Mary's heart leapt to recognize her husband. As the barge passed beneath her window, he snatched his hat from his head and waved it in her direction. Not merely a polite gesture, but a wide sweep with the enthusiasm of a boy, nearly bouncing on his toes. Through her tears Mary laughed and held the fingers of both hands over her mouth. The image of her father so long ago, doffing his cap to her beneath the terrace at Hatfield, jogged in her mind.

He loves me. Praise the Lord, he loves me.

Philip left off waving but continued to gaze up at the window. Mary continued to watch him as the barge proceeded on its way and never took her eyes off it or him until it was around the bend in the river.

CHAPTER NINETEEN

Estelle was adjusting her bosom so that enough would show but not so much as to give it all away for free, and so she wasn't seeing what Marta saw.

"Ach! Look there!" Her friend nudged and pointed, then snatched her skirts to get her hems out of the Brussels mud.

Estelle yet fiddled with her dress, a new one cut down from old cloth from a discarded gown once owned by a countess. Estelle was only the third owner, and she was thin enough and the fabric taken in enough that most of the seams were fresh. The hem had needed extensive turning and the skirt was perhaps shorter than she would have liked, but the bodice looked like nearly new fabric. Blue silk that she liked well with her nearly blue black hair. She was so proud of her beautiful new dress she could hardly breathe.

Once she was happy with the arrangement of her breasts, she peered myopically up the street. She was never any good at seeing much beyond the ends of her fingers, so seeing several houses away and by moonlight was a strain for her. Marta tired of waiting for a reply, and told her what she was looking at. "'Tis the prince!"

"King, you mean? Or is it truly the boy?"

"Philip."

"King. That one's the king now. I heard it from Johannes, and he knows all that sort of thing."

"He's not king yet, I vow."

"Well, he's the king of England in any case. How can you be certain 'tis him?"

"Trust me, my friend, there's no mistaking him. As pretty as he is, he's not one easily missed." A note of lust colored Marta's voice, a rare thing for such a whore as she.

"What's he doing here?"

"Here in Brussels, or here in Flanders?"

"In this part of town! In this street! He'll soil his fine clothing, won't he, just walking around!" Estelle still peered at the loitering men in the distance, struggling to guess what was going on.

Marta shrugged, then tugged on Estelle's arm. "Come! Hurry! He's going to the public house!"

"You're not going to follow him in there! You were kicked out last time we went in there."

"That wasn't my fault!"

"You stole that purse."

"I found it."

"You found it in that gentleman's belt, is what."

Marta made a disgusted sound but didn't argue the point further.

Estelle continued, "You're not going back in there after that adventure."

"Indeed, I am! We are! Tonight is our big chance!" She pulled harder and dragged Estelle a few steps.

Estelle hung back. "Are you mad? This is madness!"

"Crazy like a fox, that's what! Come, we're to meet the prince!" Marta gave Estelle a hard yank.

"King!"

"King of England, then, if you must!"

Estelle still resisted and dug in her heels as Marta dragged her onward. "I won't! We'll be thrown from the house! Go by yourself!"

"I need you to come with me. Together we might not be refused."

"We'll be tossed into the street, and I'll have mud all over my finest dress!"

"A dip in the river would solve that, and besides, they're not going to throw us out. Come on! There'll be money in it, for a certainty."

"I've had easier money than that's likely to be."

"But not nearly so *much*." She said the last word with a relish like the lust in her voice on sight of Philip. "They say he's generous with his gold."

Estelle was yet unimpressed, for she'd heard similar tales that had turned out to be naught but Marta's imagination.

But then Marta added sotto voce, "And I hear he's generous with his naughty bits as well. Plenty to go around, if you get my meaning."

This perked Estelle's interest. Money was one thing, but a truly good time with a well-endowed client was attractive. And was rare enough that she sometimes longed for it. She stopped pulling away and looked up the street toward the tavern. "They do say he is a pretty one."

Marta nodded. "I've seen his face. He's an angel, sure."

"Large, you say?"

Marta nodded again. "'Tis well known how large he is."

Estelle relented. "All right, then. And what're we going to say to His Grace ... His Royal Highness ... His *Maj*esty, the arrogant Spaniard who is by all accounts less than a flea on the hide of his sainted father, the emperor?"

"I'm going to say, 'Have you a private place where I might show myself a loyal ... ah ... *subject?*'"

Estelle laughed at that as the two young women scurried along the street toward the tavern. A cluster of guards and terribly well-dressed attendants blocked the entrance, and Marta tried to wend her way between them to get to the door. But she was snatched by the back of the neck by a gentleman who hauled her back and peered into her face. Estelle was so taken by the cloth of his doublet she put out a hand and nearly touched it as Marta writhed in his grip.

He said, "What're the two of you up to?" His Walloon was poor, spoken with a Spanish accent heavy enough to make it nearly unintelligible. Estelle grasped his meaning only by knowing from experience what he was likely to say. There were also his tone and posture, which suggested he hoped the girls would be willing to keep him and his comrades company. That he still held Marta by the scruff of the neck didn't seem to matter to anybody.

Marta's eyes went wide with an innocence she hadn't owned

in nearly a decade. She spoke slowly so there would be no chance of misunderstanding. "We've been summoned by His Grace." She pointed inside the public house, and Estelle wondered whether Marta thought the man might be confused as to which king she meant.

The caballero eyed the two of them, plainly uncertain whether this could be the truth. Marta eagerly elaborated with another bald-faced lie.

"A page came to our lodgings. He said His Grace was desirous"—she emphasized *desirous*, making the word as long as possible and fluttering her eyelashes at him—"of supple, willing, and *discreet* company for the evening." She toyed with a fastening on the front of his doublet, as if she yearned for nothing more than to have it off of him.

The gentleman said something in Spanish to his companion, who shrugged and replied in that language. The one with his hand on Marta's arm said to her, "Stay here. I'll return shortly." He gestured that one of the guardsmen should keep an eye on the two, then entered the public house.

Estelle was astonished they might actually be allowed inside. She couldn't help smiling and bounced on her toes in anticipation. Marta put on her professional face, so blasé and sophisticated, as if she were French. Marta wore a yellow wig she'd paid a month's income for and was ever putting on airs. She was a far better liar than Estelle, who envied her the skill, for the men seemed to like the pretense and paid heavily for it.

It didn't take long for the first gentleman to return with the message from his master that he wished to have a look at the girls. Marta took Estelle by the hand, and they followed the man into the pub.

It was a place familiar to them, but tonight it had been commandeered by the king ... prince ... whatever he was at the moment ... and his favorite courtiers. The men were playing at cards at a table, and now that she was close enough, Estelle saw which one must be Philip himself. The sight of him took her breath away, for he was the most beautiful creature she'd ever clapped eyes on. Not that she'd ever been face-to-face with royalty before. He was quite a few years older than herself, she knew, yet he did not show the wear of those years. His skin was smooth and free of blemishes and scars. He appeared to still have all his teeth. His hair shone, and his lips were full. Generous. So kissable. Even edible. His cheeks glowed with the drink she saw sitting out on the table in bottles, many of which had already been emptied. Goblets stood about, and the smell of wine and mead was thick in the warm tavern air. The hearth roared nearby, throwing light and heat unaccustomed in this place where on most nights the proprietor was stingy with his wood. Estelle looked around at the unfamiliar sights and found a mural she'd never noticed before of a naked woman lounging in a forest glade, surrounded by moss-covered trees and vines thick with flowers. The painting was obscured with what must have been decades of woodsmoke and barely visible even in this excellent light.

"Good evening, ladies," said the king. He waved off the caballero who had brought them, apparently satisfied with the girls' appearance. The attendant bowed and returned to his post outside the door.

The girls giggled and curtsied to their far better. "Good evening, Your Grace," said Marta. She glanced at Estelle with a grin and said, "We wish to present ourselves to the service of Your Grace. You'll find us loyal ... *subjects*." She glanced at Estelle again, and they both giggled.

Philip seemed to find them amusing, and a tiny, indulgent smile curled his lips as he held out a hand to Estelle, who took it eagerly and stood near to his chair. Marta's face darkened, but then the king reached out with his other hand to draw her toward him as well, and around to his other flank. The other men at the table waited patiently for their master to return to his game, and Philip took his time to enjoy the ladies who had come to entertain him. His fine smile and sparkling eyes made Estelle's heart flutter and her private parts thump. Had he asked to take her on the table before them, she would have hopped onto it and thrown her legs wide. But patience was the order this evening, and so she waited for him to express his desires.

Philip returned to his game and admonished the girls they should be his good luck charms. Which they seemed to be, for over the course of the evening the king won more than he lost. More, even, than might be accounted for by a policy of letting the master win. He offered the girls beer, and the two drank deeply of his stein. Laughter came easily that night, and the joy of reveling in the presence of royalty was quite dizzying. Everything he said was funny to them. The prospect of pain became incomprehensible. Life was a lark, and this night would never end. With the king's arm about her waist, Estelle knew she must be the envy of the entire country, and the next morning all her friends would know of it. She would make sure of that.

Late in the evening His Majesty drained his stein yet again and this time set it back on the table with a firm finality. Then he drew Estelle down onto his lap and snaked his hand beneath her skirt. Her thighs leapt apart, and she gasped. He found her damp spot, and she felt his hard one beneath her. She settled against it, and bent to kiss him, though he hadn't indicated wanting it. Nevertheless, his mouth opened and his tongue touched hers. She melted in his arms. She wished she could divest him of his fine silk clothes on the spot. She would have him naked if only his friends would give him his privacy.

Philip seemed to forget his companions as his interest in Estelle focused sharply. His fingers touched her in ways that made her breaths come fast and hard. She pressed against them and kissed him harder, ignoring the stares of his companions. The play of the cards had come to a halt, and now there were only Philip and Estelle at the center of everyone's attention. She would have the entire world know she had caught the eye of this man and only wished this were happening in the market square where the entire town could see.

Philip, apparently, didn't feel quite as much the exhibitionist and disengaged her mouth so he could speak. His voice was thin and breathy as he addressed his companions, though his eyes never left Estelle's bosom. "Leave me now, my friends. I wish to retire upstairs."

Without verbal response—and Estelle didn't glance at their expressions, for her gaze was locked on Philip's face—the other men gathered their cards and what money was left to them. Philip nudged Estelle from his lap, stood, and reached for Marta's hand to guide them both along with him and upstairs.

The first room they came to seemed occupied, though it was empty of people. Belongings littered the bed, so Philip withdrew and continued looking.

The next room seemed more accommodating and was clean, at least. Tonight it didn't smell of any previous tenants, and she knew this bed had fewer lumps than the one in the other room. Philip drew the two of them inside, shut the door, and bolted it with the iron bar leaning against the wall. Now they were safe from interruption, which made Estelle all the more eager to get on with things. Her fingers danced over the fastenings of Philip's doublet.

"May I, Your Grace?"

He grinned. "I could hardly refuse a supplicant such as yourself."

Marta giggled, and she and Estelle fell to the task of relieving the king of his silk, leather, and linen. Then, stripped bare, he toppled to the bed and lay back to receive their attention. Estelle grasped her skirts in her fists to climb onto the mattress, and knelt over him, straddling him. Marta knelt before him on the floor and burrowed beneath Estelle's skirts to take him into her mouth. The rumors were true. Philip had flesh to spare, as stiff as any Estelle had ever seen.

His hands went to Estelle's fastenings, and soon her gown and shift were pulled over her head and tossed aside. She lay atop him, her mouth on his and his hands squeezing her wherever he could find soft flesh. Sometimes he was rough enough to hurt, but then he smoothed the hurt, and she was ready for more of the same.

Moans in his throat grew louder, more insistent, until she feared it would be over for him—and therefore for them all—too soon. She reached behind to push Marta from him, and her friend stood to remove her own clothing. Meanwhile, Estelle settled over Philip's member and pressed herself against him.

He was the strongest, most magnificent man she'd ever known, and she'd known hundreds. He moved against her ever so long, until she went dizzy in ways she never did with a client. Any moment now, she was certain, he would finish, and that would be that.

But he wasn't even close. First he satisfied Estelle, then

Marta had her turn, and still he wasn't through. He took them both in other ways and was yet ready for more. It became a game for the girls to see which would bring him to climax. For more than an hour he persisted, and it was Estelle who finally received his seed with much howling and grunting. His slick, sweaty body slapped against her a few more times, then he collapsed onto the damp sheets, his chest heaving for air and his heavy breaths verging on laughter.

Panting and equally slick, Estelle and Marta lay entangled with him. Estelle gazed at his beautiful face, his hair awry and stuck to his cheeks. His eyelids drooped, and his red lips parted for breath. She wanted to kiss them, but it was too much effort to move.

"I wish to sleep." He mumbled as if nearly asleep already.

Estelle nodded and laid her head on the bed.

A moment later Philip looked at her. "I said, I wish to sleep."

Marta poked her. Oh. Right. They were to leave. With a groan Estelle sat up and looked around for her clothing. Every inch of her was sore, inside and out. She'd been well used everywhere and wasn't certain she could walk just then. She would have liked to sleep where she lay, but it was plain the king wished to be alone now. She and Marta reached for their clothing and helped each other make themselves presentable for the street.

When they were nearly ready to leave, Philip said without opening his eyes, "There is money in my purse. You may have it all."

Estelle and Marta looked at each other, not believing their good luck. All of it? Philip had won a small fortune at cards earlier.

Just to be certain they wouldn't be jailed later on, Marta said, "Truly, Your Grace? May we have all of it?"

Philip looked at them as if she'd called him a liar, and she curtsied as deeply as she knew how. "Your Majesty," she said, "we are astonished by your generosity." Marta wasn't lying. Her cheeks were flushed, and all the insouciant pretense had left her. Just then she showed herself to be a Flemish girl of seventeen who had never been anywhere but the seediest part of Brussels.

He waved off the idea of generosity. "Take it. You've both earned it. That was the best I've had since leaving Spain. English women are dull as a wooden sword."

The two whores grinned at each other, and Estelle pawed through the king's clothing to find the purse bulging with ducats. It was a *large* purse, and the drawstring could barely contain the gold. Estelle giggled as she stuffed the thing inside her bodice and arranged it so nobody would see it wasn't her in there. Philip dropped off to sleep, snoring in an instant. For one lingering moment, Estelle gazed at the gold collar and jeweled brooch resting with the clothing but shook her head for the foolish idea of taking them. Even were they to get away with them, they could never sell them. And the king's men would surely come after them the instant they were discovered missing. The girls let themselves out of the room to step carefully down the stairs.

In the public room they found the caballeros still at the table, some awake and drinking, some passed out and sprawled with their heads rested on the tabletop. One of the ones playing cards looked up and said with a tone of acute indifference, "That howl. You haven't killed him, have you?" Certainly he knew better, for he knew the king, had heard that howl before, and was only teasing. He busied himself with a solitaire game with a deck of cards, laying the cards down one by one and paying more attention to them than to the girls.

"No," said Marta. "He nearly killed us, though."

The man chuckled and glanced up before returning his gaze to his game. "Any left for me?"

Marta shook her head, and Estelle was glad. She could barely walk without waddling and did not relish the idea of taking on another client for at least a day. To be sure, with the king's purse, the two of them might not need another client for a month.

The man reached for his stein, held it aloft to them in salute, then drank. He set the stein on the table with a sharp thump. "A word of this to anyone, and you'll be arrested and never heard from again. You both understand that, *sí*?"

They each nodded. Marta said, struggling to retrieve her facade of sophistication, "We understand how it is. No need to worry about us." Estelle nodded in agreement, though she said nothing.

"Then here." He reached for his purse.

Marta's eyes went wide. Estelle realized they were in for even more money paid for a night they would have enjoyed even without it. Marta started to speak, but Estelle cut her off from accepting.

"No, we've already been paid. The king gave us some ducats."

The gentleman glanced up at them with raised eyebrows, as if he could hardly believe that he was hearing a couple of whores decline money. Then he nodded and sat back.

Marta poked Estelle hard. "Fool!"

Estelle hissed in reply, "More the fool you! We'd be arrested if the king learned we'd taken more money."

Marta thought about that for a second, then nodded in reluctant agreement.

"Go, then." The gentleman nodded toward the door. Marta and Estelle made their exit without dallying, lest the fellow change his mind and detain them for his own amusement. They left him to his cards, and he paid them no more attention.

Outside, the sun was making itself known in a lightened sky above the tall surrounding buildings. The street was slippery with mud, it having rained some more during the night, and they made their way carefully back to their lodgings. Marta began to giggle, and Estelle followed.

"Ach, did you see the size of him?"

"Oh, yes!"

They giggled some more, then broke into a scurry the rest of the way.

"Johannes!" Marta called once they were inside the house where they all lived. "Johannes, you'll never guess who our client was tonight!"

Estelle laughed out loud. So much for being discreet subjects. This story would be all over Brussels within a day.

I had letters from Philip. At first they were warm. Generous. The sort of message one would hope for from a loving husband. But over the weeks and months, they became more distant. Philip wouldn't say when he might return. Gradually the household members he'd left behind began to join him. They made their way back to their master, who needed them to replace those his father took with him to Spain when he retired. My fear grew. Apprehension filled my days. This was how it had been with my mother: small disgraces at first, then more, then larger insults. I feared the ending would also be the same. Each day I didn't receive a letter was a stab through the heart. Each letter I received healed the wound, but less and less as the months progressed. Then one day I received a letter that nearly killed me.

Niccolò Delarosa played a song of his own composition and hoped his mistress enjoyed it. He watched her out of the corner of his eye and thought he saw a bit of a smile. It warmed his heart. There had been entirely too few of those lately. The queen pined for her absent king, and that Spanish pig would not send her a letter to ease her loneliness. Today she sat with her ladies, listening to the music and gossiping in low, soft voices. Niccolò enjoyed the sound of women's voices, for it was much like music. A room full of light, female chatter soothed his soul and made the day just a little gentler for him.

A page entered, holding a small letter sealed with a surfeit of wax. The seal was large enough to comprise most of the weight of the message, and the paper sagged as the young man offered the thing to the queen. Mary took it with curiosity touched with apprehension. Turning it this way and that to watch it flop back and forth, she noted the flimsiness of the single sheet of paper and its overly hefty glob of impressed wax. She examined the seal, which Niccolò saw was unbroken. The sender was not only desirous of privacy, but he was well-connected enough to get it. Mary broke the seal.

Niccolò tried to concentrate on his playing, but couldn't help watching Mary's face for her reaction to this mysterious note. Her ladies appeared to ignore her and chatted amongst themselves, but they must also have been watching her, for they fell silent when the shadow of grief darkened the queen's face. It was all Niccolò could do to keep playing his lute and appear to be minding his own business.

Tears sprang to Mary's eyes, and her lips pressed together hard enough to make a white line around them. In a near panic, she folded the letter, rose to toss it into the fire, then ordered her ladies to follow her. The women left the room quickly and silently.

Alone in the room, Niccolò hurried to set his instrument aside and pounce on the letter that had only just begun to burn. He picked it and flipped it onto the apron before the hearth, then stepped on it to extinguish the sparks on it. Once it was out, he carefully unfolded it and read it where it lay. Only one corner had been burnt away, small parts of the paper only darkened, and the short message inside was still intact. The language was Spanish.

Your Majesty:

   Though my communications have been few, I, your loyal servant, have been carrying out your orders these past months with all diligence and in good faith. I have been reluctant to send word, for what I've found has been neither expected nor hoped for. It grieves me to inform you that your husband has been unfaithful to his marriage vows during his time in Flanders. I have from unimpeachable sources that he has taken a mistress, his cousin, the duchess of Lorraine, who is considered very handsome, and of whom he seems much enamored. In addition he has visited other women of the lowest sort. His reputation for excess grows in drinking, gaming, and other forms of revelry. Among his Flemish subjects, he attends masques nearly every night. I heartily regret being the bearer of this news, for it was my dearest wish to find my liege a faithful and loving husband.

Ever at your service,
F.W.

Niccolò had no idea who F.W. might be. He thought he knew all the courtiers, but knew nobody with those initials attached to Philip. He wondered whether Mary had commissioned a paid spy or if she'd merely requested reports from a friend in Philip's household. That this was in Spanish suggested a casual request of a compliant Spaniard to keep an eye on the king, but it certainly didn't preclude a professional engagement.

Regardless, this was bad news for everyone. Niccolò's heart went out to his queen, and he knew the next few days would be a disaster of weeping and illness. Poor Mary. The thought crossed his mind to offer himself to her use as revenge for her husband's infidelity, but shook away the idea before it entirely formed. Mary would never break her vows. Any vow, but especially her marriage, was inviolate. Even were she to find him other than a crusty old Italian, even were he a king, she would never succumb to that sort of temptation.

With a deep sigh Niccolò tossed the letter back into the fire and poked it until it had burned entirely to crushed ashes.

CHAPTER TWENTY

It was very near the end of my life and my reign that I realized there would be no happiness for me. I never knew my time was so short but knew well that all of my days would be bleak as a winter landscape and devoid of the joy I'd once thought would be mine one day. I was forced to resign myself to the fact that I was a servant of God's will—whatever plan that might be—and only my faith could guide me through the treacherous future ahead. All that was left to me was the task of ruling England, and I determined to do that as I knew I must. As my mother had done and my grandmother also, I would be the queen I was born to be, and no man would deny me my birthright and my destiny.

* * *

Mary sat at the head of the council table at the public end of her privy chamber and gazed across at the council. She allowed them nothing in the way of a hint of what she was thinking, for her mind was on Philip. She reminded herself she was still able to have children and might yet conceive if he returned from Flanders as he'd promised repeatedly over these many months. There was word of his campaigns. He was running out of money. If she suggested the possibility of using English coffers to finance the war, he might visit her for a time. Then there would be a chance of conceiving an heir. That would be something, at least.

Without a baby, the ascension of Elizabeth to the throne was inevitable. Mary blanched at the thought. A *Protestant*. Elizabeth and her affiliation with that traitorous Robert Dudley would certainly return the country to ruin and moral decay, all that Mary had worked so hard to purge from her realm.

Mary's thoughts so focused on this matter that it rather startled her when Paget spoke. "May we begin, Your Majesty?"

She glanced a bit sheepishly around at the council and nodded. "Proceed."

"We come to you on the matter of the burnings."

Mary stifled a sigh of impatience. This again. Why could this man not understand the importance of this policy? "We would have our kingdom free of those who would mislead our subjects."

"But your subjects are not sanguine about the punishments. Even the Catholics grumble over it. They don't seem particularly threatened by those you are martyring. In fact, I've heard tell the general feeling is that your Catholic subjects feel the policy is insulting to them."

"How so?"

"They feel they can withstand the heresy without succumbing to it. They think you slight them for weakness of faith."

"Nonsense. Some are weak but certainly not all. It is the few who would succumb I wish to save. Even one soul is a loss to the kingdom."

"You risk uprising."

Cardinal Pole spoke up. "I think you exaggerate, Your Grace."

Paget gave him a sideways glance of disgust, then ignored him and returned his attention to the queen.

She said, "Again, I say I have more faith in my subjects than that."

"The question is whether they have so much faith in you."

"Paget! Your manners!" said Pole. One of the other counselors muttered something and shifted in his seat.

Paget turned to Pole, his customary calm teetering on rage. "I cannot stand by and let Her Majesty's reign collapse for the sake of politeness!" He turned to Mary once more. "Your Grace, I beg you to hear me and not dismiss me as ever in error for my faith and for my past transgressions. In this thing I am well-informed. As for my loyalty to the Crown, I remind Your Majesty of my vested interest in the success of your reign. I present my advice in all sincerity of it and swear my oath to have Your Majesty's best interests at heart. I am fully committed to you. I have no desire to test my fortune on the whim of a people in revolt."

Mary nodded to indicate his point was well taken but then said, "Of course you wouldn't, were they actually on the verge of revolt."

He hesitated, took a moment to swallow his frustration, then continued. "There are many who would do away with you. There have been attempts on your life." Mary started to speak, but Paget rushed ahead, and she let him. "Many other-wise loyal subjects are unhappy with your policies. There is rebellion in Ireland. Most of England is terrified Philip will gain the Crown by force, and our realm will come under Span-ish rule."

"Nonsense. He would never do that." But Mary's voice be-trayed a sliver of doubt, for Philip had done many things she'd never before thought he was capable of.

"Come," said Paget, a hard note of condescension in his voice, "you must admit it's possible."

"Anything is possible. The sun could fall out of the sky to-morrow. However, it is highly unlikely, and if we live our lives according to every possible but unlikely event, then we would never live at all."

Paget pressed his lips together, then took a slightly different tack. "Good Catholics have spoken against you. There have been ballads sung, the words distributed in print. Rhymes. Lewd tales, ridiculing yourself and the king both."

This Mary couldn't deny. She'd seen some of them herself, and they were deeply alarming. A group of players in the north were reported to draw large crowds with a performance of a play lampooning the Crown. Her cheeks burned even now to remember reading it.

Paget continued. "The worst of them glorify the martyrs burned at the stake. The commons have begun to spew hatred at the Crown for the burnings. They sing of incompetent exe-cutioners and atrocities committed against the condemned even as they died. Witnesses weep now at sight of the martyrs, and even the Catholic majority have no stomach for it."

"That cannot be true."

"It is absolutely true, Your Majesty. Would that it weren't, but I cannot lie to you."

"If they would tolerate heresy in their midst, then they cannot be counted among true Catholics. They must, in their hearts, be faithless heretics themselves."

Again Paget's frustration rose, and he looked away for a moment.

Pole took the opportunity to speak again. "The error must be purged."

"But at what cost? How will it benefit England if the queen is overthrown and possibly executed? Is conformity of worship worth that price?"

"Yes." Something in Mary snapped. All this self-serving debate over what should have been obvious to them all wore her patience to nothing. Her voice rose to a pitch of near hysteria. "Yes, it is worth it!" She would brook no argument.

The men fell silent to stare at her, as if they'd only just then realized she was in the room.

She continued before either of them could dismiss her words. "The souls of our people are worth whatever cost might be required of us, for they are all any of us has of any real value. They are ourselves, and we have been made by God to be their leader and protector. We are made as we are for his purpose. If we deny that—if we abrogate our responsibility and our honor— then we are nothing in this world. If we bow to evil because it might win, then we are less than nothing. We become evil ourselves.

"My mother taught me that faith is more than daily prayer. It is more than reading Scripture and participating in the sacraments. It is living by God's law every day. It is being what one is meant to be, and never allowing one's honor to be compromised for any reason. It is holding spiritual matters more highly than matters of the world and the flesh. I would go to the block happily and without hesitation rather than allow my subjects to descend into error and lose their souls."

There was a long silence. Then Paget opened his mouth to speak.

Mary cut him off. "This meeting is finished, gentlemen."

"Your Gr—"

"*Finished.* Good day." She waited for them to clear the room, but nobody moved. Mary continued to wait, not moving a hair, until finally Paget rose from his seat, bowed, and made his exit. Then the rest went, hesitantly and in silence. Mary said nothing as they left. Then, once the room was hers again and there were only women around her, she closed her eyes and prayed. Afterward she sat in silence for a moment.

"Please leave me," she told her attendants. Her eyes remained closed as she listened to the soft footfalls of the women's slippers as they left the room. Even after the door had closed and all was silent, except for the sounds of London commons drifting up from the river below, she sat and tried not to think. Too much thinking made her sick. Too much pondering led her thoughts to things that kept her from doing any good. She calmed her mind before she attempted to work out what to do.

Paget was more than likely right that there was much unhappiness in the land over the burnings. Executions always brought comment, and many executions could bring outrage. She'd seen that during her father's reign and the executions of those who held fast to the old religion. It was only natural that there should be unrest in response to the purging of those who would disseminate error.

The heart of the question was whether the feeling was strong enough to be a danger to the realm. It was plain she needed to weigh that against her mandate to return her people to spiritual health. She knew God could only want peace and prosperity for England, but there hadn't been either of those things for a good many years. The Lutheran heresy her father had used to his own ends had plunged the country into economic and moral bankruptcy. Crops failed more years than not. Riots and risings flourished, and though they had each been put down in good order, they also each had a monstrous influence over the general welfare of the land. Over the decades her subjects had learned to be disruptive, untrusting, and selfish. They'd learned to flout authority.

Philip, though he had little stomach to burn his English subjects, felt it an effective solution to the Protestant problem on the Continent. Mary also felt that Paget's concerns were exaggerated because of his natural fear of one day being burned himself. Unlikely, for he never preached and had little direct influence over spiritual lives, but he couldn't be blamed for having an aversion to seeing his fellow Protestants go to the stake. His opinion on this matter had to be taken with some reservation.

At the heart of it, Mary couldn't bear to forfeit her honor for the sake of political expediency.

She opened her eyes. Her path was clear. The burnings would continue, for it was the only measure that would rid the land of the evil that had suffused it since the advent of that horrible woman. Perhaps Anne herself should have been burned rather than beheaded. Then the evil might have died with her.

In any case, it was up to Mary now to rid her kingdom of the heresy that so plagued it.

*   *   *

The burnings continued, and I never again questioned them. Unbeknownst to me, my time was short. And my husband commanded all of my attention as fleeting hope once again entered my life.

Now that Philip ruled over his father's lands, he looked toward war against France and Italy. He hated the French as heartily as his father had and now asked me to support him in his efforts. Though his promises to return to England had ever proved empty, when he sent his pages, stable, and armory, I knew he must be sincere and would finally return to me. When he asked me for troops to protect the Netherlands from the French, I sent him six thousand foot and six hundred cavaliers.

Once more England would go to war with France.

Bells rang all over London. Mary sat in her privy chamber, her heart in her throat and her breaths short and tight. Philip had arrived. His barge sat at the dock below, and his entourage was at that moment escorting him to his chambers in the palace. Mary could hardly contain herself, so powerful was the urge to run to him. But she refrained, wishing to maintain the dignity of her station. It wouldn't do for her to scurry through the halls with her skirts in her fists like a commoner, nor could she leap upon her husband with the joy that inflamed her. So instead she sat as still as possible, her cheeks aglow and her heart thumping wildly in her chest, waiting to be summoned to his presence.

An hour passed before one of her ladies came to inform her

the king was ready to see her. It seemed he should be the one to visit, but the question of precedence was a sticky one for him and in some instances she was willing to let him take the higher place. This was one of them, for Mary was only glad to have her husband back in England.

Her women escorted her to Philip's privy chamber, past the anteroom where his gentlemen milled about in quiet, tired conversation after their long boat ride up the river. Mary passed them without much notice and entered Philip's chamber.

He stood near his altar, probably having just finished a prayer. A candle burned there, flickering amongst the others kept to light the room.

His visage shocked her. Something had gone from his eyes during his time in Flanders. He'd always seemed preoccupied, but now there was a jaded air he hadn't owned before, as if he'd aged ten years since leaving England. He was no longer the pleasant, handsome young prince but rather the grave king weighted with the responsibility of his possessions and the prospect of a costly war.

Even worse, she could see in his eyes she was not what he'd expected, either. By her mirror she knew the strain of recent events had lined her face so that she appeared even older than she was. Before, there had been some vestige of beauty left in her, but now she must seem an ancient hag to this man who was not yet thirty.

Once the shock of seeing changes in each other had passed, Mary went to him and kissed his mouth. A hug was out of the question, though she longed terribly for it. She stepped back and saw no such desire in his eyes, nor in his posture. She bit her lips together, then said, "Welcome home, my husband."

A shadow passed over his eyes, and she knew it was because he didn't consider England his home. Nevertheless, he replied, "Thank you, my wife."

She wished to be alone with him but also wished to appear dignified, so she waited for him to indicate they should sit in chairs nearby.

They sat. She waited for him to speak, and he did.

"I've missed you."

She didn't believe it, but felt her chest loosen a little anyway. It was good of him to say it, at least. "I've missed you, as well." More than he could ever know. But she couldn't say so. Instead, she took his hand in hers. His grip was noncommittal. He neither squeezed nor pulled away.

They chatted some about his trip. He told of the weather on the channel and the sighting of some French ships that made their joining with the English escort at Dover a relief. They touched on the situation with the French king, and Philip expounded on some of the diplomatic pros and cons of the impending war. Mary understood his words were little more than a campaign for more aid from England than was provided in their marriage contract. It was a disappointment they were not words of love, and his talk was unnecessary, for she would give him what he wanted. If only he knew she would give him nearly anything for the sake of his affection.

Too soon the conversation wound down and came around to the small details of settling back into the palace. Philip's household needed to be assigned rooms. Then he said the last thing she wanted to hear. "I've brought the Duchess of Lorraine."

A hollow sickness yawned in Mary's gut. She struggled to keep from her face that she knew of his mistress, but by the flicker in his eyes, she could see she'd failed. He looked to the floor, and she closed her eyes for a moment to clear the hurt from them. Then she looked at him and said, "Where shall she sleep?"

"Wherever you like," he replied. As if he didn't care a fig about the woman. "I think, though, for the sake of protocol you'll wish to put her somewhere better than a scullery cot."

For some odd reason his rather wobbly joke made her smile. It was one of the things she loved about him, even if the subject was not a pleasant one. She said, "I'll see personally to her accommodations."

Scullery cot, indeed.

He came to her room that evening, bringing hope for an heir and the comforting knowledge he wasn't visiting his mistress. But that was all he brought. Gone was the passion he'd once had, just as his youth was gone from his eyes and voice. His lovemaking that night was perfunctory. And when he'd discharged his duty, he rolled over to sleep. Mary lay awake most of the night, cherishing this time with him and wishing it could be like before.

When she awoke the next morning, she found him gone from her bed. She rolled back over to stare at the wall and prayed for conception.

Philip stayed in England only long enough to secure the troops and money he needed to wage the war against France, then returned to the Continent. I never saw him again.

CHAPTER TWENTY-ONE

When my belly began to swell, I thought myself pregnant. But this time my hope truly was for naught. The illness was a fatal dropsy, and I soon died, never knowing until the very last that my life was over. In the end, I died knowing that my life had been a failure.

Simon Renard heard the bells and knew the queen was dead. A great shouting rose in the streets, and he went to a window in the gallery to look out over London. People were cheering for the new queen, who would be Elizabeth. A travesty, for she would return her kingdom to the moral confusion of the reigns of her father and brother.

He turned away from it, only glad he would one day go home and leave these ignorant people to their decay.

Peter Barnacle stopped in the middle of the street, his back burdened with wood on its way to market, when he heard the bells. For a moment he hoped the news was of a birth, but knew it was unlikely. Then a herald came within hearing, shouting of death. The queen was gone. Protestant Elizabeth would be their new queen. He set his wood on the ground, unable to go a step farther, for his knees had quite given out on him. The world shifted. How could God have allowed this? What would become of them now?

Niccolò Delarosa knelt in the anteroom outside the queen's privy chamber, hugging his lute, and wept.

EPILOGUE

The figure in the mirror gazed at the children around her and smiled at their little girl snores. It was true. She could take one of them with her. But she wouldn't. She never had. People only thought she had.

Mary considered her past. All three of her father's children had ascended to his throne, one by one. Edward and his council had attempted to destroy the Catholic faith, and they had failed as abysmally as she had in restoring it. It was Elizabeth who had taken the path of moderation, who had allowed both to survive and encouraged tolerance in the kingdom despite her own beliefs. She'd made her way through the pitfalls she'd seen demonstrated by the rulers who had gone before her. It was also Elizabeth who had been allowed to live for more than six decades and ruled for most of that life. She had been the one to bring peace and prosperity to her kingdom wearied by a generation of death, destruction, and poverty.

Mary returned to the mirror and looked out on the world. Her life was what it was. She'd been what she was made to be, for there was nothing else for her. She no longer had any rancor for Elizabeth, for her sister was also part of God's plan. And Mary was at peace with that.

"Thy will be done," she murmured. Then the spirit returned to her God.